P9-CRT-414

Advance Praise for *The Secret Thief*

"Judith Jaeger (is) a powerful and exciting new voice in fiction...
utterly compelling and psychologically astute... I found myself
diving into the book as I would a dish of my favorite ice cream."
- Marc D. Feldman, M.D., Clinical Professor of Psychiatry,
University of Alabama, author of *Playing Sick?*

"*The Secret Thief* is a work that successfully walks the tightrope
between humor and pathos. The voices of all of her characters
are rich and distinctive. Ms. Jaeger has written a multi-layered,
emotionally complex, riveting coming-of-age saga."
-Neil Landau, screenwriter and playwright; Visiting Assistant
Professor, MFA Screenwriting Program, UCLA School of Film
and Television

"...moving and entertaining, and the tone of Jaeger's writing hits
the right note all through...The humor was wonderful,
alternately light-hearted and caustic at the right
moment...Connie's voice is so complete that she succeeds in
inviting the reader along with her into a grim situation. We go
willingly, because the writing is multi-faceted — smart, well-
modulated, agile, creating indelible scenes without a lot of
fanfare or overworked imagery."
-Mariana Romo-Carmona, author of *Living at Night* and *Speaking
like an Immigrant*

"With skillful precision, Judith Jaeger weaves us into the mind
and body of a young woman on the verge of exploding with
pent-up rage and denial. This sustained, unsparing journey to
the core of the narrator's self-loathing and out the other side
makes an utterly compelling read. *The Secret Thief* announces the
arrival of an important new novelist."
- Eric Darton, author of *Divided We Stand: A Biography of New
York's World Trade Center*

For him – May you always be guided by Truth and Love. Enjoy!

The Secret Thief

by
Judith Jaeger

Judith Jaeger
June 6, 2006

Behler
PUBLICATIONS

California

Behler Publications
California

The Secret Thief
A Behler Publications Book

Copyright © 2006 by Judith Jaeger
Author photograph courtesy of Rob Carlin
Cover design by MBC Design – www.mbcdesign.com

All rights reserved. No part of this book may be reproduced or transmitted in any form or by any means, electronic or mechanical, including photocopying, recording, or by any information storage and retrieval system, without the written permission of the publisher, except where permitted by law.

This is a work of fiction. Names, characters, places, and incidents either are the product of the author's imagination or are used fictitiously. Any resemblance to actual persons, living or dead, events, or locales is entirely coincidental.

Library of Congress Cataloging-in-Publication Data is available
Control Number: 1933016280

FIRST PRINTING

ISBN 1-933016-28-0
Published by Behler Publications, LLC
Lake Forest, California
www.behlerpublications.com

Manufactured in the United States of America

For my parents, Ray and Judy

For my husband, Trevor

And for the Jaeger family, the best around

Acknowledgments

I owe a large debt of gratitude to Eric Darton and Neil Landau, who helped shape not only this book, but also me, as a writer.

To Behler Publications, especially Kristan Ryan and Karla Keffer who shepherded my manuscript through publication with careful attention and patience with a new author.

To my Mom and Dad, Judy and Ray, my sister Mary, and my nieces Jill and MaryJo for their unending enthusiasm and support.

To Flo and Paul, Russ and Martha and Kay and Stephen, Rita, and all of my coworkers in Clark University's Public Affairs Office who cheered me from the sidelines and provided much needed distractions.

Especially to Kay, who willingly read more drafts of this manuscript than any friend should have to read and always found something encouraging and insightful to say about it, and to Martha for lending me her medical expertise.

To my husband and best friend, Trevor, who helps me be the person who can write books like this and, more importantly, keeps me laughing through life.

1

I close my eyes and whisper, "Disappear. Disappear. Disappear."

I've tried this trick about a thousand times since I was five years old and it never works. But I still give it a shot in desperate situations.

When I open my eyes, Grandmother is on the porch looking in my direction. Standing there, with her arms crossed and her feet placed together, she looks like a nail sticking out of one of the porch floorboards. Her long white hair is wound in its usual bun on the back of her head. She pulls her hair back so tightly that her eyebrows are permanently arched. Loosening that bun just the slightest bit would put her in a much better mood.

She's looking in my direction, but not right at me. There's a difference. I sit very still.

Then she waves a few fingers at me. I sag in my seat. Grandmother stays on the porch, waiting for me to place a light kiss on her cheek.

"What happened to your car?" she says.

The edges of my ears burn. I look at the damage for the first time. The left headlight is smashed, and there's a crater the size of a watermelon above the front tire.

"I had a little accident."

"Oh no!"

"Just a little one."

"What happened?"

"I hit a lawn mower."

"How in the world did you hit a lawnmower?"

"Someone was driving it across the street and I hit it. By accident."

"I hope you didn't hurt anyone."

Note that she didn't ask if I was hurt.

"Look at your car—it's awful!"

"It's not so bad."

She *tsk-tsks*. "What will your mother say?"

My ears burn so hot; they must be glowing red. How am I going to tell my mother that I already wrecked the new, previously owned car she just gave me for my college graduation?

"It's fixable. I can get it fixed."

"Before your mother sees it, I hope," Grandmother says. She sighs and shakes her head. "What a shame." Then she goes inside, letting the screen door slam shut behind her, right in my face.

I reach for the doorknob, an old wooden one that people pay a lot of money to have in their restored farmhouses. Amber and black swirl beneath its shiny surface. *How much could I get for it?* I wonder. I reach toward it slowly, as if it could be charged with electricity. My fingers graze the knob. I take a deep breath, grab it and yank the door open.

Grandmother walks by, pauses, and marches back to the door.

"You're letting the bugs in."

"I'm sorry," I say, not sure to whom I'm apologizing.

A few months ago, Grandmother decided to sell the family homestead and move to the new assisted-living complex in town. It's called something corny like Modern Living or Pleasant Vistas. The exact name doesn't matter. They all mean the same thing — Wrinkle City.

This is the house Papa and Grandmother lived in their entire married lives. It's the house my mother and her sisters grew up in. Grandmother didn't tell them, and then announced at my college graduation party that she'd sold the house. Apparently I was hogging all the attention. My aunts went into hysterics. "How could you do it?" they wailed. "That's our home! How could you?" I wanted to tell them to get a grip; it's just a house. My mother gracefully shuffled my aunts and their husbands into our small dining room to spare the few non-family party guests from witnessing the scene. My mother hates it when people make a scene. She shooed me from the room, leaving me to watch my bratty cousins.

A few days later, my mother told me about my pending trip. It was after dinner, and I was well into one of my favorite movies. I love those bad 1980s movies, where the cute-but-outcast high-school girl ends up with the object of her crush, usually the star quarterback. Dreamy. This movie was a particular favorite. Everyone forgets the cute girl's birthday because her horrid older sister is getting married.

"You'll be going soon," my mother said.

"Where?"

"To your grandmother's."

"Why would I go there?"

"Don't be fresh," she said. "She needs help packing up the house. Your job doesn't start until September—"

"August," I said, sitting up in my chair. "I have to be there in mid-August."

"Fine, mid-August. You're still the only one with nothing to do for the whole summer."

The first twang of pain sprung up deep in my belly, a little burning itch. I crossed my arms and pressed down. In the movie, the boy just arrived at the cute girl's house to confess his secret crush on her – the best part.

A certain kind of person would say my mother interrupted my favorite movie on purpose. But I'm not that kind of person.

"I was planning to get a job for the summer," I said.

She knelt down in front of me, trying to make it look like she was begging me. As if I had a choice. She pulled one hand away from my stomach and held it between her palms. The hair on my arms stood up. I held my breath.

"I'm not asking you to do this for her," she said. "Do it for me. Because you love me."

The next morning, Grandmother called.

"You don't have to come," she said. "I'm sure you have better things to do."

"No. It's fine."

There was the long pause so typical of our conversations. We don't talk to each other so much as interrupt the silence now and then.

"I'm sure I can do it myself, if you'd rather not come."

My mother scrutinized me from across the kitchen in her usual stance, back against the sink, arms crossed. I chose my next words very carefully.

"It'll be better if I help."

I left the next day, as late in the day as possible. In protest, I left my mother's clean clothes in a laundry basket in her room instead of folding them and putting them away. I ran the dishwasher, but didn't empty it. I didn't make my bed. And, on top of all that, I gave her the lightest possible kiss before climbing into the used sedan she bought me for my college graduation gift. Even though it's used, it still has that new car smell. They must make it in a spray. We shopped for it together, all through the spring of my senior year of college, looking for just the right style—sporty, but not flashy—the right mileage, the right color red. My mother made a big deal of our Saturdays car shopping. After visiting several dealerships, she'd treat me to lunch and an ice cream.

"Isn't this something?" she said on the Saturday we'd found the perfect car. We were sitting on the patio outside Friendly's, eating our chocolate ice cream cones. "You're graduating from college, getting your first car." Her eyes filled then. She sniffled into a napkin. "There was a time I wasn't sure you'd live to see your high school graduation."

I put my hand on her arm. "I know, but I'm better now. I made it. You got me through," I said.

My mother smiled. Her tears dried instantly. "You bet I did."

On the three-hour drive to Grandmother's, I breathed in that new-car smell and thought about my mother's fountain pen. The body of the pen is tortoiseshell—classy—with a black grip. It has a tortoiseshell cap with a gold clip and trim. I gave it to my mother for her birthday last year—$39.95 at Staples. Free for me. Just ask the attendant to take a pen out of the display case. Examine it quietly for a long time, like it's a tough decision. Inevitably, someone else will come to the counter for help. When the counter is good and busy, walk away with the pen tucked away in your purse.

My mother likes writing with a fountain pen. She says it makes her feel smart and rich. Ballpoints are for the commoners. She must've been so mad the next time she went to write a check and found the penholder in her wallet empty. She hates to lose things, the time spent searching, that feeling of going crazy because she swears she saw the missing item two seconds ago, in its place, where it belongs. "Everything in its place," she always says, which makes her even angrier when something goes missing.

Green Hill looks exactly like its name. The main road into town climbs a small hill—small for those parts anyway. The locals call the surrounding granite peaks "hills." Where the meadow grass ends some distance from the edge of the road, a forest of evergreens begins. The center of town and the outlying neighborhoods, small clusters of little white houses among the trees, are visible from the top of the hill. Beyond the neighborhoods, the trees become thick in every direction, a green felt blanket broken only by the sharp peaks of the mountains jutting out of the earth like daggers. The hill is long and steep down the other side, heading into town. Perched at the top, I have a perfect view of Mount Washington.

It may be beautiful, but Green Hill is still a black hole in the White Mountains. When people ask me where it is, I tell them to climb a tall tree and look north—Green Hill is just beyond the edge of the planet. There is nothing in Green Hill. Not even a pizza place. It doesn't have a supermarket, just the sad little Green Hill Grocery for milk, butter, eggs and a wide selection of Pez dispensers—$1.69 each, but free for me. The nearest supermarket is forty minutes away. The nearest *anything* is forty minutes away. It does, however, have its own movie theater, The Mayflower, which plays the worst movies, the ones real theaters refuse, ones that aren't even worth the three bucks to see.

Lending an air of the bizarre to the whole place are the Hassidic Jews. They flock to Green Hill every summer. Motels put screens of blue tarp up around their pools so Hassidic guests can swim without revealing themselves to members of the opposite sex. Most of the inns have signs in both English and Hebrew. No one knows why they come. The dominant theory is that the cool, mountain air makes their heavy clothing more bearable in the summer. They all wear wool or polyester, the kind of fabric that makes me hot just looking at it. The women and girls wear thick nylons, and the older women wear wigs to cover their hair. It's the custom, I think, for Hassidic women to grow their hair long and then cut it off when they get married and cover it with a wig. Something about their hair being a gift reserved only for their husbands.

The Hassids were far from my mind that day as I started down the hill toward my destination—the black hole's vortex, a white Victorian house on Grove Street.

"It'll be different this time," I said to myself. "You're an adult. You can't be pushed around anymore. You're in charge. If she tries to make you do something you don't want to do, stand up for yourself. Say 'no.' What's the worst she can do to you? Send you to your room? Ground you? Make you scrub the floor with a toothbrush? She can't bully you now. You're bigger and stronger. And she's old and weak and—"

Wham!

My brakes squealed and I came this close to slamming my head on the steering wheel. My eyes were shut tight. And when I had the courage to open them again, slowly, there was a riding lawnmower attached to the left front fender of my car.

"Are you O.K.?"

A man stood at my window. He smiled at me, revealing a gap between his two front teeth. My hands were clasped over my gaping mouth, so all I could do was nod.

My pine-tree air freshener still swung with the impact. It was ninety-nine cents at Wal-Mart, but free for me. My U2 CD skipped on the CD player. The CD was $11.99 at a used music store. Free for me.

"You sure you're O.K.?"

I nodded again. So smooth.

Beyond the man at my window, four or five other men watched the scene. They all wore torn, dirty clothing and heavy boots. A short, stocky man leaned on his shovel. Two younger men, their age betrayed by the smooth skin on their cheeks and chins, mumbled to each other and chuckled, nodding now and then at my cracked-up car. A tall black man took a kerchief from his pocket and wiped the sweat from his bald head. They were either a group of convicts on work release or a construction crew.

The man at my window waved at the men, and the short, stocky guy and tall black guy—the two strongest looking of the group—came over to unhook the mower from my car. It made this awful metal-on-metal scratching sound that made my teeth hurt. There was the crunch of more glass breaking off my headlight. The man rested his forearm on my window. It was muscular and tan. It was a really nice arm—not that I was looking.

"We'll get this piece of junk out of your way."

I remembered something about my registration and insurance information and reached for my glove compartment.

"Don't bother. That thing can barely cross the street anymore—obviously, right? You probably just increased its value." The man laughed. He was a young guy, my age, maybe a little older. He looked familiar, but I didn't look at him long enough to place the face.

"You're all set," he said. The mower was on the side of the road. I pulled away without even saying "thank you."

* * *

After Grandmother scolds me for letting the bugs in the house, I finally step over the threshold. The stairs to the second floor loom in front of me.

"Take your things up to your room," Grandmother says, with all the warmth and affection of a prison guard. I'm ready to be strip-searched.

My room looks the same. Smaller and dustier, but still the same. The same yellow quilt, which matches the yellow curtains, covers the bed that stands against the wall opposite the closet. The lamp, with Humpty-Dumpty perched on its base, is on the nightstand. The same figurines—a rocking horse, a gray kitten and a little girl—are on the bureau in the corner near the door. The room smells stale, like the stacks in a library where the only air is trapped between the pages of old books.

I pick up the figurine of the little girl. She wears a green dress and holds a basket of flowers. The girl looks back at me with her fixed porcelain smile and blank stare as if to say, "Nothing has changed here."

Instead of helping Grandmother prepare dinner, I explore the rest of the house. In the living room, pink roses bloom on the walls but are hidden in most places by cabinets, display cases and shelves — all of them full — crowded in around the two pink love seats and a coffee table of dark brown wood. Unlike my bedroom, every surface is shiny. The cleanliness, along with the careful arrangement of the objects, gives the impression of order, but the clutter still closes in on me. I feel like I'm budging into a cocktail party ruined by too many people and too much noise.

Two glass cabinets hold Grandmother's collection of perfume bottles. One of my chores used to be washing the glass doors on those cabinets. When I was small, I used a stepstool to reach the very top.

Hidden in the rows of delicate bottles decorated in endless patterns of swirling color are the dozen or so perfume bottles my mother has made me give Grandmother over the years. The only one I find is a tall, slender bottle of clear glass edged in gold that I gave her for Christmas that year. It's tucked in the back corner of the lowest shelf. It was $24.95 at Sadie's Curiosity Shop back home, but free for me.

Two more cases hold a zoo of porcelain animals. The top shelf of each case is a memorial to Blue, my grandparents' long-deceased beagle, who is buried in the flower garden in the backyard. No two of the dogs are alike; none sit, sleep or stand in the same way as any other. The creativity reflected in this collection of dogs amazes me. Or maybe it's the stupidity of it. It's hard to say. In any case, it's a marvel, really, how many different ways a beagle can be cast in porcelain.

Among them is the one I've seen in my mind over and over again for years. Tail straight out, one forepaw lifted off the ground, the dog looks off into the distance, its ears cocked forward, listening. The line of the crack runs from the top of the dog's back, down around its belly and up the other side — a clean break. One ear is chipped and the tip of its tail is missing. It had slipped, jumped right out of my small hands onto the hardwood floor. I'm not surprised that she kept it. Like the pewter goblets and crystal candy dishes on the rest of the shelves in the room, Grandmother collects her grudges, polishes them and puts them on display.

My family looks down at me from the mantel, smiling faces framed in silver. My four little cousins are in the center — of course. There's a picture of the twins, Teddy and Zach, wearing matching gray shorts, matching white button-down shirts, matching red bow ties and brown hiking boots. Matching. They look about two, their heads covered with white fuzz that will grow into the Grey family white-blonde hair, full of curls. Grandmother calls them the Two Peas, as in Two Peas in a Pod. I hate peas.

They share the center of the mantel with my other cousins, Heather and Iris. The Two Flowers, Grandmother calls them. How precious. A five-year-old Heather, bouncy white-blonde curls falling to her shoulders, and a three-year-old Iris, her curls still coiled close to her scalp, sit in small wicker rocking chairs. Their pink dresses are full of ruffles and bows. Teddy and Zach belong to my Aunt Audrey, the Two Flowers to my Aunt Elizabeth.

The family grows out from the center, with pictures of Elizabeth and Audrey in high school and college, at their weddings, then in the hospital with their purple, prune-faced newborns. In each picture, their hair changes in length and style to match the fashion of the decade. Even Papa had blonde hair, although the pictures on the mantel were taken long after it had darkened to the color of wet sand. There are pictures of Papa standing on the porch with Grandmother, standing beside his first and only new car—a blue truck—with Elizabeth and Audrey and my mother. My mother always tells me if I'm going to cry, smile instead. So I smile and touch my fingers to the image of Papa's face.

At the edge of the mantel is one picture of my mother. It's her high-school picture, the same one she keeps in our dining room in a drawer under the cloth napkins and quilted placemats. I pull it out once in a while, usually just before setting the table for another big family dinner my mother feels compelled to host a hundred times a year. In the picture, she has long brown hair, flipped back away from her face in feathered curls. She wears a dark blue sweater vest over a bright yellow shirt with an extra long pointy collar. She smiles in the picture, which is maybe why I take every opportunity to peek at it. I always bury the picture back under the placemats before she catches me.

Tucked into the corner of the frame of my mother's picture is another small photograph, me at one day old. An eight-by-ten-inch version is on the wall in my mother's bedroom at home.

Around it hang my school pictures, one goofy face for each grade. My mother framed one for herself and one for Grandmother every year.

Except for my mother, the Greys look almost exactly alike. Elizabeth and Audrey are identical twins who look just like Grandmother. They have her long face, pointed chin and close-set eyes. They have her tall narrow frame, long arms and long fingers. My mother says she got her looks from Papa's side of the family. I like to think I get my looks from him, too. I touch his face one more time and then continue creeping through the first floor of the house, smiling.

The dining room showcases three sets of china. Shelves and shelves of figurines, most of them little girls and boys, line the walls in the den. In Grandmother's bedroom, the empty glass eyes of her porcelain dolls stare back at me, as if the dolls were corpses. The drawers and cabinets in every room hold more dolls, china and figurines.

After a silent dinner of egg salad sandwiches — which I hate — Grandmother takes me through the house and shows me what needs to be done.

"I hope you'll be careful with everything," she says.

"I will."

"Many of these things are very valuable."

"I know."

"And you know how easily they can be broken."

How I wish I'd been able to catch that porcelain beagle before it hit the floor.

In addition to all the collections on the first floor of the house and the stuff in the bedrooms upstairs, I have to clean out the basement. It's a musty hole full of boxes stacked neatly on top of each other in a dungeon maze. Three bare bulbs struggle to cut through the darkness, which is almost as thick as the moist air. A pile of lumber, left from a project Papa didn't get to finish, lies on the dirt floor. I open the top drawer of his tool chest, where he kept his finer carving implements. His favorite knife, a short blade with a wooden handle, is still there.

Grandmother takes me to the attic last. Her attic is not the typical crawl space accessed through a trap door in the ceiling. It's a full-size room down the hall from the yellow bedroom that takes up half of the second story of the house, one giant receptacle for the remnants of the five lives that make up the Grey family. Piles of junk, old suitcases, bulging trash bags full of god-knows-what, racks of old clothes, and toppling stacks of boxes leave only a tiny patch of bare floor in front of the door. "What's all this?" I say.

"I hardly know anymore. Baby clothes, I imagine. Old furniture. Toys. Things that belonged to Elizabeth and Audrey."

"To my mother?"

"You'll have to sort through it all."

I want to ask her why we don't just put a dumpster under a window and heave it all out.

"I'm sure I'll want to keep some things, and Elizabeth and Audrey will want whatever belongs to them. There's probably some things for your cousins, and some of it can go to Goodwill."

And some to my mother, I want to add. But Grandmother is down the hallway already, starting down the stairs. I take a tentative step into the attic, afraid that the slightest vibration could send the whole mess toppling down on top of me. None of the polished order of the rest of the house is evident here. The categorical display of the porcelain animals, and the careful placement of the perfume bottles that allow a clear view of each one, do not apply. Even in the basement, the boxes are stacked edge-to-edge in neat rows.

But the attic is a free-for-all, where layers of dust have dulled everything to a sepia tone. Even the cobwebs gathered thick in all corners of the ceiling are covered in dust. The windows are black with it. How can a person like Grandmother, so meticulous with her things, live with such chaos swirling behind closed doors?

Oh, yeah. I forgot. I don't care.

Later, in the yellow bedroom, I try to sleep. My stomach hurts, and there's so much to do. Everything that needs to be packed and cleaned and sorted swirls through my mind. I count backward from one hundred for a few hours, and then I must fall asleep because I jolt awake.

It's always the same dream. I'm in the hospital with this blinding pain in my stomach and no one will help me. My stomach is huge and I'm crying because I don't know what happened. My mother stands at my side, looks down at me and then walks away without saying anything. I'm scared, frantic, in such pain.

The dream is so real that when I wake up, I run my hand over my stomach just to check. Flat, thank god, but the pain is still there. The bottle of Pepto-Bismol whispers to me from the bathroom down the hall. It's on the bathroom sink next to a box of pills, the latest prescription for my serious attacks. My mother picked it up for me, like she always has, before I left. I debate whether to take the Pepto or the pills. Even half asleep, I place my pain at the correct level in the hierarchy I've developed over the years. With chronic pain, the general rule is that if you're even considering the prescription, take it.

With sleep now completely out of reach, I go to the attic and find an empty patch of floor just big enough for me to sit down and lean my back against the wall. A box poking out from under a trash bag catches my eye. It's a large shoebox, much like the one my mother uses for her receipts. Every time she spends a dime, the receipt goes into that box on top of the refrigerator. The box in my lap is full of receipts, too, but of a different sort.

The first photograph I take from the box is just a distorted blur—orange turned to yellow, red to pink. There's a person's chin and neck. Many of the pictures are like this, a flash of movement in front of the camera lens. Some are either too dark or fiery white to reveal anything. Others aren't so bad, though.

There are several of Papa and Grandmother standing on the porch—outtakes from the picture in the living room. Papa looks much younger. His belly hasn't yet grown round and soft. His skin is smooth. Grandmother must be equally younger, but it's hard to tell in the black-and-white picture. Her hair is white as ever and her face already bears the furrows and creases from her permanent scowl.

In every shot, Papa stands on the porch, smiling, while Grandmother is caught mid-march down the porch steps, finger pointing at someone in front of her, eyebrows pinched together, mouth half-open, no doubt barking instructions to the photographer. I put a couple of them aside. Grandmother could easily be cut out of them.

Deeper down in the box are treasures—pictures of my mother at her high school graduation, holding up her diploma next to Papa. He has his arm around her shoulder, squeezing her close to him. In a similar picture, my mother kisses Papa on the cheek. There is one of my mother flanked by Elizabeth and Audrey. There's one of my mother and Grandmother, standing side-by-side, close, but not one part of them touching. There's even one of my mother at her graduation party—I can tell because she's still wearing her mortarboard—opening a gift from a pile of presents. None of these are in any of Grandmother's photo albums.

There are pictures of birthday parties, Elizabeth and Audrey, their blonde curls tied in fluffy satin bows, sitting at the head of the table with a big frosted cake in front of them. Grandmother stands behind the birthday girls in these pictures, leaning in between them to help blow out the candles. Balloons, streamers, party hats and presents crowd the images.

My mother always told me there weren't any pictures of her as a baby or a little girl. No one was ever interested in taking her picture, she says. But there she is, sitting alone with her birthday cake. Her face is so round. She has chubby cheeks, made chubbier by her grin, and a bowl cut that makes her look like one of the Campbell's soup kids. Her birthday cake is big and fancy, too, made in the shape of a bunny rabbit.

I find pictures of the three little girls together: playing in the sand at the ocean, sitting by a camp fire with toasted marshmallows skewered on the end of sticks, on their bikes in front of a meadow covered in waves of purple and deep pink lupines, holding out handfuls of feed to goats at a petting zoo. Years of yesterdays are in the box, all the Easters and Christmases, Thanksgiving dinners and Fourth of July cookouts. In one picture, the three girls stand in a row in front of a Christmas tree. My mother looks about twelve, which would make Elizabeth and Audrey three. They wear matching robes. The way the quilted fabric of the robes stands away from their bodies, the girls look like a set of three little bells. Grandmother's robe matches the girls'. She crouches between Elizabeth and Audrey, with an arm around each of them, her chin resting on Elizabeth's shoulder. They all smile at the camera, except for my mother, whose eyes are on Grandmother and the twins. My mother could never compete with the twins' inherent cuteness.

The story behind this picture is a holiday favorite in our house, right up there with *It's a Wonderful Life* and *A Christmas Carol*, retold every Christmas night after my mother and I commiserate over Grandmother's lousy gifts—a set of kitchen utensils for my mother, a hairbrush for me. A coffee mug for my mother, socks for me. One year, she gave me a used board game with missing pieces. But the best was the year she gave me a pack of new underwear—just what every kid hopes to find under the Christmas tree.

Our Christmas ritual included a game in which we each had to find a creative use for these gems. One year, I made us wear the underwear on our heads, my mother banged her new wooden spoon on the bottom of a pot, and we marched around the house in a demented Christmas parade. After we collapsed on the floor laughing from whatever creative use we'd found for Grandmother's idea of presents, my mother would tell the story of "The Christmas Robes." Elizabeth, Audrey and Grandmother all had pink robes. My mother's was blue. "They thought it was so grand how they all matched," she'd say.

There is a story like this for almost every picture in the box. How Grandmother had just a few people over for cake and coffee when my mother graduated from high school, but there was a big party for the twins. How my mother never got the same attention on her birthday as the twins did on theirs. How Grandmother gave my mother all the chores on those vacations, leaving Elizabeth and Audrey to play.

My mother has a name for these stories. She calls them "The Slights." It's a multi-volume collection.

With them lined up in front of me on the floor, I see why the pictures were left in the attic. In each shot, someone's eyes are closed, or someone is caught mid-smile with a lopsided mouth. Some are out of focus, and most of the others have flesh-colored corners where the photographer's finger hung down into the frame.

There's something else about these pictures. My mother is rarely at the center of them. Only in a few birthday shots and at her high-school graduation is she in the middle of the group. The rest of the time, she is off to the side, at the edge of the family. For the first time, I see "The Slights," my mother's own hierarchy of pain. What do they prescribe for that?

By the time I finish sifting through the box, my stomach still hurts but feels much better. Sunlight filters through the attic windows, edging the boxes and suitcases in gold dust. A car goes by, and then another a few minutes later. Grandmother wants to see any photographs I find. So, I take the best of the pictures, the ones I want and the ones I know she'll want, and hide them in a drawer under my socks.

The pain in my stomach is still bad, but not bad enough to stop me from pulling on a pair of black nylon running shorts, a white sports bra — to hold my flat chest in place — and a white cotton-spandex shirt. The shirt is supposed to be tight fitting, but is almost loose on my bony frame.

I tie the laces on my new running shoes. They're expensive shoes, and my mother often scolds me for spending so much on them, but I ignore her. They're snug, and over the course of a few days, maybe a week, they'll become a second skin. They are thin and light, and when I take them off, they hold their shape. Every time I bring home a new pair, my mother throws a fit. "How can you spend so much on them?" she says, holding one shoe up between her thumb and forefinger, too expensive even to touch. "There's nothing to them!"

A certain kind of person would purposely buy the most expensive running shoes just to get under her mother's skin. But I'm not that kind of person.

I don't buy them. They are expensive after all — $95 at most shoe stores — but free for me.

Shoes are the easiest. Put them on and wander around until the store gets really busy or the staff is helping other customers. Then walk out.

Sometimes, stores put those big plastic anti-theft tags on shoes that expensive. If you can't convince the clerk to remove the tag so you can try them on properly, then you slip them into the foil-lined shopping bag you carry with you through the mall for just such an occasion. The foil blocks the sensors, and one hit with a hammer will remove the tags at home.

The new shoes feel good, already conforming to my feet as I jog up Grove Street and along the side streets that wind through Grandmother's neighborhood toward Main Street.

I pass the old train station first. The shack that was gray for so many years is now bright yellow with green and rust trim. A sign on the door says, "Welcome to the Green Hill Youth Center." Just past the train station is a big red building with paint peeling off the clapboards. There was an ice-cream shop there once. Papa and I used to walk there after dinner for soft-serve cones. The ice-cream shop is gone now, replaced by a video store. The Laundromat next door is still there. A pile of white bubbles painted on the storefront windows illustrates its name — Mountain O' Suds.

On the flat part of Main Street, I pass more antique shops than I remember, and a new ice cream and pastry shop. The steeple on the Methodist church is gone. There's a new playground on the common, next to the big sunken rectangle the town fills with water in the winter for a skating rink. I run past it all, the dance studio, the Grocery, the big brick shoebox of a Post Office. Past three more churches, their steeples intact, still pointing the way to eternal salvation. Past the coffee shop, where old men still sit at the counter nursing mugs of coffee. Past the fire station — a garage big enough for one engine — the elementary school, and the row of ancient maple trees that line the far end of Main Street, at the bottom of the hill. Beyond the trees and a margin of well-groomed lawns are the old houses, standing prim and proper like respectable Victorian ladies, elaborate gingerbread trim climbing up to their roofs like lace collars.

There are two styles of houses in Green Hill, the old Victorians, and the 1970s ski lodges, square, squat and sheathed in weathered cedar shingles.

I run up the huge hill of Main Street, keeping a steady pace. Blood pulses through my veins as my legs slip into rhythm. *Don't — shame — your — mother.* The words flow in and out of my mouth, carried on my breath. Two on the inhale, two on the exhale, one foot hitting the pavement with each word. The pain fades as the muscles in my legs, my arms, my back press against the back of my skin and surge as one up the hill.

As I near the top of the hill, I run faster, too fast. My legs and lungs burn. I feel like a little kid, outrunning monsters up the dark stairs to bed at night. The hill grows longer and taller under my feet. When I pass the Catholic Church at the top of the hill, I can't breathe anymore, but I can't stop. Something is about to grab my ankles.

I recklessly tear down the other side of the hill to the edge of town and the sign declaring that I am now leaving Green Hill. I pause at the sign, glare at it, stare it down. *I'm going to turn around and go home.* My eyes fill up. I wipe at them with the back of my hand, smearing sweat into them at the same time, making my eyes sting and water even more. *I swear to God, I'm going to turn around and go home.*

Beyond the sign, Route 302 winds west, toward Vermont.

I run back to Grandmother's.

Grandmother is waiting for me, nailed to her spot on the porch. She wears a tailored navy-blue dress that comes down to the middle of her shins. It's short-sleeved and cinched at the waist with a matching belt. Her hair sweeps into a French twist instead of its usual bun. She holds a small clutch purse and her hands are clad in white cotton gloves. She's dressed and ready to leave for Mass. As I rush up the steps, she pushes back the cuff of her glove and peers at her watch.

"Sorry," I say, as I brush past her into the house.

I rifle through my clothes. There are three pairs of jeans—$60 each, but free for me. Four pairs of gym shorts—$26.95 each at my college bookstore, but free for me. A pile of T-shirts from the Gap, Old Navy and Banana Republic—they average about $25 a piece. Free for me. My everyday work sneakers, which cost $50, but were free for me. A hooded sweatshirt, socks, underwear, pajamas—free, free, free and free.

The family dress code for Mass is no shorts, no jeans, no T-shirts, and no sneakers. But that's all I have. What happens if I break the dress code? Forget God, what would my mother say? Forget my mother *and* God; an even higher power waits for me on the porch.

"Oh, no," Grandmother says when I scurry down the stairs. My shirt is sticking to my skin, still wet from a quick shower. My damp hair hangs limp around my face, the ends just brushing the top of my shoulders. Grandmother looks me up and down. "Is that the best you can do?"

"I packed work clothes." I sit on the bottom step to put on my sneakers. Sneakers in church will surely earn me a seat on the express to Hell.

"Well, it won't do." She marches down the hallway. A door opens and then slams shut.

"Put this on." Grandmother holds out a lacy white cardigan. "And button it."

I put the sweater on and push the little pearl buttons through their respective holes. Grandmother, almost out the front door, looks back at me.

"Better," she says.

The Catholics have the only stone church in town, made from hunks of granite cleaved from the New Hampshire soil. Granite is so dense that heat can't penetrate it. So, while the Congregationalists, Methodists and Presbyterians sweat it out on the few hot summer days in Green Hill, we Catholics enjoy God's own air conditioning.

The heels of Grandmother's navy pumps click on the stone floor as we walk up the center aisle. Dim light filters through stained-glass windows that line the long walls leading up to the front of the church. The saints depicted on the windows watch us as we make our way to an empty pew just a few rows back from the altar. Grandmother lets me in first, giving herself the aisle seat. She pulls the kneeler down and lowers herself onto the maroon vinyl padding. I kneel down next to her, hands folded and eyes closed, and pray, as I've done so many other Sunday mornings. Grandmother always sat to my right, a sliver of space between us, and Papa on my left, holding out the misselette so I could follow along with the hymns.

The front of the church faces the mountain, which rises up out of the earth right in the center of a massive stained glass cross that takes up most of the wall behind the altar. Unlike the windows of the saints, with their intricate patterns of dark glass, the bulk of the cross is made of pale yellow glass, decorated with just two small bunches of purple grapes and two green grapevine leaves, so it's easy to see the mountain. Someone planned it this way, of course. They had the forethought to buy the land directly in front of the church to prevent a future building from blocking the view of the mountain, which is meant to remind God's flock of His capacity for great beauty and love. But it's also a reminder of His wrath. Lots of people die on that mountain.

The last time I was in this church, we sat in the very first pew with my mother and aunts. There were so many people that even God's own air conditioning failed—and who do you call to fix that? Audrey nearly fainted, and I was doubled over with the worst stomachache a ten-year-old has ever been known to suffer, before or since.

That was my first time in the church without Papa. This is the second. I put some missalettes on the seat beside me—anything to fill the empty space. Even through the white lace sweater, the bones in my spine press against the back of the wooden pew as I slouch in my seat, trying to make myself smaller next to Grandmother. Why did she have to dress up so much, with her white gloves and clutch purse?

A little boy wearing striped shorts and a Hawaiian shirt slides down our pew. The rest of his family shuffles in behind him. They all break the dress code, and with the most criminal violation—flip-flops. Just like all the other people who fill the pews around us, until it's Grandmother who looks out of place. Other old women are dressed in their Sunday best, but even they've given up the gloves.

The priest, a short middle-aged man with a potbelly, keeps the Mass short, which must just frost Grandmother's cake. "Jesus doesn't get time off in the summer, why should we?" she mutters as the closing hymn ends.

Back at the white Victorian, I start in the attic.

The first bag is full of shoes, Grandmother's, I can tell. The shoes are plain leather in dark colors with low heels. Just like the navy shoes she wore to church this morning. She owns a pair of shoes to match every outfit in her closet. Grandmother calls that "proper," as in "You have to learn to dress like a proper girl" or "I expect you to act like a proper girl." It's one of her favorite words.

Not one pair of shoes in the trash bag would pass for proper anymore. Not even for the church thrift store. They're bent into strange shapes from being smashed together so long.

They all have holes in the soles or broken heels, and they all stink like sour milk. The next bag contains baggy cotton sweaters with bright stripes and geometric shapes, the kind high-school girls wear in those bad 1980s movies I love so much. Since Grandmother wouldn't be caught dead wearing anything so cheerful, and since there are two of each sweater, they must have belonged to Elizabeth and Audrey.

By late afternoon, the hallway is almost completely blocked with fat, dusty trash bags headed to the thrift store for some other unfortunate family, or to the dump, and still only a small semicircle of floor has been freed. I haven't found anything that belonged to my mother.

At the end of the day, Grandmother and I sit down to Sunday dinner — roast turkey, mashed sweet potatoes topped with marshmallows, broccoli, asparagus and my most hated vegetable, turnip. All that and only two places set at the dining room table, where we eat surrounded by cabinets full of Grandmother's best china. For Sunday dinner, we use the good silver, cloth napkins and the good china, the white plates with pale pink flowers around the edge. It's some famous Japanese porcelain that was cheap when Grandmother and Papa got married and has since appreciated in value. Papa used to hold a plate up to the light and wave his hand behind it to show me how you could see through it. I make a sparse arrangement on my plate of a small slice of white meat and a little glob of sweet potatoes.

"That's all?" Grandmother says.

"I'm not hungry."

"You want more turkey?"

"I'm fine."

"You can't have just that. It's not enough. No wonder you're so thin."

"It's enough," I say, covering my plate with my hand. Our eyes lock for the first time in two days, Grandmother balancing a slice of turkey on the serving fork, me blocking my plate with my hand. Eventually, she gives in, puts the turkey on her own plate and begins cutting her food into tiny, polite bites. I nudge my sweet potatoes with my fork and push a bite past my lips, careful not to let anything drop on the white tablecloth. During another, similar dinner, years ago, Grandmother let a few drops of juice from a bowl of cranberry sauce drip onto a white tablecloth. After the meal, Grandmother spent hours scrubbing the stain out, using every brush and cleanser in her arsenal under the kitchen sink. She took a break from it only to put me to bed.

The next morning, I found the tablecloth in the trashcan. It's funny how she kept that broken beagle but not the tablecloth.

"You should have some broccoli," Grandmother says, lifting the lid off a glass dish that holds a broccoli crown, a steaming green brain sitting in a puddle of water.

"No, thank you."

"Just a little." Grandmother digs a large silver spoon into the green brain and drops a hunk of it on my plate. To an outsider, a dinner guest, the gesture would appear so benign. Grandmother seems so nice, so kind, but I know better. This is not a doting Nana, making sure her granddaughter is properly nourished. This is the witch from *Hansel and Gretel* fattening me up for the kill.

"And how about asparagus?" She pushes the post-lobotomy broccoli aside to make room for another steaming glass dish. "You have to try this asparagus," she says, placing several spears onto my plate. "And turnip, too. It's so good for you."

Grandmother does all this from her regular post at the end of the table closest to the kitchen, a habit from when Papa was still around. She'd never let him leave the table to get anything during a meal.

I sit in my old spot on the side of the table to her right. I imagine Papa sitting in his chair at the other end of the table, grunting his approval of the turkey and sweet potatoes and vegetables, especially the turnip, his favorite.

After every Sunday dinner, I'd clear the table and wash the dishes and pots and pans while Grandmother spent about half an hour wiping down the stove, the sink and all the counters. She'd use a sponge and hot soapy water first, then Windex and paper towel, and then a dry cloth. She scrubbed the sink with Comet, too. Salmonella never had a chance in her kitchen.

When we were done, I'd climb into Papa's lap to eat dessert, a layer cake or a pan of brownies Grandmother baked from scratch—not for me, though, for Papa, who liked something sweet after dinner. Grandmother always scolded me for sitting on Papa's lap while we ate. Not proper. But Papa never shooed me away.

After this meal, we finish the Sunday ritual the same way. I clear the table and wash the dishes and pots and pans. Grandmother takes her sponge and a bucket of hot soapy water to the stove and starts wiping down the kitchen.

That night, when the pain won't let me sleep, I take those pictures out from under my socks in the bureau drawer. There's one of my mother's birthday cake. It's big and fancy, just like her sisters' cake, and there are just as many balloons in that picture of her. In the one of her high school graduation party, there are lots of people watching my mother open her presents. She always told me she didn't get any presents, that Grandmother told people not to bring gifts. And it looks like some of the people in the picture have plates of food — real food, not just cake and coffee. In the vacation pictures, my mother is riding her bike, too, playing in the sand, and roasting marshmallows over the campfire. In each one of them, she's smiling, like she's enjoying herself.

A certain kind of person would see how the photographs don't exactly match her mother's description of her shunned childhood, would notice when things don't quite add up. But I'm not that kind of person.

2

The best way to survive life with Grandmother is total avoidance. My mother learned this a long time ago. After she had me, she tried to live with Papa and Grandmother. She waitressed at the coffee shop and helped Grandmother with Elizabeth and Audrey. She cooked and cleaned and did the laundry, and took care of me most of the time. That lasted a few months, until my mother finally realized that she wasn't a little girl anymore and doing everyone else's chores wasn't going to win her mother back. She took out some student loans, found a part-time job and took me to Massachusetts so she could finish her degree. She wanted to be a nurse and ended up working in the billing department in a health insurance company.

I was exactly one year old when my mother brought me back to Green Hill. During the summer, she needed to work full time and take a part-time job in order to make enough money to pay for her classes in the fall. Papa offered her money, but she wouldn't take it, and there was no one to take care of me while she was working all the time. So, at the end of May, my mother made the three-hour drive with me to Green Hill and then drove back home alone. My mother says I screamed and cried the whole way, harder and harder the closer we got to Grandmother's.

"I swear you were doing it on purpose, just to make me feel bad," my mother says.

By the time I was four, I'd learned not to cry.

It was an annual trip for ten years. Then Papa died and I begged my mother not to make me go there anymore. I told her I'd clean the house and cook dinner every night and get a job somehow. Surprisingly, she agreed. I was getting sicker and sicker by that time anyway, and my mother wanted me close by so she could take care of me, monitor my food and medications, and get me to the specialists. I still cleaned the house, cooked dinner every night and worked in my mother's office filing and shredding papers three days a week. When I think of it now, it seems like a lot to ask of a sick ten-year-old. But I offered, right?

To be honest, I would have been happy gutting fish all day or cleaning crappy toilets, as long as I wasn't with Grandmother. When Papa died, I promised myself I'd never go back.

So much for that.

Grandmother and I settle into a routine so that we need to interact with each other only once or twice a day. I run first thing in the morning, rain or shine, and then work in the attic all morning before it gets too hot, while Grandmother works downstairs, packing her valuables and cleaning.

In the afternoon, when Grandmother goes to work at the library, I work downstairs and finish what she started packing that morning. When she comes home from the library, I poke around in the basement and she repacks what I finished that afternoon. I go for another run or a walk after dinner, making sure to be home before dark, of course. And that leaves just an hour or so to suffer with each other in the den. I watch TV and try to ignore her ball of cotton string rolling in the bowl at her feet while she crochets. That woman cannot sit still, never could. Her hands, at least, are in constant motion. I wouldn't be surprised if they keep moving while she sleeps.

We see each other at lunch and dinner and at church on Sundays. And that is more than enough.

After a few weeks of this, the hallway outside the attic is stuffed with trash bags for the dump. There's still hardly any place to walk in the attic, so I basically have to claw my way over to the small chest of drawers in a back corner of the room. It's white wicker with pink knobs on the drawers. I open the first drawer very slowly, in case a mouse comes flying out at me, or worse, in case a mouse is lying dead in there. I've already found two dead mice up here. Grandmother gave me a dustpan to scoop up the bodies and then showed me where to toss them in the woods in the back yard. It was a bonding moment.

There's no mouse, but the little bureau does hold small things, like baby clothes. The top drawer holds pajamas—flannel nightgowns printed with pastel flowers, plaid farm animals, shooting stars and crescent moons, and knitted buntings with those little flaps that cover the baby's hands. I always loved dressing my doll in those.

The next drawer is full of tiny little pants and shirts in bright colors and patterns, made from the softest materials. The next drawer holds dresses, all ruffles and bows, ones the Two Flowers would wear. Others are plainer shifts with butterflies and flowers, ladybugs and bumblebees dancing along the hems and around the sleeves. I can tell by the tangle of thread and knots on the inside of the dresses that they were embroidered by hand. Factory-made stuff is all neat and tidy on the inside. I know handmade clothing when I see it—even clothes made so well no one is supposed to know they're handmade.

Growing up, if I wasn't wearing something my mother had made from scratch, then I was wearing something she bought at Goodwill and remade. My mother and I spent hours in the Stitches in Time fabric store looking at the pattern books and choosing the material for my mother's latest creation for me. We always went after one of my doctor appointments, which meant we were there almost every week.

"You need a new sundress," she'd say. "And how about a matching hat?"

I'd show her a pattern for handbags or capes or nightgowns, and she'd pull them all from the big file drawers that held the pattern envelopes.

"Oh, yes—you need that," she'd say. "Anything for my girl."

At home, she had boxes and boxes of patterns and enough fabric, buttons, zippers and Velcro to sew continuously for a decade without having to go back to Stitches in Time. Most of the patterns remained unused, as she stuck to the old standbys in my wardrobe—calico smock tops, elastic waist pants and skirts, and loose-fitting sundresses. I asked her once about a pattern we'd bought for a gray wool cape with special metal clasps.

"You think I have nothing better to do than sit home and sew for you," she said.

One time, though, she did get adventurous and make me a bathing suit. Now, I loved everything my mother made for me, especially those calico smock tops. I wish I could still wear them. But everyone can tell a homemade bathing suit. They never look right, all saggy in the butt and bunched up under the arms. How I longed for a store-bought bathing suit that year. I asked my mother for one.

"So, now you're too good for my sewing?" she said. She took the bathing suit she'd made and threw it in the trash. I couldn't go swimming for the rest of the summer because I had nothing to wear.

The dresses in the attic look like something my mother would make for me. I find a small white tag sewn inside. On the rectangle of white cotton, someone embroidered a red heart and the letters "C.G." in black thread. My initials.

All the clothes have the tag. They're all mine, made by my mother. They must have been left behind by accident, or maybe my mother gave the clothes to Elizabeth and Audrey to use with their dolls.

I shuffle backward, pulling the chest of drawers toward the attic door. I turn around and—

"Jeez!"

"I didn't mean to startle you," Grandmother says.

"I didn't hear you come up."

"I guess not, when you're dragging that piece of furniture like that. You should take the drawers out, pick it up and carry it. You'll scuff the floor."

I want to tell her that the floor hasn't seen the light of day in a hundred years, but she is already poking through the trash bags in the hallway. She opens a bag and pulls out a handful of tangled ribbon, lace and thread, one small portion of the giant nest of string in that bag.

"Why is this going to the dump?"

"It doesn't seem usable anymore to me. It's all knotted up."

She grabs more handfuls of it. "This is very good ribbon, perfectly good yarn and crochet thread. Someone could use it. Did you try to untangle it?"

"Yes," I say, nodding for emphasis so she'll believe the lie.

"Well, that's a shame," she says, moving to the next bag. It's the shoes.

"Now why are these going to the dump?"

"I went through them all. They're no good."

"None of them is any good?" she says, picking through the bag. Her perfect grammar does not escape notice. "This is a perfectly good shoe." The heel is still on, but the toe is bent up at a ninety-degree angle and there's a hole the size of a quarter in the sole.

"There's a hole in it."

"What's a little hole? Pay the cobbler to fix it and it's still cheaper than buying a new pair of shoes."

I want to tell her that cobblers died out somewhere between the dinosaurs and those newspaper barkers who used to yell "Extra! Extra!" on every street corner. But she is already flinging shoes out of the bag and onto the floor.

"These can all go to the thrift store at the church. Someone will be very happy to have them."

I can just picture it—some poor single mother on welfare, wondering how she's going to feed her six kids that day, crying tears of joy in the middle of the thrift store over Grandmother's bent-up brown shoes with holes in the soles.

"And what's in there?" she says, pointing to the chest of drawers.

"Just some baby clothes."

She yanks open a drawer and then stops. The woman who never stops moving turns into a statue for a full minute. Unheard of.

Grandmother slowly takes a dress in her hands. It's red gingham with a white lace collar and red ladybugs embroidered all over the front. Some of them have their wings open and are trailing a dotted line of black thread to show that they are flying. She holds it up in front of her.

I shouldn't say anything. Don't say anything.

"Those are mine. I think. Aren't they?"

"What makes you say that?"

"They have my initials in them." I lift the skirt and show her the tag. "My mother made them."

Grandmother folds the dress and puts it back in the drawer. "Heather and Iris can wear them."

Don't say anything. Just let it go.

"But they're mine."

Grandmother slides the drawer of dresses shut. "You have no use for baby clothes. Give them to your cousins."

Never hide things together. I learned this the hard way.

When I was in elementary school, the bus dropped me off at my mother's office every day, and I'd sit in the reception area practicing my spelling for the next day's test until it was time to leave. I liked to impress my mother on the way home with my knowledge of the silent "t" in the word "scratch" or the two different "g" sounds in the word "garbage."

"You are such a smart girl," she'd say.

Mr. Shine's office was next to my mother's. He was an older man whose bald head went so well with his last name. That's why I liked him. That, and the candy dish he kept on the front of his desk. The round, clear glass dish, cut like crystal, held red-and-white spiral peppermints and gold butterscotches. "Take a candy, sweetheart," he'd say, and I did, pulling on the ends of the wrapper and popping the round disk of sugar into my mouth. Then, when he turned back to his work, I'd slip another one or two into my pocket.

I stashed the candies in the bottom of my bag of doll clothes, someplace my mother never looked—until the day she cleaned my room, pitching toys I apparently didn't need anymore. She dumped the bag of doll clothes onto my bed and about 200 candies rained down, a mountain of peppermint with veins of gold butterscotch. She made me eat them all that night, without sucking on them.

"Chew it!" she yelled.

Not that any of them were worth savoring after number twenty. My stomach still turns every time a waiter tosses a handful of those pinwheel mints on the table with the check at the end of a nice dinner out. My mother usually holds one out to me.

"Mint?" she asks, and smiles at her own joke.

I puked up that red, white and gold syrup all night. My mother came with me to the bathroom every time, held my hair back, put cold compresses on my neck, soothed me. Every time, she asked me, in a comforting way, if I'd learned my lesson. I nodded and made a mental note to myself: *Don't hide everything together. Ever.*

At home, in my room, I have things stashed in holes behind the baseboards. Some of the floorboards in my closet lift up. All of the drawers in my bureau and my desk have false bottoms or false backs. I have things taped underneath my nightstand, my bookshelf. I've sewn things, small things, into clothing before, hidden them in the lining of jackets and coats.

With my mother nosing around my room all the time, I've
had to be clever. I've had to create spaces that are beyond her
reach and that only I know about. It's a little different with
Grandmother, who rarely came to the yellow bedroom when I
was a somewhat cute little kid, let alone now that I'm a big ugly
adult. Still, I don't like keeping everything together. I put the
three dresses—a blue stripe, the yellow check and the red
gingham—in the inside pocket of my suitcase and zip it shut.
Then I push the suitcase all the way to the back of the closet,
where Grandmother can't see it.

3

The church thrift store used to be a carriage house for the rectory, a white Victorian much like Grandmother's, across the parking lot from the church. A sign on the door reads, "Helping Hands," the words surrounded by little handprints stamped in bright colors. A Sunday school project for sure.

More than half the stuff I tagged for the dump is stuffed in my car for the thrift store. Grandmother refuses to throw anything out. Who does she think is going to use just the base of a blender? Who does she think is going to want pocketbooks with broken straps and busted zippers? Why does she insist that children's books with half the pages missing are still "perfectly good"? God is going to strike me down for trying to pass this trash off as charity.

There has to be a box or a bin outside where I can leave this stuff. There's always a bin. The Salvation Army has a bin. St. Vincent DePaul has a bin. Where is the Helping Hands bin?

Stupid Green Hill. They don't even have a bin.

The store is dark inside, mainly from all the clothes and bookshelves and boxes crowding out the light. It's as crammed as Grandmother's attic, but much more organized. The clothes are grouped by color on several racks that run almost the length of the store. All books are on a set of shelves; all glassware, grouped by color like the clothes, is on another set of shelves. Even the toys are sorted—one bin for stuffed animals, another for action figures and another for blocks and Legos, with puzzles and board games stacked on the floor nearby.

The store has the stale, mothball musk of old clothes. I know it well from all those late-summer shopping excursions with my mother. We hit every Goodwill and Salvation Army in the county searching for clothes she could remake for me to supplement the clothes she'd made from scratch.

"Helloooooooo!"

I stand still.

"Is someone there?"

Don't make a sound and no one will know I'm here.

"Ah-ha!" calls a woman from a brightly lit doorway behind a row of jewelry cases. She is short and round and wears a bright blue dress. The blousy top and full skirt make the woman look like a blueberry. She has short curly gray hair, cut in the style old women pay a hairdresser to refresh every few days. "I knew you'd come!"

The blueberry woman takes a couple of steps and then moves her cane forward. *Shuffle, shuffle, thud. Shuffle, shuffle, thud.* She waddles toward me, her legs no longer strong enough for her roundness. As she struggles to walk toward me, I slowly step backward. By the time she reaches me, I'm pressed up against the shop door.

"My goodness, my goodness!" the woman says, pressing her cheeks between her hands, which lifts her glasses off the bridge of her nose. "I knew it was you! I saw you in church, and I just knew it was you. Let me look at you." She puts her hands under my hands and lifts my arms the way a mother does when she wants to get the full effect of the wedding gown her daughter has just put on. She looks me up and down.

"You're so skinny. And your hair—it used to be so short! You look so different—but that only makes sense, right? You grew up! But I still knew it was you. You can't fool me!"

She lets go of my hands but continues to look me over, shaking her head, patting her cheek with her hand, sighing.

"Turn around, turn around."

"Excuse me?"

"Turn around, so I can get a good look at you."

Obedience has always been my best quality.

"Such a beautiful girl, a beautiful, beautiful girl," she says, as I slowly turn and come back around to face her. With the long blue dress draped over her roundness, the chubby cheeks that push her glasses off the bridge of her nose when she smiles, and the sing-song lilt of her voice, she reminds me of Cinderella's Fairy Godmother. She holds my face in her hands. They are warm and large, and I am overcome with the urge to rest the whole weight of my head in them. Then she wraps me in both of her arms. I freeze in her embrace. A trapped mouse comes to mind.

When she releases me, I feel like collapsing.

"Now," she says, holding me at arms' length. "Do you remember me?"

I can tell by the sound of her voice and her smile that she wants me to remember her, but I have no idea who she is.

"Oh, my," she says, her smile drooping just enough to let her glasses slide back down on the bridge of her nose. "You don't remember me." She waves her hand, shaking off her disappointment. "That's all right. It was a long time ago, and you were so small then. You just come with me."

She leads me back around the jewelry cases full of old necklaces and clip-on earrings. I pause by the case. A couple of rhinestone pins look promising.

I follow her into a large back room. Using her cane for support, she lowers herself into an old wooden chair and starts digging through a black leather bag with about fifty different pockets. She opens and closes one pocket after another, muttering to herself.

"Ah-ha, here it is. Look at this."

She holds out a small, square piece of paper to me. A photograph, the color slightly distorted with age. Two young women sit on a porch. I recognize the steps leading up to the porch, the gray floor, the white trim and the red screen door behind the women. The woman on the left wears her hair pulled back away from her face and a dark dress. Long, dark curls fall on the other woman's shoulders. She is chubby and wears a bright green dress. They sit close together and hold a baby between them. Both of them are smiling at the baby.

"That's you," the woman says, "and that right there is me." She points to the woman in the green dress. "I was still dying my hair, a losing battle even then." She chuckles at her own joke. "Now do you remember your Aunty Mable?"

"My aunt?"

"Well, not your real aunt. More like an adopted one."

"Oh," I say—my alternative to "what the hell are you talking about?"

"Your grandmother and I used to sit out on the porch all afternoon and sew and knit and talk while you slept or cooed in the pram."

"That's not my Grandmother."

"Yes, it is."

"No," I say, handing the picture back to Mable. "That's not her."

"Why do you say that?"

"That woman looks happy."

Mable's whole body starts to shake. Her glasses are way off the bridge of her nose. Out of her mouth comes this "hoo-hoo-hoo" sound, like an owl hopped up on caffeine. She slaps her knee a couple of times.

"She looks happy—that's rich!" Mable says. She lets out one last, long "hoooooooo" and wipes the corners of her eyes. "You're funny, you know that?"

I look behind me to see whom she's really talking to.

"Your grandmother and I were very close then, the very best of friends. Didn't she ever mention me?"

"No. She doesn't have friends."

"Everyone has friends. Even cranky old crones like your grandmother," Mable says. I want to laugh. "I'm sorry. I shouldn't say such things. It's not very nice. And your grandmother, she's had her share."

What does that mean, I wonder, "Had her share?" And who is this Aunt Mable—my Grandmother's friend? None of this fits together.

"Pull up a chair," Mable says. "Come sit." She has one hand on her chest and one on my wrist. I'm desperate to pull my hand away from her. She looks me in the eye, but not like Grandmother, whose X-ray vision penetrates my brain looking for errors, faults, and weaknesses. Not like my mother, whose eyes always deliver the full weight of her love for me. A baseball hurtling at my forehead at 95 miles per hour comes to mind. *Whack.*

Mable's eyes are soft, like the rest of her, and watery. Still, it makes me very uneasy.

I tell her where I went to elementary school and high school. I tell her about running and all my championships, about college and my job and why I am back in Green Hill. I give her everything I know about myself. It takes about five minutes.

"That's wonderful. Really wonderful." She shakes her head a few times. "I'm so glad."

She could cry. *Please, don't cry.*

"I really need to unload my car. I have some things for the store," I say.

"Oh, yes. I forgot—you're here for a reason." Mable uses the cane to hoist herself out of the chair. I offer my arm as extra support. "Let's see what your grandmother has so generously donated to us this time. You know, someone needs to tell her that shoes with holes in them are not the same as 'Holy' shoes."

I try not to, but I can't help it.

I smile.

4

Running was never about exercise or staying fit with me. It's a necessity. The habit started when I was seven, running home from school at the end of each day, my scrawny legs propelled by an overwhelming feeling that someone was chasing me, someone was going to catch me. Even during those summers in Green Hill, I ran, to the Grocery for Grandmother, to the Post Office, the Library. When Grandmother sent me to run an errand for her, that's what I did.

By the time I was in junior high, I spent my summers at home and running was part of a training regimen prescribed by my junior varsity track coach and strongly recommended by one of my many doctors. The running kept the ulcer under control better than most of the medications. Stress aggravated the ulcer, one doctor told my mother, and the running released the stress. My mother left the appointment asking me, "What do you know about stress? What stress can you possibly have?"

After one year of junior varsity track and cross-country, I was bumped to the varsity team in eighth grade—the youngest kid in school history ever to make varsity. My mother still tells people that fact. I picked off the top runners on my team one by one, and then toppled the top runners in our district, the county and the state. By my sophomore year in high school, no one could touch me—and not just in distance races. I could sprint, too. I never fully shook that feeling of being chased.

I'd taken three state championships and every other top title by the time I graduated from high school, a fact my mother shared with everyone she met. At the supermarket, she'd just blurt out my latest win to whoever was near her, to total strangers. She told every teller at the bank about all the colleges and universities around the country courting me with full scholarships. "Guess I won't be needing that college fund after all," she'd say. And I'd close my eyes and whisper my little chant. "Disappear, disappear, disappear."

When it came time to choose a college, I wanted to get out of New England. But my mother wouldn't let me leave Massachusetts. I wanted to go to a big school. We visited the state university, where the student center was more like a bustling city train station. There were so many different people there, and not just different from each other or me—I mean, just *different*. A guy with a head full of long dreadlocks, for example, girls dressed in Army fatigues, another guy with a giant bar code tattooed on the back of his neck. My skin tingled with the prospect of losing myself in all those people and emerging as someone else, someone new.

"I'm not letting you go to a school full of freaks and losers," my mother said as we left the campus tour. She had someplace else in mind, a college that had everything she was looking for—small, elite, and all girls.

At "The Convent," as I called it, I took hard classes and earned good grades—my scholarship was never in jeopardy. Never, or I'd be in purgatory right now and my mother would be serving a life sentence for murder. I majored in English. I read all the time anyway—everything from trashy romance novels to the classics. Victorian novels have always been my favorite. They're just a more crafty version of those romances, the emotion made all the more intense for its repression in Victorian drawing rooms. My mother let me study English, but only if I also got a teaching certificate.

Don't get me wrong—I had choices. My mother told me I could go to college for teaching, medicine or law. Anything else was a waste of money.

I earned my teaching certificate and also added a lot of shiny trophies and medals to the case in the lobby of The Convent's athletic center and to the one in my mother's living room. When she remodeled our house a couple of years ago, she had a special cabinet made to hold all of my winnings.

Those trophies and medals nearly extinguished the ulcer. And now I'm back in Green Hill.

Every morning, my stomach is on fire. So, I get up, get dressed and put on my running shoes.

I have my favorite paths through Green Hill. Some days, I turn left at the end of Grove Street and run through the relatively flat condo complex, where skiers spend the winter and golfers spend the summer. If I'm out early enough in the morning, I hop the stone wall that separates the condos from the golf course and run the rolling hills of the course before the golfers are up. At the Grocery and the Post Office, the buzz is that a bull moose with a full rack has been spotted on the course several times in the last couple of months.

Papa and I saw so many moose together — along the roadside, even in the woods on our walks — but never a bull. Ever since he died, I've had this idea that Papa will one day appear to me as a bull moose.

Most often, like today, I turn right at the end of Grove Street and head toward the hill on Main Street. It's a long and difficult route, and on clear days I'm rewarded with one of the best views of Mount Washington. My legs move to the rhythm of my mantra: *Don't — shame — your — mother. Don't — shame — your — mother.*

No one but me is crazy enough to run up Main Street. But I swear I hear another pair of feet hitting the pavement behind me. I run a little faster.

"Hey!" a voice calls behind me. I keep running.

"Wait!" The voice is closer. It's the guy with the lawnmower, the one with the gorgeous arm. Arms. There are two of them.

I keep running.

"Wait!" he calls again, his huffing and puffing tugging at my sympathy. I slow down and jog in place until he catches up. He stands bent forward with his hands on his knees, breathing hard. Judging by the way he runs, clomping up the street in heavy work boots, at the way he needs to work at breathing, jogging is not something he does regularly. Still, he looks fit. He finally straightens up, and I am about eye-level with his chest. It's a nice chest, well formed like those beautiful arms. He has nice legs, too. He must play soccer. In high school, soccer players always had the best legs. His right leg, though, is badly scarred from the knee down, like it's been burned or chewed up in some machine. Not that I'm looking; not that I ever looked. I'm definitely not looking. I'm much more interested in that car going by, my hands, my shoes, that gum wrapper on the ground. Is that Wrigley's or Juicy Fruit?

"I know you," he says, still a little out of breath. He smiles, revealing the gap between his two front teeth. Some people find that appealing. Lauren Hutton built an entire modeling career in the gap between her teeth.

"I know you from before," he says.

During those long summers in Green Hill, I had two respites from Grandmother's constant scrutiny: Papa and this boy I used to visit on the two afternoons each week Grandmother worked at the library.

Ethan Matthews.

He had that gap between his two front teeth even then.

"You're Connie Grey," he says. "It's me—Ethan."

"Yeah," I say. "I'm really sorry about the other day."

"Forget it," he says, waving me off. "I've been racking my brain for two days trying to put a name with your face. And then, just now, I saw you go by the coffee shop and it finally hit me who you were. How long has it been? Ten years?"

"Twelve."

"Wow, twelve years," he says, shaking his head. "It doesn't seem that long ago we were out hiking through our back woods, does it?"

I just smile and nod.

"What are you doing back here?"

"I'm helping my grandmother move."

"That's right, I heard she was moving. Well, that's great. That you're here," he says awkwardly. "How long are you staying?"

"I don't know." My feet start to move in place—small steps, not quite jogging.

"We should get together sometime, to catch up, you know."

"Yeah," I say, my legs starting to carry me away. "I don't know. I'm pretty busy."

"Well, I live in town, right next door to my parents, actually," Ethan calls after me, as I jog away. "Come by anytime."

I wave to him and continue down the other side of the hill, toward the edge of town.

I see him everywhere now. He's behind me in line at the Grocery whenever I stop to buy Grandmother's milk and eggs.

He's at the Post Office when I drop off Grandmother's mail. He's at the hardware store when I need more packing tape.

And, more often than not, when I stop at the top of Main
Street to look at Mount Washington, I also see Ethan Matthews
trudging up the hill. "Hey," he says, or "Hey, Connie." If it's
sunny and dry, he says "Nice day for it." You can't do anything
anywhere in New England on one of those beautiful days
without someone saying "Nice day for it." It's a law.

Sometimes he just nods, and other times he asks, "How are
ya?" Then I know he wants me to stop and chat. Naturally, I run
for my life.

Every time I see him, all I can think of is smashing into his
lawnmower. The memory of it gets worse and worse until just a
hint of the thought of it makes me break out in hives. When I
spot him in the Grocery, I crouch down in one of the aisles and
pretend I'm reading a cereal box label just to avoid him. When I
see him out jogging, I keep running to the edge of town, to the
sign that says, "You are now leaving Green Hill." I pass him on
my way back to the top of the hill, when he's on his way to the
sign.

I replay the accident over and over in my mind, redoing my
encounter with him until our conversation goes exactly the way I
want, with me as the epitome of cool. In my latest version, I give
him a check right there, on the spot, for a new mower, top of the
line.

"But that's too much," he says.

"It's nothing, really," I say. "Please take it. I insist."

Imagine that—me, insisting on something. Wow.

My mother would want me to pay him for the damage I
caused. She'd want me to mail him a check. But what if the check
gets lost in the mail? That would be bad, right? My mother
wouldn't want that. I decide to take a walk on a Monday night,
hoping Grandmother will forget about it by the time she has her
weekly conversation with my mother next Sunday.

After dinner, I change into a clean pair of shorts and a plain
white T-shirt. I leave my hair down and look at my reflection in
the window, tucking and untucking my hair behind my ears
about a thousand times before deciding to leave it tucked back
away from my face. If only Grandmother had a mirror somewhere
in the house. She probably has one in her bedroom, but I'm not
about to stroll into the lion's den and start poking through her

stuff. But it doesn't even matter. No one cares what I look like anyway.

Grandmother sits in the den. A ball of cotton twine rolls in a bowl at her feet as she works it into a web of lace between her fingers. The bottom of the stairs and the front door are behind her. I creep to the door, not making a sound, and slowly push the door open. It creaks. Traitor.

"Where are you going?" she says, not even bothering to turn around.

"Just for a walk."

"It'll be dark soon."

"Not for a while."

"Soon enough," she says. "You shouldn't be out alone after dark."

Right, I want to say, *because a gang of Hassids might jump me at dusk.*

"I'll be back before dark."

"Where are you going?"

"Just to the center of town and back."

The ball of cotton comes to a rest for a moment. Then it starts rolling again.

"Don't be long."

My hands clench into fists and then release over and over again as I walk up Main Street. It's a cool evening, but I'm sweating. I smell my armpits a couple of times just to make sure I put on deodorant. I feel inside my pocket every five seconds, as if the check could jump out at will. I wrote it in my bedroom after dinner, with my mother's fountain pen.

At the town common, a large oval of grass with tall maple trees around the edge that splits Main Street into two roads, I go left onto Rocky Brook Road. Like just about everything in Green Hill, the road is named for what it is. After about twenty feet, the pavement turns into rutted dirt. I watch my step. I can't go home with a sprained ankle.

Trees form a tunnel over the road. There's a curve, and just beyond the curve, a brook gurgles from one side of the road, through a big metal pipe to the other side. The brook's voice bubbles up from the water running over and around the rocks and pebbles that line the streambed.

The Matthews live on the other side of the brook, around another sharp bend. The house is dark, except for the porch light. A cloud of moths and mosquitoes swarm around it. Oh well, no one home. Too bad. Guess I'll just leave the check in the door. But there's also a barn, separated from the house by a wide patch of dirt. The windows above the barn door are bright. Music spills outside. It's old-fashioned music, like big band jazz. A figure passes behind one of the curtains. I dart behind a tree. The sky overhead grows deeper and deeper shades of purple as I debate whether to stay behind the tree or walk across the street and knock on his door like a normal girl. It's always such an effort for me to act like a normal girl.

I have all the social skills of a nuclear physicist and even fewer than that when it comes to interacting with members of the opposite sex. Under normal circumstances, when people approach me, I forget how to speak English. My vocabulary shrinks to a paltry collection of grunts: "wow," "yeah," "oh." I punctuate these by nodding my head and trying to chuckle. Sometimes, I snort.

When faced with a boy, I just about go catatonic.

I was never allowed to be around boys, really. My mother does not allow boyfriends, and no boys as friends either because boys as friends lead to only one thing—boyfriends. Other girls have similar rules about boys, of course—only most of them have a time limit. No boys until high school. No dating until the age of sixteen. My mother's rule, however, doesn't have an expiration date.

Growing up, boy-girl parties were out of the question, which just about killed whatever shreds of a social life were still in my grasp. My only girlfriends were either on the track or cross country teams, or girls I tutored. And they weren't really friends, just people I happened to be with because we did the same thing. I tried to go out with them socially once. We went out for ice cream. A group of boys stopped at our table to say hello. My mother, who'd been watching us from her car in the parking lot, grabbed me by the arm and marched me out. She didn't say a word to me for days.

The only sex education I received was in school, during gym class. They split up the girls and boys one day in fourth grade and showed each group a seventies-era film about puberty. It was called *When Budding Girls Blossom* or something equally corny and sick. Everyone snickered and giggled in the dark as we learned about menstruation and maxi pads. Gross. That film was so stupid, trying to make it look like having your period could actually be fun. At one point, the film showed a girl riding her bike. When she stopped, she said, real cheery, with dimples in her cheeks, "Wearing a maxi pad makes riding my bike so much more comfortable."

The only sex education I received from my mother was through ABC *After-School Specials* involving abortions that ended badly, with either the girl dying of blood poisoning or the boy committing suicide. And after the show, she'd always tell me that if I ever got myself pregnant, she'd kill me.

I don't want to be afraid of boys for the rest of my life. I do not want to grow up to be the official Crazy Cat Lady of whatever town I end up living in. But I stay glued to the tree where I'm hiding. And I'd hate to think what my mother would do if she found out I went to Ethan Matthews' apartment alone, at night. She will find out with Grandmother watching my every move. I knock my forehead into the tree a few times. The bark is rough. It hurts. It scratches.

I run back to Grandmother's, just to stop my body from shaking.

Just for kicks, I think I'll change my running route. My evening walk reminded me what a nice spot Rocky Brook Road is. It's shady and quiet, no traffic, perfect for a jog.

5

The stairs are my favorite place to eavesdrop. At home and at Grandmother's, the stairs are close to the kitchen phone. I can sit on the stairs, shielded by a low wall, and listen as long as I want. My mother has called Grandmother every Sunday of my whole life. I was six when I first snuck out of bed and crept halfway down the stairs to listen to my mother talk to Grandmother. By the time I was seven I was addicted. Listening to my mother tell Grandmother how wonderful I was gave me a fix that's better than an endorphin high after a marathon or even after eating a whole bag of Pixy sticks.

"She's such a good girl, so bright and talented," she'd say, and a wave of relief and pure joy would wash over me. My whole body felt tingly and alive. That must have been what it was like to be just a little bit drunk.

But there were other kinds of conversations, like when my advanced physics grade slipped from an A to a B or when someone beat me on the track. Everyone has a bad day now and then, right?

"She doesn't even try, doesn't even care," my mother would say. "She's so lazy I want to strangle her sometimes. I want to kill her."

And then there were all of my medical problems. I've always been a sick kid — food allergies, the ulcer and all kinds of other gastrointestinal problems. When I was a baby, my mother said I had such bad respiratory problems I'd stop breathing. She took me to the emergency room about once a week, and they had to resuscitate me at the hospital half a dozen times. It wasn't easy for my mother, taking care of me alone, rushing me to the emergency room, dealing with the doctors and nurses, pushing them to take care of me properly and find out what was wrong with me.

"You don't know what it's like," she'd whimper to Grandmother. "I have to be on all the time, taking care of her all the time. I try so hard to be a good mother. What did I do to deserve this?"

At Grandmother's, I have the chance to hear the other end of the conversation, but she always lets the kitchen door swing shut—on purpose, no doubt. I strain to extract words from her mumblings.

"Constance!"

She's the only one who calls me by my full name. I hate it.

Before I go down the stairs, I take a few steps in place to make it sound like I'm coming down the hall from the attic. It gives me some time to think about what I will say when my mother starts grilling me about that walk I took last week. Grandmother must have told her about it, how I'd changed my clothes, how I'd run into the house and straight upstairs afterward, how rude and secretive I am.

"How are you?" my mother asks. There's enough sugar in her voice to make my teeth hurt.

"Fine."

"And how is everything going? Are you working hard?"

"Yes."

"Are you doing what she says?"

"Yes."

"Exactly what she says?"

"Yes," I say. "I'm doing what she says."

"Good girl," she says, and that wave of relief hits me. "Just do everything exactly the way she wants it, and don't get into any trouble." She knows how Grandmother sets her snares. "And how are you feeling? How's your stomach?"

"It's all right," I say.

"Connie," she says, her voice taking that tone that says she thinks she's caught me in a lie. "I know when you're hurting. It's bothering you, isn't it?"

"Yes," I say, conjuring up some pain for her.

"You're probably not eating right, are you?" she says, frustration rising in her voice. "I swear if I didn't watch your every meal, that ulcer would've eaten through your stomach by now."

"I'm sorry."

"You have to be more careful," she says. "So, have you found time to have any fun while you're there?"

"Not really – but that's all right."

There's a pause. My stomach flutters for real this time.

"You're still mad at me, aren't you?"

"No, I'm not mad at you."

"After all I've done for you – all I've sacrificed – this is the thanks I get," she says, her voice breaking with anger, or maybe sadness. "You know I can't stand it when you're mad at me. I just can't stand it."

I swallow and arrange the words in my mind. "I'm not mad at you. It's fine, just lots of work. I'll be home before you know it."

"I love you," she says, softly.

"I love you too."

"I'll talk to your grandmother about your diet."

I'm about to hang up when she says my name again.

"Did you happen to see my fountain pen anywhere before you left?"

"No."

"Damn it," she hisses under her breath.

"Sorry," I say coolly. "Your favorite pen, too, right?"

"I love that pen. And you know how I hate it when I can't find something. It was right there and now it's gone."

Grandmother is in her chair in the den. The web between her fingers has grown to about the size of a dessert plate. I walk quickly past her to the stairs.

"What did your mother have to say?"

The question makes me realize that my mother didn't ask me about my walk. And she still hasn't asked me about my car. It's been weeks since the accident, and Grandmother has had plenty of opportunities to tell my mother about the dent.

"Nothing really," I say. Grandmother is looking in her pattern book, not listening. I scoot up the stairs.

Just before the phone rang, I came across a box in one of the many corners of the attic. Although it's just a big square room, the attic has way more than four corners in which to hide things. The cardboard box, large enough to hold one of those mini fridges, was sealed up with packing tape and buried under piles and piles of old clothes and smelly blankets. I cut the tape with my car key.

A lump immediately forms in my throat and it's hard to breathe. I want to laugh. I want to cry. Papa is here with me right now, and yet he is gone. His absence is a lead weight on my chest.

Papa made the oversized toy train in the box. It was waiting for me when I arrived for my fifth summer in Green Hill, which is my first memory of being left here. I stood in the driveway at the white Victorian, holding my mother's hand with the grip of someone dangling over a cliff. My mother took two steps toward Papa and Grandmother, who were standing on the porch. I didn't budge. At five, I knew what was going on. My mother knelt in front of me.

"You know there's nothing else I can do," she said, smoothing my hair and tucking it behind my ears. "Just don't cry. I hate it when you cry. Be my good girl."

She stood and took a step forward. I still didn't move. But when I realized that my mother wasn't going to turn back to comfort me again, I followed her up the driveway and across the lawn to the house. Papa came down the steps, kissed my mother on the cheek and took my hand. Grandmother stayed on the porch.

I didn't cry that day, not even when Papa and I waved to my mother as she pulled out of the driveway. I didn't cry because I wasn't thinking about her driving away without me. When Papa took my hand just minutes before, he whispered to me that there was something special for me in the backyard.

Papa made the train during the winter. He loved woodworking and had his own shop full of saws and carving knives and vises and sawhorses. I loved to watch him work in the shop. He could make anything, from tiny little birdhouses to complicated rocking chairs and walking sticks with troll faces carved into the handle. He taught me to whittle one summer. The dull knife he gave me to use is still hidden in my room at home, under a floorboard in my closet. It was our secret. If Grandmother ever caught me playing with a knife, she probably would have stabbed me with it just to prove that knives are dangerous. I especially loved the power saw, though. I loved the sound of it and the smell of fresh sawdust.

The train has an engine, three cars and a caboose. The cars are basically open boxes, big enough to hold dolls, stuffed animals and a good load of pebbles or sticks or sand. Each car is painted in a bright, solid color — blue, yellow, green, black for the engine and red for the caboose. The train is as bright now as when I last saw it, years ago. The wheels, the large, white-walled kind used on toy wagons, still turn smoothly. Even the metal clips and loops that connect the cars are shiny silver.

The day Papa gave me the train, he had it all set up, the train cars linked together and a new doll sitting in the green car ready for a ride. She has short brown hair like mine was and a pink gingham dress, just like one I had. She looks good as new, although a little misshapen from being smashed in the bottom of the box — poor thing. Grandmother probably did that to her on purpose, hoping it would act as a voodoo doll. I fluff her dress and again find my mother's tag sewn into the side of her body, the red heart and my initials in black. She and Papa must have planned it together then. He made the train, and she made the doll to look just like me.

The soft knocking sound of a ball of cotton string rolling in its bowl tells me Grandmother is still busy with her lace. I creep back to the attic and quietly set up the train on the floor. I put the Connie doll in the green car and slowly pull the engine forward. The wheels rumble on the wood floor, so I stop. Nervous that the noise has caught Grandmother's attention, I start to take the train apart.

There's a *thud, thud, thud* on the stairs. I pull the cars apart as fast as I can. Her shoes are clicking down the hallway toward the door. I throw it all back in the box.

The door flies open. I hide the Connie doll and the open box behind me.

"What are you doing?"

"Nothing," I say. "Just cleaning up a few things."

"Well, it's getting late. I think it's time to stop."

"Sure."

Grandmother turns to leave, but I don't move.

"I said it's time to stop. Come downstairs."

"Sure," I say. "Sure. I'm coming." And as I say the words, I drop the Connie doll into the box behind me, praying for a soft landing. I'll come back for her later.

6

I walk out Grandmother's front door, carrying an overstuffed trash bag for the Helping Hands. I strain to look around the bag at my feet so I don't trip.

"Hey."

I peek over the top of the bag, but I already know who it is. Ethan is here every Friday morning to mow Grandmother's lawn, trim the shrubs and weed the flowerbeds. So far I've been able to avoid him. If I'd remembered what day it was, I would have avoided him today, too. I haven't showered yet. My hair is greasy and I smell.

He has that smile on his face. The gap between his front teeth makes him look a little goofy, but in a nice way. It makes him look like someone who loves to laugh. He has a nice face, too, clear and warm and open. A friendly dog comes to mind. It's a face to be trusted.

"Hey." I walk down the porch steps and head for my car.

"How are you?"

"Fine," I say, without turning around.

Grandmother comes out the front door.

"Ethan!" she says, greeting him with a big smile and a handshake, the two-handed kind. I've never even gotten that from her.

I spot a leatherman on the tailgate of Ethan's pickup truck.

Papa carried a leatherman everywhere. Sometimes he'd let me play with it. I loved pulling out all the tools. I thought it was the neatest thing, all those different screwdrivers and pliers wrapped up in one contraption small enough to fit in your pocket. Magic.

Papa's was red. Ethan's is black.

Now, any normal girl would just talk to the guy, maybe even ask him out for coffee. Not me.

The leatherman finds its way into my pocket.

Ethan and Grandmother are still chatting on the porch. Ethan nods and smiles at me as I try to scurry by. But Grandmother grabs my arm and yanks me toward her.

"Ethan, you remember Connie, don't you?"

I want to run away, but Grandmother holds me in place, her fingers digging into my arm.

"Sure, I do," he says. "We've run into each other a couple times already." He winks at me. My mouth goes dry, and all the blood in my body drains to the bottom of my feet.

"That wasn't you she hit on her way here, was it?"

A sudden thunderstorm would be good right now. Just one strike of lightning would put me out of my misery.

"No, that wasn't me," Ethan says. "Sorry to hear it, though. I hope you're all right."

"She's fine," Grandmother says. "I'm just glad it wasn't you. I would have felt terrible if it were you."

"Well, I better get to work," he says. I turn to go back inside. "Nice seeing you again, Connie," he calls to my back. I let the screen door slam shut behind me.

When I go back out to my car a few minutes later with another trash bag for the thrift store, a shiny new lawnmower is in the driveway, and Ethan is poking around the back of his truck. An open toolbox is on the tailgate. Half the tools are strewn on the truck bed. After I stuff the second bag into my back seat, I lean against my car and watch him search.

"Lose something?" I ask.

"I can't seem to find my leatherman," he says, crouching to look under the truck.

"Leatherman?"

"Yeah. It's kind of like a Swiss army knife, but with more stuff on it. It was right here, and now I can't find it." He puts his hands on his hips and shakes his head. "Gotta get a new one, I guess."

"Sorry," I say.

"Oh, well. These things happen. Especially when you're a slob like me," he says, standing and brushing off his knees. There's no hair on his leg where the gnarled scar is. "Hey, isn't that you I see running by my place every morning?"

"Me? No."

"Really? I swore it was you."

"It's not me. I don't run that street. It's too flat and rutted up. I prefer Main Street, more of a challenge."

"Well, you must have a double in town then. You know what they say, everyone has a twin."

"Sure," I say. "My double."

"Hey, I hope you don't mind my little fib to your Grandmother. I figured if you didn't already tell her, she didn't need to know."

"Yeah, thanks."

I think of the leatherman tucked away upstairs. I wish I could just ask him out for coffee.

It's a hot day, with no clouds in the sky to block the sun even for a short respite. It's a good day to be on the mountain, which is outlined perfectly against the blue sky at the bottom of Main Street. An old Hassidic man is trudging up the hill. Sweat pours down his face, which he keeps wiping with a handkerchief after every few steps. I wonder where he's going, why he's walking in this heat under all those heavy clothes. Talk about commitment.

The Helping Hands is dark inside and cool, thanks to the church's shadow. I recognize things in the thrift store now. Those bad 1980s sweaters are stacked on shelves with the other sweaters, a column of color among the stoic grays and browns. Grandmother's old raincoats are hanging with the other coats. Most of the sheets and blankets were good enough to resell, and even a few pairs of Grandmother's old shoes made the cut. A woman is trying on a navy-blue pair. She is short and small. She has long black hair, parted in the middle and pulled into a long braid down her back. She's wearing a bright pink T-shirt and black leggings.

Everything about her shouts "poor," her old-fashioned hair, her unstylish outfit, the creases etched into her face long before the age of wrinkles, the way she looks in my direction but never makes eye contact. I can almost smell her failures on her as I press by to get to the back room.

Mable stands at the ironing board, pressing a blue-and-white striped shirt. She's a tomato today—red dress, red shoes, red necklace and earrings. No navy blue, or brown, or gray for Mable.

"There's my girl!" she says. I know she wants me to hug her, but I back away.

"I've got more to bring in," I say.

When I bring in the last bag, she is sitting in her usual chair. I stand across the room.

"Come sit. Visit with me a while."

I sit down in a chair equally as far away from her.

"Give an old woman a break and come here by me, would you? I can barely see you all the way over there." She laughs.

I pull my chair closer to her, but not too close.

"I hope your Grandmother isn't working you too hard."

"There's a lot to do."

"On a day like today, you'll end up with heatstroke."

"I'm fine."

"Make sure you drink plenty of water. She lets you drink water, doesn't she?"

I want to laugh, but all I do is blink a couple of times.

"I'm joking," she says, patting my knee. Her hand is warm. Part of me wants to hold it against my skin, let it warm me to the core. "Such a serious girl." She nods at the pile of junk I just unloaded in her already cramped workroom. "You've been busy. Your grandmother must have you working all the time."

"Pretty much," I say, relishing the sympathy just the littlest bit. "There's nothing else to do, anyway."

"This must be just a terrible bore for you, living with your Grandmother, not knowing anyone. I imagine you must just about hate it. Oh, but you do know one person, don't you? You must remember Ethan Matthews."

"Yes," I say. "I remember. We've met."

"Oh, how wonderful!" she squeals, squishing her cheeks between her hands. "He's such a nice boy!"

Mable tells me what a great guy Ethan is, how he took over his dad's business when his dad got sick with Parkinson's and how he lives in that apartment in the barn at his parents' house to help his mother and father. How he takes care of the church landscaping for nothing.

He's obviously flawless, perfect.

"He was a wonderful skier, too. Won all sorts of races, was on his way to the Olympics even." She sighs and shakes her head.

"Then what?" I ask.

"He was in a terrible car accident. His leg was hurt very badly. You've seen the scar, I'm sure. He can never ski again."

"That's terrible," I say, trying to imagine what my life would be like if I couldn't run anymore.

Mable looks at me out of the corners of her eyes and grins. "He's a handsome boy," she says in her singsong voice. Heat flares up behind the skin on my face. "And he's *sing*-gle."

"I don't have time for anything like that," I say, standing up to leave.

"Oh, I wasn't suggesting anything at all," she says. But I can tell by the way she winks and looks at me, trying to be sly, that she is suggesting something that I can't even begin to consider.

"I have to go," I say, my stomach roaring.

"Oh, stay. Don't rush off."

"I have to. Too much work to do."

"Well," she says. "I suppose I have work to do, too." She hoists herself off her chair and waddles over to the ironing board. "Don't work too hard," she calls as I leave.

The lights are on in the Matthews' house this evening. From behind my tree across the street, I watch Ethan and his parents have dinner. I hear his father's voice. He gets up from the table now and then. Sometimes Ethan gets up to help him, taking his father's elbow and guiding him out of the dining room to a darker part of the house.

There are only three of them at the table, only one more than the gathering around Grandmother's table a little earlier. But it sounds like more. The way they talk and laugh so easily makes it sound like ten people. I wish I could get closer, to hear what they say to each other.

Ethan helps his mother clear the table and then helps his father out of the dining room. His dad is stooped a little, and he takes small shuffling steps. It takes them a while to get out of the room. A light goes on in the front room on the other side of the house. Ethan deposits his dad in a chair and turns on the TV. He goes to leave the room, but his dad stops him. Ethan bends down, so his dad can wrap his arms around him. His dad's arm shakes uncontrollably. I hardly notice it, though, over the contact between father and son.

About every inch of my body is covered with mosquito bites by the time Ethan comes out the front door of his parents' house and walks toward the barn and his apartment. I dart behind my tree and step on a twig. *Snap!*

Ethan's footsteps stop.

I close my eyes tight—because that helps so much. I hold my breath so there's no possibility of making a sound.

"Hello?" Ethan calls.

I close my eyes even tighter.

His feet start moving again. They get louder.

"Hello?" he says again. He can't be ten feet from my tree.

In my head, I whisper, "Disappear. Disappear. Disappear."

His feet start moving again, getting softer this time. He clomps up the stairs to the door of his apartment. The door opens, and then shuts. I peek around my tree. The lights are on inside, and he is nowhere to be seen. I wait a while longer though, until the stars poke through the darkness, before I run away.

7

I am curled on a bed with this pain in my stomach. I cry and cry, pound my fists into my belly. The pain makes me cry, but there's something else, too, something very wrong.

Everything is too white, blinding. The bed is cold, with metal railings so high I have to climb them to get out. The floor is ice on my bare feet. The pain in my stomach is so bad I can't stand up straight. I'm afraid to even look at it, because it could be an open gash, it hurts that badly. I make it to the door of the room. I call my mother, call and call.

I look down the bright hallway, down the white walls lined with more white doors. I scream to my mother. She looks at me and then walks away down the hall. I want what's in her arms. She holds it carefully, something wrapped in a yellow blanket. She holds it like the most delicate piece of porcelain. I call to my mother to come back and give it to me. Give it back.

She looks at me again before disappearing down another hallway.

I want to run after her, but the pain pulls me down to the floor, pulls me into the tightest ball, my forehead touching my knees.

I wake up curled into this ball. Sweat soaks into my nightshirt. I remind myself to breathe. I have to breathe in order to get up and get to my pills. I make my way down the hall, stooped and shuffling like Ethan's father. The pill goes down easy. I lay on the cold floor for a while, recovering from the dream as much as from the ulcer. What is in my mother's arms? The way she hides it from me, I can't help but think it's mine.

When the pill starts to work, I get up and go to the attic.

That day I'd uncovered a metal filing cabinet, the short kind with two drawers. The top drawer is locked, so I start with the bottom one. I pull it open very slowly, so Grandmother won't hear. The sour smell of moldy paper fills my nose. It's packed with school papers from Elizabeth and Audrey. Their entire academic career is archived here, starting at the front of the drawer with yellowed newsprint filled with crayon scrawls and smears of crusty finger paint. Farther back, the crayon is replaced by pencil, then pen. The newsprint turns to lined notebook paper and that onionskin paper once used in typewriters.

I flip through every folder, checking their grades and reading teacher comments. Elizabeth can't spell. Wite-Out makes her term papers for senior English look like an astronomy project. The rest of her tests and papers bleed red pen. Audrey was a consistent D student in math. I like looking at her tests, figuring the unfinished problems in my head. Neither of them were stellar students. My chin goes up half an inch thinking about how much better a student I am than they were. From the way my mother complains about their total perfection, and the way Grandmother fawns all over them, I never would've guessed they were so...average.

My mother's schoolwork is, of course, absent. I wonder what kind of grades she earned, what the teacher comments were. I bet she was as good a student as I was—probably even better.

That top drawer won't budge. Fortunately, Grandmother wears her hair in a bun every day, a French twist for special occasions, both of which require lots of bobby pins. She keeps them in every room of the house, so she can capture and restrain any stray strands of hair. She'll be washing dishes, a few loose strands will fall into her face, and, mid-wash, she'll open the kitchen cabinet in front of her, take a bobby pin from a small pile on the shelf and pin the hair back. Even with her rubber dishwashing gloves on.

I slide one of the silver bobby pins into the lock and slowly turn it, twist it, jiggle it a little, until I hear that satisfying "click" of the lock giving way. The drawer opens.

More papers. Bank statements this time, cancelled checks and tax returns. It's just like Grandmother to hang onto Papa's payroll checks from thirty years ago. And not just in a random box, but neatly filed, chronologically, just in case the IRS ever dares to audit her.

There's a box sitting in the bottom of the drawer beneath all those hanging folders. It's a thin rectangular box made of wood with a brass plate on the front. A keyhole is cut into the brass plate and is surrounded by an elaborate design etched into the brass. It's a nice box, heavy. And of course, it's locked.

With a few twists of the bobby pin, the lid pushes up beneath my thumb.

The letter "S" is on top, cut from navy blue felt and dotted with four gold pins in the shape of footballs. It reminds me of the purple and white "B" hanging in our living room at home. My letter has a lot more than four pins, each one carefully arranged by my mother. "So they look their best," she said. The "S" must have been Papa's, although I don't remember if he played football. He was tall and broad and very strong, so I imagine he did.

Underneath the "S" is a puzzling collection, a metal rectangle with some kind of military symbol attached to one side and the words "Semper Fi" engraved beneath it. I lift the lid—a lighter. I never knew Papa smoked either.

There's a green pocketknife bearing the Boy Scouts insignia. I pull out the blades one by one. They look brand new.

A small silver cross, so tarnished it's almost black, hangs from an equally tarnished chain. Only the bottom tip of the cross still has enough shine left to glint in the dusky light coming in from the newly freed windows.

There's also a gold locket, without a chain. It's shut tight, so I use the pocketknife to pry it open. It finally gives, sending the locket flying, the knife jabbing dangerously close to my thumb. Imagine me bursting into Grandmother's bedroom with the stump of my thumb spewing blood everywhere. Good morning!

When I find the locket on the floor nearby, Grandmother looks back at me from the small black-and-white photograph inside. I don't recognize her at first, the smooth, slightly plump face, and the relaxed smile. She can't be much older than twenty there.

All that's left is a dark blue box, the kind that usually holds expensive jewelry. Surprisingly, there's no lock on it. A star rests against the velvet lining. Its five points are beveled, to give it depth. A second, tiny star, sits in its center.

A ribbon is attached to the star's top point. The ribbon is striped, a thin blue one down the middle, wide red ones on each side and slivers of white separating the colors and finishing the edges. I slide my fingers underneath the star and let it rest against my palm. It hasn't tarnished, but I rub it with the corner

of my nightshirt anyway. I put the box down on the floor with
the lighter, the pocketknife, the cross and the locket.

They must be Papa's things from the Army. No— what is
Semper Fi? The Marines—I just saw a bumper sticker for the
Marines with that slogan. I knew Papa had been in a war, but I
never knew which one. He never talked about it much and I was
too young to know what questions to ask. When he died, I was
still in grade school, learning about the Pilgrims and Plimoth
Plantation.

My father was in a war, too. David Hobbs. A boy my
mother met at the start of her second year of college. Love at first
sight, she said. After only a month, David Hobbs told my mother
he was going to propose to her someday. I can't imagine what
my mother must have felt when he said that. It was probably just
like that movie where that redheaded guy finally gives those
diamond earrings to the girl who's truly loved him all along.
And so what if she dresses a little weird and plays the drums?
He loves her anyway.

Before the end of my mother's sophomore year, David
Hobbs was gone. He'd had enough of college. He wanted to do
something real, my mother said. So, he enlisted, and was killed
just about as soon as he set foot in Vietnam. My mother didn't
offer any more details than that.

A month after she got the news, my mother was back in
Green Hill, telling Papa and Grandmother that she was
pregnant. She told them after one of Grandmother's big Sunday
dinners. My mother says Grandmother didn't say a word, just
marched up to my mother's room, the yellow bedroom, and
started packing up my mother's clothes. The way my mother
tells it, Grandmother quietly removed each drawer out of the
bureau, dumped the contents into a trash bag and put the
drawer back. She emptied the closet, took everything off the
bureau and the night stand—the figurines, my mother's jewelry
box, the book she was reading—and put them in the trash bag,
too. She stripped the bed and took down the curtains, erasing
my mother's presence.

When she started tearing at the wallpaper, trying to rip it
off the walls, Papa grabbed Grandmother's wrists and shook her
a little. "Enough," he told her.

Grandmother looked at my mother, who was curled up against the doorjamb, making herself as small as possible. My mother's red face was wet with tears, but she made no sound. She hid her face in the crook of her arm. Grandmother looked back at Papa. "Enough," he said again, and Grandmother marched out of the room.

My mother tells me this story all the time, usually after her third martini.

"What I went through for you," she says.

What my mother remembers most about that night is that look from Grandmother. Her eyes weren't blue anymore, my mother says, but solid black. At first, my mother was amazed that a person's eyes could change color like that. She saw all of Grandmother's fury swirling in those black eyes like a gathering storm. But that wasn't what made my mother look away; that wasn't what made her cry all night long, even while she and Papa put her room back together. It was when my mother saw all that fury dissipate and disappear that she couldn't look at Grandmother anymore. It was when she saw Grandmother's face relax, when her forehead became smooth, when her jaw released, when her eyes turned from black back to blue. My mother watched all the feeling drain from Grandmother's face and knew that her mother didn't feel anything for her anymore, not even hate. My mother always says, given the choice, she'd take hate over nothing.

What I remember most from the story is that all of my mother's clothes, all of them, even the essentials—underwear, socks, shoes, pajamas—fit in one trash bag. I think of it now, as I sit amid the ruins in the attic.

By contrast, my mother only told me about my father once and with so little detail that I wrote it down as soon as she left my bedroom.

David Hobbs. When my high school class went to Washington, D.C. for our senior trip, I asked my English teacher to please make a rubbing of his name on the memorial for me. I keep the rubbing and the story of my father, the papers folded up small, under a floorboard under my nightstand, somewhere my mother would never think to look.

I like to imagine that my father was a lot like Papa, that he smiled a lot and had a similar low, soothing voice. And in a way,

I'm kind of glad he was killed so soon, before he had a chance to kill anyone else. I don't like the idea of my father killing anyone. I prefer to think of him as the kind of man who would spend an entire winter building a big wooden train for his daughter.

I wish I had more of my father, something more than just the rubbing of his name, something that belonged to him — a key chain, his watch, or a favorite baseball card. If I had things like that of his, I sure wouldn't keep them locked away. I'd keep them close to me, in my nightstand maybe, instead of under it, just to feel my father near me, watching over me while I sleep, there with me when I wake up.

Judging by the way she had it all locked up, Grandmother doesn't want anyone to know she has this stuff, which means she won't say anything about a missing piece. That's the great thing about stealing from people who hide stuff — they can't even admit that something's been stolen. It's a special kind of torture for them, because they can't ask for help, can't rant and rave about what they've lost.

I take the star, and the lighter, too, just because it's so cool.

Grandmother stirs downstairs. She sets the teakettle on the stove, starts the toaster and pulls a chair out from the table. She will soon find the box full of bank papers I left in the hallway, the wooden box used as a paperweight on top.

"Constance!"

I trot halfway down the stairs and look at her over the railing. She stands just outside the kitchen with her arms crossed, her lips pursed into a wrinkly prune. She's wound tight this morning, just like her hair, which is already wrapped into a perfect bun. She probably ironed her bathrobe before putting it on this morning.

The box is by the front door, at the opposite end of the hallway.

"Yes?"

"Come down here please," she says. I walk the rest of the way down, one arm over my stomach. It's time for another pill. They don't seem to be working very well.

Grandmother nods her pointy chin at the box of papers. "Where did you find that?"

"There was a filing cabinet up there. I thought you'd want to look at the papers before I just threw them away."

"Not the papers. I mean *that*," she says, jabbing her finger at the wooden box. "Where did you find it?"

"You mean this?" I say, picking up the box. It's hard not to smile.

"Yes."

I walk toward her with the box, and I swear she moves backward. So, I move closer and closer to her, until her back is up against the kitchen door. She crosses her arms tighter and alternately looks at the floor and some point down the hall behind me.

"This was under all the papers. It's locked, so I don't know what to do with it."

"It was locked when you found it?" she says.

"Yes. But I couldn't find a key, so I can't open it." I shake the box gently from side to side. "Sounds like something's inside."

"I'm sure it's nothing important. Probably little baubles that belonged to Elizabeth."

"Then I can just throw it out, right? If it's nothing important?"

The tension in the air between us could support the box if I took my hand out from underneath it.

"No," Grandmother says, snatching the box from my hand. "Don't throw it out. There could be something valuable in there—something valuable to Audrey, I mean."

"I thought it was Elizabeth's box."

"Right. Did I say Audrey? I meant Elizabeth. Something valuable to Elizabeth. And it's a nice box. I'm sure one of them will want it." She backs into the kitchen door, pushing it open. "I'll figure something out."

Up at the Helping Hands, Mable is ironing, as usual. I take what is becoming my seat, a molded plastic chair with metal legs. Vintage mustard yellow public-school furniture, it would probably fetch a couple hundred dollars on EBay. As Mable babbles on to me about the weather, I wonder how I can get the chair out of here without getting caught.

"How close were you and my Grandmother?" I ask.

"Very close, very close. She was like a sister to me."

"So, you probably know a lot about my Grandmother?"

"Probably."

"And about my grandfather?"

Mable stops ironing. The look in her eyes makes me sit very still, as if a monster is standing right behind me about to dig its fangs into my neck.

"Who?" she says.

"My grandfather. Papa."

She laughs a little, pats her chest with her hand. "Oh, yes! Your Papa. Of course." She waddles over and sits in the chair next to me. "Your Papa was just about the nicest man I ever knew."

"I was just wondering if you knew anything about him and the war."

"Oh, not much," Mable says. "He didn't talk about it. Nobody did back then. It's not like now, how people talk about all their problems and figure things out. People just kept it all in and kept on going." She pulls a handkerchief from under her watchband and dabs her forehead with it. "It's better now, I think. Although some people still hang on to their silly secrets."

"So, you don't know anything about Papa and the war?"

"Just that he was in the Army."

"You mean, the Marines."

"No, I'm pretty sure it was the Army," Mable says.

"But I found some stuff in my Grandmother's attic, some of his things from the war. There was a lighter. It says *Semper Fi* on the side. *Semper Fi* — that's the Marines."

"Huh," Mable says.

"There was a varsity letter with his pins on it from football. Did you know he played football?"

"No." Mable wipes her upper lip with her handkerchief.

"And a Boy Scouts pocket knife, a silver cross, a locket with Grandmother's picture in it."

"How nice," she says, with about as much enthusiasm as a rock. Only rocks don't sweat like Mable's sweating now.

"And some kind of medal."

Mable puts her hand on my knee. It's warm against my skin, almost hot. Drops of sweat run down her forehead. "What kind of medal? What did it look like?"

I describe the star to her, the beveled points and the small star in the middle, the striped ribbon pinned to the velvet lining of the box.

"But what color is the medal?" she asks.

"It's sort of coppery, but not quite the color of a penny."

Her hand falls from my knee, and she looks away from me.

"A Bronze Star," she says.

"Yeah, bronze is the right word. It's bronze."

"What? Yes, bronze," she says, turning back to me. "I mean no, not bronze star—Bronze Star—capital B, capital S. The military medal. For bravery or something like that."

"Bravery." My chest expands to accommodate the louder, bolder pounding of my heart. "What did he do to get it?"

"I don't know." Mable wipes the handkerchief over her whole face, which is so red it's starting to turn purple to match the color of her dress. She breathes heavily.

I rest my hand on her arm. Her skin is warm and a little moist. "Are you all right?"

"I'm fine," she says. "Just a little warm. It's so hot today, you know. The heat gets to me sometimes." She closes her eyes and takes a few deep breaths, wipes her upper lip again. "Could you please turn off that iron for me? It's heating up this room something awful."

I turn the dial on the iron until the red light goes out. I open the door on the other side of the room. Mable's dress billows in the breeze. She smiles, her eyes still closed.

"You should ask your grandmother about that star."

"I can't ask her about something like that."

"I bet she'd love to talk to you about your grandfather," Mable says.

"She doesn't like to talk to me about anything."

"Have you ever tried asking her?"

Now, I'm the one starting to sweat, even with the breeze coming through the door.

"No," I say. "It would be pointless anyway. She'd just get upset and then be mad at me for making her upset, and the two of us would be even more miserable together."

Mable gets up and waddles back to the ironing board.

"It's better if I just don't say anything to her," I say, trying to explain.

"You don't know if you don't try," Mable says.

She might have known Grandmother once, but she doesn't know her now.

At the coffee shop, I slide into an empty booth. My skin squeaks as it rubs against the red vinyl covering the bench seat. The coffee shop is vintage 1952. There's a counter with a Formica top speckled with silver, a dark wood base and aluminum trim. The stools at the counter are shiny aluminum with red vinyl seats to match seats on the booths, which are made of the same dark wood as the base of the counter. Old pictures of Mount Washington hang just above the wood paneling that covers the bottom half of the walls. There are ladies in elaborate dresses waiting to take a horse and buggy up the mountain, a tank-like vehicle called a Tucker Sno-Cat crawling across the mountain's snow-encrusted summit cone, the famous snow arch in Tuckerman's Ravine, climbers gathered at the AMC huts preparing to make their ascent, people being carried down the mountain after being rescued. There are nineteenth-century maps of the presidential range and yellowed pages from *Among the Clouds*, the old summit newspaper.

I come here in the afternoons to have a cup of coffee and read, while Grandmother thinks I'm at the Helping Hands or the dump. The owner, a small man with short, white hair and glasses in heavy black frames, doesn't even ask me what I want anymore. He brings me a white ceramic mug of coffee, a little pitcher of cream and some sugar packets. I watch the cream expand like a thunderhead pushing up through the dark liquid and stir three sugars into the mix.

My mother has told Grandmother what I can and cannot have. Coffee is on the "no" list taped to Grandmother's refrigerator door. It's one of my trigger foods. Picture my stomach as a bed of hot embers. Sometimes the embers lay dormant, but given the right fuel, they flare into a roaring fire that leaves me curled in the fetal position on the cold bathroom floor.

Coffee is often the right fuel, along with deep-fried foods, like French fries and onion rings, and pizza, spaghetti, nachos, with or without salsa, and a million others—basically anything worth eating.

I've always had to be careful about what I eat. Beyond careful. For a while, growing up, I had horrible food allergies. I was maybe five or six and had just gotten past all my respiratory problems when the food allergies started. In fact, the doctors started to think that maybe my respiratory problems were caused by food allergies. I was allergic to all the typical stuff like nuts and shellfish, but then I started getting these awful rashes or fits of vomiting whenever I ate any fruits, or sometimes certain vegetables would do it, or just regular meat—chicken, beef, pork, it didn't matter. The doctors took me off protein for a while, and then they thought it was glucose. Glucose is in almost everything, which means I was pretty much allergic to food in general. The doctors used my body like a human pincushion, pricking my flesh a thousand times to try to isolate the allergy. I can still feel the raw, stinging ache on my skin. Multiply one tiny paper cut by a thousand.

After every session with the needles, my mother took me shopping for new doll clothes and new sets of dishes and fake foods for my toy kitchen. She'd grab doll dresses and pajamas off the shelves by the handful, throw giant boxes of toy kitchen accessories into our shopping cart.

"Anything for my brave girl," she'd say, holding my hand as we cruised the aisles for more toys. "You were so good at the doctor today. I really think we're getting somewhere now."

The allergy tests always came back negative. But that wasn't good enough for my mother. There was something wrong with me, and she wasn't going to stop until someone paid proper attention to my illnesses.

"You've got to help me," she'd say to the next doctor. "She's such a sick kid. Please help me."

My mother has had to watch my diet, first to keep my histamines from sending me into anaphylaxis, and then to stop the ulcer from eating through the walls of my stomach. For the ulcer, she keeps me on a bland diet of toast, dry turkey sandwiches, white rice and plain broiled fish and chicken. Doesn't sound too bad? Try eating it every day of your life for ten years and get back to me then. It's all just tasteless paste in my mouth now. In some ways, I preferred the feeding tubes. My mother pressured each doctor, insisting that I'd starve to death if they didn't give me a feeding tube. Eventually, they each succumbed to her entreaties, slitting my skin—cutting into me—to insert the tube. At least then I didn't have to put another spoonful of plain white rice or dry chicken in my mouth for a few weeks. This thick liquid just went straight through the little tube and into my stomach. If only the incision didn't get infected so easily and so badly, I'd probably still have one now just to avoid the whole eating thing. The infections left the patch of shiny wrinkled skin on the right side of my abdomen, just below my ribs.

Even though I'll pay later, a cup of coffee, light and sweet, is heaven to me. I take a sip and swirl it around in my mouth. It tastes like coffee ice cream.

The only people in the coffee shop at this time of day are a few old men who sit at the counter, toward the back, sipping from their own mugs. The little white-haired man chats with them as he cleans the grill behind the counter and prepares for tomorrow's breakfast rush.

My booth is about halfway back. I always take the seat facing the front of the shop and its storefront windows.

I open my book and am instantly sucked into the world kept between its covers. Is this the day Mr. Darcy declares his love for Elizabeth Bennett? Or when she finally realizes she's in love with him? I have to know. I already know, since I've read this book about eighteen times. But all the suspense and intrigue in the quiet English drawing rooms still kills me. That's what I love about nineteenth-century novels. They're nothing but soap operas in disguise.

"Hey, I thought that was you."

I jump a little in my seat, jolted back to reality. Ethan has already slid into the other side of the booth.

"Mind if I join you?" he says.

I keep my book open, and shake my head a little. He takes this to mean that I don't mind, rather than "don't sit here." I'm not sure what I meant by it.

Ethan waves to the white-haired man behind the counter, who is chopping buckets full of potatoes and onions for tomorrow morning's hash browns. He wipes his hands on his apron and pours a mug of coffee for Ethan.

"Is this guy bothering you?" the white-haired man asks me as he puts the mug and another little pitcher of cream on the table in front of Ethan. The hint of a French accent in his voice reveals his Canadian origins.

"No," I say, laughing a little.

"You call me if he gives you any trouble, eh?" he says, punching Ethan in the arm. They exchange smiles.

"Go back to your potatoes," Ethan says.

Ethan pours the cream into his mug, slowly stirs it and takes a sip. I keep my head down, nose in my book.

"I think this is the first time I've seen you sitting still," Ethan says, after a long silence. I look up from my book. "Not running, I mean."

"Yeah, well," I say, and go back to pretending to read.

"You're some kind of runner, I hear," he says. "Your grandmother. She tells everyone in town about you."

I look up. "I don't believe that." I say, shaking my head, laughing a little at the thought of it. "That doesn't sound like her."

"Well, believe what you want, but I can probably name every trophy and medal you ever won. Youngest person ever to run on the varsity cross country team at your school, right?"

How could he know that? Ethan breaks into that big grin.

"I'm right, aren't I?" he says, nodding really big.

"I thought you would've forgotten about me by now," I say.

"It's been hard to forget about you with your grandmother telling me all about you all the time."

I want to ask him if we're talking about the same woman, the old, bony white-haired woman who lives on Grove Street.

"Besides, how could I forget you when we had so much fun?" Ethan says. "I couldn't wait for summer because finally there'd be another kid my age in town."

We both laugh. Half of my brain is engaged in the conversation. The other half is busy reminding me that my mother is several hours away in Massachusetts. She cannot possibly be watching me; she will not come marching into the coffee shop and drag me out.

Ethan talks about all the Indian toys he used to have, headdresses and rubber tomahawks and plastic spears, drums and belts with pouches for stones and feathers and whatever cool stuff we found in the woods. None of those toys are very politically correct now, but then, we'd tie on the vinyl headbands, the bright blue, red and yellow feathers—very authentic—sticking up around our heads, pick up the spears and tomahawks and head for the woods. We spent hours out there, pretending to hunt or setting up forts. One summer, Ethan read a book about the California gold rush and we spent weeks wading in the brook down the street, panning for gold in his mother's aluminum pie plates. We'd save the shiny grains that settled into the bottom of our pie pans, planning how we would spend our treasure.

"You were always going to buy a buffalo," I say.

"And you were going to buy a pony."

"Yeah, well," I say. "I really wanted a power saw, like my grandfather."

"That's way better than a pony."

We talk about those afternoons when Ethan's mother sent us into the woods with a backpack full of sandwiches and cookies—everything allergy proofed—and two canteens filled with juice.

"What is it about drinking out of a canteen?" I say.

"I know. When you're a kid, it seems so magical."

We'd hike all afternoon, careful never to go beyond the low stone wall left behind by a farmer years ago. We'd pretend we were on an expedition to Mount Washington, hike for a couple of hours, and then sit on top of one of the big boulders in the woods and eat our sandwiches and cookies. One day, we spotted a deer through the leaves. We held our breath until it spotted us and ran.

"I don't think we moved for another hour after that, hoping it would come back," Ethan says. The memory of the two of us frozen on the rock makes me smile.

One afternoon during my tenth summer in Green Hill, Ethan and I were playing in a camping tent his mother had set up in the front yard. We'd made it into our Indian fort. We were in the tent telling stories, when the zipper on the tent door ripped open. Grandmother jabbed her hand in my face, the charms on her gold bracelet jingling in front of my nose. She pulled me out of the tent on my knees and marched ahead of me to the car. I ran to keep up. Ethan's mother said something to us about Papa.

Not long after that, Papa died.

That was the last time I saw Ethan Matthews.

"I always wondered what happened to you," he says. "You never came back, not even to visit."

"My mom needed me at home," I say.

"Well, hey, you should come by, you know?" Ethan says. "My mom and dad would love to see you."

"Maybe. I don't know. I'm really busy at my Grandmother's."

"Are you telling me you couldn't use a little break?" Ethan leans in closer to me, his beautiful arms so tan against the white tabletop. His handsome face so close, I almost want to touch it. "I work for her, remember?" he whispers, winking at me after the last word.

I laugh, but something in the window at the front of the shop catches my eye. A shock of white, and the air is sucked right out of my lungs.

Grandmother is watching me through the window. When our eyes meet, she quickly looks away and marches down the sidewalk.

Ethan is saying something to me, but I can't hear him over the blood pounding in my ears. I leave a dollar on the table for my coffee and stumble out of the booth.

"Hey," Ethan calls, as I run out the door.

Out on the sidewalk, I look up and down Main Street, but Grandmother is gone.

She is hanging up her purse in the hall closet when I burst through the screen door after running all the way back. She must've sped home, because I never even saw her car on the road.

"Yes?" she says.

"It wasn't planned," I say.

"What wasn't planned?"

"At the coffee shop, just now. I was there alone, and he came in and sat down at my booth."

"I don't understand."

"I didn't plan it," I say, slower this time, so she gets my meaning. "When you talk to my mother, make sure you tell her I didn't plan to meet him there."

She shuts the closet door and stands there a moment before slowly walking over to me. She starts to say something, but stops, starts again, trying to find the words.

"You're an adult now," Grandmother says. "What you do is no concern of mine."

The corners of her mouth twitch as she looks at me. Then she turns and goes to the kitchen, where she has been packing all of the antique plates and kitchen utensils that decorate the walls.

I think my mother was wrong. No feeling at all from Grandmother isn't so bad.

8

Someone should do a study on Green Hill, New Hampshire, to find out why it's such a magnet for misfit losers. Not only is Green Hill the Hassidic capital of the world during the summer, it's also the lesbian capital of the world. And while the northern migration of the Hassidics remains a mystery, the lesbians flock here because of the retreat center—The North Country Womyn's Center. Yes, that's "women" spelled with a "y" — because "men" have no place in the word.

Now, I have nothing against the Hassids or the lesbians, or gay men for that matter. I lived among lesbians for four years at the Convent, ate with them, even shared a bathroom with them, and it never bothered me. Frankly, I don't care what two people do with each other behind closed doors.

On one end of the spectrum are the Hassidic women, who wear fancy dresses and heavy nylons all the time, and who cut their hair off as some symbolic act when they get married and then wear coiffed wigs to hide their shorn hair. And on the other end of the spectrum are the lesbians, who wear baggy shorts and boxy shirts, who don't shave their legs and who cut their hair as short as possible just to prove they can.

Both ends of the spectrum have converged in the Grocery today, with me somewhere in the middle, the only true misfit loser in the bunch. But at least I'm making an effort to blend in.

Grandmother needs more Comet and Windex. Johnson Wax should give her stock for keeping them in business all these years.

There are two cans of Comet and three bottles of Windex left. I put all of them in the plastic grocery basket. It's tough to take the five-finger discount on five big bottles of cleanser, even for an expert like me. I wander through the store looking for something else. I put my basket on the floor and sneak long glances at Hassidic women and the lesbians while I pretend to be searching for the right color of blush from what seems an endless amount of choices. What's the difference between "buff," "nude" and "soft suede?" And I'm no make-up expert, but why would someone wear nude-colored blush? Isn't the point of blush to make your skin pinker or redder or something? Color doesn't matter to me, anyway. The mirrors are what count, and there aren't many. My hand roves the rack, hovering a moment over each compact until I find just what I'm looking for, a round green compact of "bubble gum pink" powder with a mirror in the lid. I hold the mirror up in front of my face and watch everyone behind me. Mirrors are great for looking at other people.

A woman behind me to the left surveys the selection of pain relievers. Her hair falls on her shoulders, but I can tell she's a lesbian. I went to a women's college, remember?

I'll be working with a lesbian at the academy. Faith McGuire was one of the hundred people who interviewed me on my second visit to the academy this spring. She's the dean of students. And since I'll be living there as a residential assistant in one of the dorms in addition to teaching, she needed to interview me, too, along with every English teacher on the faculty, the assistant headmaster, the kitchen staff and the groundskeeper.

Dean McGuire is a big woman, taller and wider than me, but not fat. Just solid. When she stood in front of me with her hands on her hips, she resembled a very sturdy wall. She had long straight red hair that she wore without bangs. On the day we met, her hair was unrestrained, falling down her back and over her shoulders. They were the shoulders of a football player or at least a professional swimmer.

Dean McGuire is the Lesbian/Bisexual Association advisor at the academy. She also counsels girls who are coming out and runs workshops about safe sex. She gave me all that in the first five minutes of my interview.

"And I'm gay, in case you haven't figured that out yet," she said, "and in the true sense of the word. I'm both happy and homosexual." She laughed.

I wanted to tell her that a sense of mystery could be a very powerful quality in a person.

"So, what made you choose a women's college?" she said.

"I liked the environment. It's a safe place to be, a good place to learn."

That's my standard answer. What was I supposed to say —
"my mother told me to?" Was I supposed to say that my mother
just about wrote my application essay for me, that she insisted
on sitting in on my admissions interview? Was I supposed to say
she called the track coaches every week with my latest times?

If I told people this, they wouldn't understand. My mother
only does these things because she wants the best for me. I
wanted to go to college in Florida or California, but my mother
said the best schools are in New England. She's right. I wanted
to go to a big university, but she said a small school would be
best for me. And I graduated *magna cum laude*. The college my
mother chose for me really was a safe environment and a good
place to learn, even if she did remind me that I could've learned
more. There is one level of honors higher than *magna cum laude*.

And there were other considerations, namely the ulcer.

"You need to be able to come home if you're sick, so I can
take care of you," she said. "And I need to be able to bring you
the right foods."

She even considered moving to an apartment near campus,
so she could cook all my meals. Then she got promoted at work
and decided it was best to stay home and keep her job. Instead,
she made me come home every weekend, so she could monitor
my diet and medications and give me a supply of bland food to
bring back with me. While the other girls got chocolate chip
cookies and homemade brownies in their care packages, I got
Saltines, two bags of rice and a six-pack of Pepto-Bismol.

My mother cried all summer long before I moved to college
for the first time. "I can't believe you're leaving me," she said.
"Who's going to take care of you? Who's going to make sure you
eat right?"

The day before I packed for freshmen orientation — when I
was still naïve enough to call new students at a women's college
freshmen and not first-years — I packed the car with all my
things. My mother couldn't help me in her condition — collapsed
on my bed crying her eyes out. "I won't help you leave me!" she
said.

When I finished loading the car, I went to her. The shades in
my room were drawn, the lights off. She was sprawled face
down on my bed. Her back rose and fell with her breath. I
thought she was asleep.

"What do you want?" she hissed.

"The car's packed."

"Is that all?"

"Yes." I waited, hoping she would at least look at me. Then I started to leave the room.

"Don't go," she said, sitting up. "Please, don't go," and the sobbing started anew. I rushed to her side "I'm sorry," she said. "I'm sorry I didn't help you. I should have helped you, and now you hate me."

"I don't hate you," I said, putting my arm around her. A hard ache grew in my throat. I felt nauseous. "I love you, Mom."

"You do?" She took my face in her hands. "You love me? You do?"

"Yes."

She grabbed me, wrapped both of her arms around me and cried. She held me so tightly I almost couldn't breathe.

"Then don't leave me!" she cried. "Please don't leave me!"

"But, Mom—"

"No, Connie—don't go. It'll kill me. If you love me you won't go!"

"O.K., O.K.!" My body shook with a kind of coldness I cannot describe. "I won't go! I promise I won't go!"

My body kept shaking, but hers stopped. She relaxed against me. Her arms went slack. She pulled away from me and held my face in her hands again. She smiled at me, this strange, sickening smile. I wanted to look away, but I couldn't with her hands holding my face.

"It's O.K., Connie. You can go. Tomorrow, you will go to college."

"But, you don't want me to go."

"Yes, I do, silly girl," she said, smoothing my hair. "Of course I want you to go—now that I know how much you love me."

I didn't tell Faith McGuire all that. A sense of mystery can be a very good quality in a person.

I squat down next to my little grocery basket and fiddle with the Windex bottles, pretend I'm checking the price, while I slide the compact under the waist of my shorts and pull my shirt over it. I could pay for it. I have the money. I just don't think I should have to. It's the chronic pain, always there, stealing from me every day, time, pleasure, and freedom. Don't I deserve to take something back?

I step up to the counter to pay for the Windex and Comet. The man behind the cash register has a bushy brown beard and mustache and shaggy brown hair that hasn't been washed in a couple of days. It's shiny and clumped together, sprinkled with dandruff flakes. He wears a black T-shirt with a wolf head on it. Red suspenders keep his jeans up around his fat belly. He's a Santa reject.

"Looks like someone's planning to do a little cleaning," Santa says. His small teeth are crooked and yellow. "Is that all now?"

The compact is pressed against my stomach, right in front of him. Regular price $4.69, but free for me.

"Yes. That's all." I smile at him.

I walk out the store with that compact tucked in the front of my shorts. He would have noticed the odd-shaped bulge in my belly if he'd been paying attention.

Just as I'm about to put the Windex and Comet under the kitchen sink, I hear this strange grunting, growling noise. Grandmother is home, but it can't be her. She'd never make such a sound. When she was in labor with my mother and my aunts, she probably didn't make a peep. I picture her on the operating table with her hair wrapped neatly in a bun, no trace of pain or sweat on her face, and her hands folded on her belly. No—her hands would be moving, her hands are always moving. She was probably quietly crocheting a doily, with the doctors and nurses scurrying around her. If she had her way, Grandmother probably scoured the entire delivery room herself when they were done.

The sound comes again, more of a frustrated yelp this time, and it definitely comes from Grandmother's room. Her door is open just enough for me to see her sitting on her bed with her back to the door. Her shoulders slouch forward and her head hangs in front of her, exposing the bones in her neck. I can almost count them. Then she throws her head back and looks up at the ceiling.

Her hair is a mess. The usually large, tight bun is just a small, loose knot on the back of her head. Wild white curls fall almost all the way down her back and over her shoulders, and a cloud of thin wisps hovers around her head. Grandmother pushes all ten of her pointy fingers into the mass of curls and knots until it looks like what's left of the bun is going to completely fall out. I hold the doorjamb and bite my lip to stop myself from running up behind her and catching her hair before it falls.

She slowly drags her hands out of her hair and looks down at her lap again. Her arms start to move, her shoulders jerk, her arms strain against something. She makes that grunting noise again. She struggles like this for a few minutes before flinging the box on the bed. It's the wooden box I'd found in the filing cabinet.

Too bad she never learned how to pick a lock.

Back in the kitchen, I make a lot of noise, crinkling the paper bag from the Grocery, putting the Comet and Windex down hard in the cabinet under the sink, slamming the door shut.

By dinnertime, Grandmother's hair is all pinned back in place. How does she do it without a mirror? She must have a little hand-held one somewhere in her room, tucked in a drawer. No one can make a bun that perfect, pull her hair back so smoothly, without a mirror.

Tonight, she's made plain broiled chicken and white rice. There are string beans, too, but only enough for her. Green vegetables give me hives. The food is already on my plate. Just looking at it starts the gag reflex in my throat.

"Is there any butter?" I ask.

"Your mother said no butter," Grandmother says. "Too rich for your stomach."

I pick up the saltshaker.

"Not too much," Grandmother says. "Too much salt isn't good for you."

When she looks down at her plate to cut her chicken, I violently shake the salt all over my food. It's the only thing on my plate with any flavor.

"Constance," she says. "I wanted to tell you that I think you're doing an excellent job with the house."

The statement stops me from jabbing my fork in her eye for calling me by that name yet again.

"You've been very thorough and efficient and careful with everything. I told your mother so the other day."

She's stunned me into paralysis, like a poisonous snake.

"You've been very thorough, and I've been looking for something and I wonder if you've come across it in all of your cleaning and packing."

"What?"

"Do you remember the bracelet I used to wear? It was a gold bracelet, with charms on it."

I want to tell her that the bracelet is the center of my only memories of intimacy with her. Grandmother didn't exactly shower me with hugs and kisses. My mother always said that was just her way, that Grandmother wasn't an affectionate person. Then my cousins were born and I watched Grandmother smother them with hugs and kisses. She pinched their cheeks and held their hands.

I was ten years old the last time I felt the warmth of Grandmother's body near mine. At night during those summers in Green Hill, I'd crawl into Grandmother's lap before bedtime. Something must have come over her when I did this, because she didn't shoo me away. She'd stroke my hair instead, or rub my back in slow circles. And I'd play with her charm bracelet, slowly turn it around her thin wrist, pausing to hold each charm between my fingers. The one I liked best was a little gold book that really opened.

"I haven't worn it in years," Grandmother says, laughing a little, only Grandmother doesn't really know how to laugh so it comes out like little choking sounds. "I can't for the life of me remember where I put it. I thought maybe you'd seen it somewhere."

Crickets chirp outside the window.

"Have you seen it?" Grandmother says. She stabs some string beans with her fork.

"No."

"Are you sure?"

"Yes, I'm sure. I haven't seen anything like it."

Grandmother drops her fork on her plate, making that big clanking noise that sounds so out of place at the dinner table. She smoothes the napkin in her lap.

"Well," she says, "if you see it, please put it aside for me."

After dinner, after all the pots and pans are scrubbed spotless and the dishes are washed and Grandmother is well into wiping down every surface with the Windex I bought that day, I go to my room just to check.

The charm bracelet is still there, rolled into a pair of socks that I pushed all the way to the back of the bureau drawer.

9

Grandmother and I are in the driveway trying to figure out a way to get all of this furniture to the Helping Hands. Some chairs, a folding table, bookshelves, step stools and old wooden crates fill her little garage. I'd found two children's desks in the attic, as well, both painted pink with white drawer fronts and pink knobs for the drawer pulls. They matched, so of course they belonged to my aunts. I have instructions to bring those home, somehow, to the Two Flowers.

I tell Grandmother that I can make several trips to the thrift store. My stomach hurts, and I am desperate to end the discussion and do the work so I can drink a glass of Pepto and lie down for a minute.

"It's too bad we don't have a truck, so it can all go at once."

On cue, Ethan's big green pick-up truck pulls into the driveway.

"Good morning, ladies," he says, strolling up the driveway toward us.

"Good morning, Ethan," Grandmother says. She's wearing a church dress, even though it's Friday and not Sunday, and her hair is in a French twist.

"Looks like you've got quite a collection here," he says. I can feel him standing behind me.

"We don't know what to do with it," Grandmother says. "We need to get it to the thrift store, but Constance can't put much of anything in that tiny car of hers."

I want to punch her in the arm for calling me that name in front of him.

"I can take it in my truck."

"Oh, no," Grandmother says, and I swear she bats her eyelashes at him. "We couldn't impose on you like that."

"You're not imposing."

"But it's such trouble."

"No trouble at all. It'll take ten minutes."

"Well, if you insist," Grandmother says. "But Constance will help you."

"O.K., then," Ethan says. "Let me just empty my truck first."

Ethan walks back to his truck, but I don't move. My face is hot and clammy at the same time. Nausea comes over me like a lead apron. I stand very still and swallow back the saliva pooling in my mouth until it passes.

"Constance!" Grandmother hisses at me from the lawn. "Don't just stand there—help him."

She watches from the porch as I help Ethan empty his truck bed and load all the furniture onto it. Ethan whistles the whole time, just random notes, no melody, and no order to the tune at all. Who whistles like that?

When everything is in the truck, I walk back toward the house.

"Constance!" Grandmother hisses at me again. "Go with him!"

Can't she see my arm is crossed over my stomach to hold it together? I feel gray. I must look gray. Can't she see that?

"Go with him and help," she says again.

My mother would not want me to go with Ethan, although maybe that's changed now since I'm out of college. Rules can change, right? My mother would see how sick I am and take care of me.

Grandmother scowls down at me from the porch. I slowly turn around and plod back to the truck.

"You don't need to come," Ethan says as I climb into the cab.

"Yes, I do."

I sit as far away from him as possible, and still try to look natural. I was much more comfortable at the coffee shop with a whole table separating us and we weren't confined to such a small space. One bad pothole and we could jostle right into each other. My fingers tap on the armrest on the door. My right knee bounces nervously. If the truck door opened right now, I'd bolt out like the Road Runner, leaving nothing but a poof of dust in my place.

Now, why didn't that stupid puberty film they showed us in elementary school include some useful information about this sort of situation? Tampons and maxi pads come with instructions, after all. It would've been much more helpful to learn something about how to act around a boy.

Out of the corner of my eye, I see the chewed up skin of his scar. I steal glances at it, while Ethan is focused on the road.

"Bad car accident," he says.

"What?" My ears burn. I look straight ahead.

"The scar. I got it in a car accident."

"Oh. I hadn't noticed. I wasn't looking."

Ethan laughs. "It's O.K. Even I stare at it sometimes."

"I heard you were a big skier."

"I was," he says.

"What happened?"

He taps the steering wheel with his fingers and clears his throat a couple times.

"I was stupid. Driving too fast at night. There was alcohol, a moose. It would've killed me. But I swerved off the road and right into a boulder."

His cheeks are flushed, his hands clenched around the steering wheel.

"I loved skiing," he says. "I gave up everything—friends, girlfriends, college, everything to ski."

It's one of those moments when you can't say anything that will meet the required standard of profundity or provide any kind of comfort, but you still can't help yourself.

"Well, at least you're alive," I say. The words have the same effect as a gas attack at a funeral. So, I continue. "That's something, right?"

Ethan does one of those silent laughs, a small burst of air out his nose. "That's what I tell myself, anyway."

We pull up to the Helping Hands. Ethan gets out of the truck and heads toward the store.

I wish I could take his hand in mine and tell him that I know how he feels about skiing, because I don't know how I'd live without running. Instead, I root through his glove compartment and find a digital watch without the watchband. It's not worth anything, but it's his.

Mable is already giving Ethan one of her big bear hugs. Even though I don't like her crushing embraces, I feel strangely hurt to see Mable hugging someone else.

"There's my girl!" Mable says, spotting me over Ethan's shoulder. "There's my girl," she says again, wrapping her arms around my neck and pulling me toward her. I hold still until it's over and Mable holds me at arm's length, giving me her customary once-over. She looks at me like she hasn't seen me in years, instead of a couple of days.

"How are my two most favorite people?" Mable says.

"We brought furniture," I say.

"Oh good!" Mable says. "Bring it in."

On every trip out to the truck, I take more than I can really carry, the pain in my gut pushing me to get the job done as quickly as possible.

"That's all of it," I say, when Ethan brings in the last bookshelf. I am at the door, my hand on the doorknob. Saliva floods my mouth and I feel gray again. I am a shell of ashes on the verge of crumbling.

"Come visit with me, then," Mable says.

"Can't. Gotta go." My stomach hurts so badly, it takes all my energy to stop myself from curling up in the fetal position right there on the floor.

"I'll give you a ride," Ethan says, walking toward me.

"No, I'll walk."

"Are you sure?" Ethan says. They are both looking at me, and I want them to stop. I want to tear their eyes out, so they never look at me again.

"Maybe you should let Ethan drive you," Mable says. "You don't look so good all of a sudden."

"I'm fine. I just want to walk." And I'm gone.

I run down the other side of the hill toward the edge of town. The mantra beats in my head: *Don't – shame – your – mother – Don't – shame – your – mother.* My legs are numb at first, but I push harder and harder until I start to feel my calf muscles, my quadriceps, each individual tendon back in its place, my veins and the blood flowing through them, all moving under my skin, this feeling now stamping out the pain.

At the sign, "You are now leaving Green Hill," my stomach isn't burning so bad anymore. And then I puke and feel even better.

Back at Grandmother's, Ethan is spreading mulch in a bed of yellow and orange marigolds along the side of the garage. He smiles and waves at me. I wave back before going inside and starting up the stairs.

"Constance!"

Grandmother marches down the hall.

"Where were you? Ethan came back without you, said you didn't want a ride."

"I went running."

"But he offered you a ride," she says.

"I wanted to run."

"Well, you should have taken his offer. It was rude not to," she says. "Luckily, he's not offended."

"I didn't mean to offend anyone," I say. My legs shake beneath me. The effect of running wears off so quickly now. My hands grip the stair railing so hard that my knuckles are white. "Can I go now?"

"Yes," Grandmother says, and I start to slowly trudge up the stairs. "No, wait."

I stop, but Grandmother doesn't say anything.

"Well?" I say.

"That box, the little wooden one you found. It was locked when you found it?"

I take a few steps back down the stairs.

"Yes."

"And you couldn't unlock it?"

"That's right."

"There was no way to open it?"

"There's no key, so how could I open it?"

"Right. How could you open it? That's it exactly," she says. "That's all I wanted to know. Thank you." She starts to walk away.

"Why do you ask?" She stops. "Is something missing from it?"

"No—I mean, I wouldn't know," she says. "I can't open it either without the key."

"Of course. What was I thinking? No key."

"No key," she says, and walks away.

Grandmother makes broiled fish and mashed potatoes—no butter—for dinner, but she shouldn't have bothered. I can barely force two bites down. Just the thought of food resting on the fire in my belly makes me queasy. The diet my mother prescribed isn't working. I have to take more and more pills every day, and the more I take, the less effective they become.

I need to move. While Grandmother wipes down the kitchen after the meal, I sneak out.

Ethan and his parents are in the living room, sitting in the blue glow of the television. They are talking and laughing. When it's dark enough, I leave the safety of my tree and cross the street. I hunch down and move quickly and quietly. I sit with my back up against the front of the porch, with my knees pulled up. The living room windows are just above and behind me.

Ethan and his mother talk during the commercials. Just small talk, "Was that a good dinner, or what?" "Would you look at this commercial?" "What's up for tomorrow?" Simple stuff. At least it sounds simple, the way the words just fall right out of their mouths.

When the show is over, Ethan says, "Come on, Dad, let's get you to bed." Ethan's heavy footsteps and his father's light shuffle move across the floor and fade away. I strain to hear them talking deeper inside the house.

The front door swings open and Ethan steps onto the porch.

"'Bye, Ma."

I hold my breath and shut my eyes tight. Inside my head, I whisper "Disappear. Disappear. Disappear."

They kiss and then Ethan hops down the porch steps. The only thing separating us is a juniper bush.

"Sleep tight," his mother calls.

"You, too."

The door shuts and Ethan scuffs his boots on the dirt driveway between the barn and the house. He thuds up the stairs. The door opens and then shuts behind him.

I peek around the juniper bush. The lights are on in his apartment. I crawl away from the porch and across the lawn, just in case Mrs. Matthews is near one of the front windows. I creep across the street back to my tree.

Ethan walks up to one of the windows at the front of his apartment and looks outside. Then he turns on the television, takes something from the refrigerator and sits down. I can't watch him long before I start to get creeped out. There are living creatures in the woods all around me, and one of them is probably a crazed mountain man looking for something to kill. But it's not the living things that make me run. My stomach does. I run to the end of the road, being careful not to twist an ankle in all the ruts, and puke on the corner, far enough away so Ethan can't hear me.

"Where were you?" Grandmother says. She stands behind the screen door with her hands on her hips.

"I went for a walk," I say, pushing by her. Not even she can keep me from my pills in the upstairs bathroom.

"You shouldn't go out like that without telling me," she says. "Not when you don't feel well."

"I'm fine," I say from the top of the stairs.

"I know you don't feel well," she calls, as I head to the bathroom. I need to throw up one more time before I take my pill. "I can tell."

I slam the bathroom door and turn the shower on so she won't hear me retching.

10

It takes only a little more than a month of living with Grandmother for my stomach to turn into a giant, festering open sore that someone throws acid on from time to time. I can't even run. I lie in bed, listening to the rain on my window, until the last possible moment and then drag myself into the shower. After the shower, I sit on the toilet for a while, wrapped in my towel, gathering strength for the next stage—dressing. I put on my underwear, and then sit on the bed and rest. I put on a shirt, then rest. Jeans. Rest. I get up off the bed one last time and walk down the stairs.

Grandmother waits by the door. She looks up at me and shakes her head.

"You look awful," she says. And I wonder if she's commenting on my hair or my clothes. "It's your stomach, isn't it?"

"It's nothing. I'm fine."

"You should stay home. Go back to bed."

"I'm fine. Let's just go."

Grandmother runs through the rain to the car, so it doesn't mess up her hair or spot her beige linen dress. I walk, trying to stand as straight as possible. The rain is cool on my hot skin.

During Mass, I focus on the mountain behind the stained glass cross. Clouds and rain shroud the summit. Sometimes, the shape of the mountain emerges a little, and then fades back into the mist. It's a bad day for a climb, so easy to lose the trail and end up hurt, or worse. All it takes is one mistake. That's how people die up there.

I hope whoever's out there is smart enough to turn back and get below the tree line. People never turn back when they should.

It's cool in the church, but I'm sweating. My mouth is dry. I'm not even interested in taking what I want from the collection basket today. It doesn't matter. By now, I probably have enough tucked into the lining of my suitcase to fix the dent in my car.

Just the thought of getting my car fixed, so my mother will never know what happened, makes me feel a little better.

Grandmother keeps glancing at me, but I just watch the mountain. If I look at her, she might try to touch me in some comforting way.

After communion, she takes my arm. Her bony fingers dig into me as she pulls me past our pew.

"Come on," she says. "We're going home."

I don't fight her. It's rude to talk in church. My mother never allowed it. Not even to ask to go to the bathroom. Not even if I had to go so bad my eyeballs had started to float.

Grandmother tries to make me go to bed.

"You need to lie down."

"No, I don't. I'm fine." I go to the living room and bring an empty box over to the cabinet that holds Grandmother's perfume bottles. The bottom shelf still needs to be packed up.

"What are you doing?" Grandmother's hands are on her hips. Her little white purse dangles from her wrist. She hasn't taken her gloves off yet.

"I'm packing these bottles."

"Why?"

"They need to be packed."

"Not right now, they don't."

I decide right then that there's no way I'm going to lie down in bed like a sick, helpless animal. I don't care if my stomach turns itself inside out and my head explodes with fire. I will not allow her to see me broken. I will not give her the satisfaction of telling my mother that I'm weak and helpless.

Pulling one finger at a time, Grandmother takes her gloves off and slaps the pair in the palm of her hand. I take a bottle from the cabinet and slowly wrap it in three layers of white tissue paper. I put it in the bottom of the box and look at her. Nails would probably come shooting out of her mouth now, if she opened it. But she doesn't. She turns quick and marches out of the room.

I keel over and rest my forehead on the Oriental carpet.

I've won.

It takes me most of the day to wrap up the bottles. Keeling over every five seconds makes for slow progress. When I finish,

Grandmother comes and wipes the whole glass cabinet down with Windex—three times. The cabinet is trimmed with brass. And while Grandmother cleans the glass, I polish the brass.

"You don't have to do that," she says.

"It's fine," I say, rubbing the brass a little harder.

"I wish you'd go lie down."

"I don't need to."

When we're done, so is dinner. And I've made it through the whole day without going to my room.

Grandmother made broiled chicken, baked potatoes and steamed carrots for dinner. The carrots are only for her, though. Orange vegetables give me diarrhea. I load my plate with chicken. I even go to the refrigerator and put a huge glob of butter on my potato.

"Want any?" I ask Grandmother.

"No," she says, without looking at me. "Thank you."

I clean my plate, just to show her I can. The chicken is dry as sawdust, the baked potato thick glue on my tongue. Not even the butter helps.

I do all the dishes and the pots and pans. And only when Grandmother is well into her second swipe of all the kitchen surfaces—only then do I say, "I think I'll go take a shower."

She doesn't respond, too deep in her Windex-induced trance.

I calmly walk up the stairs and down the hall to the bathroom. I turn on the shower water and vomit.

When I come back downstairs. Grandmother is on the phone.

"Wait, here she is," Grandmother says and holds the phone out to me.

"Your Grandmother says you don't feel well," my mother says. "It's your stomach, isn't it?"

"What else would it be?"

"Don't be fresh," my mother snaps. "I'm trying to help you."

"Sorry," I say.

"I worry so much about you. I do everything to try to help you, and then you're so fresh to me."

"I know. I'm sorry."

"Is it bad?" she says.

"Yes, but it's been worse."

"Are you watching your diet? Is your grandmother making the right foods?"

"Yes."

"And you're taking your medication?"

"Yes."

"I don't know what this is, then," my mother says, in the tone she usually takes with the doctors and nurses, all business. "When you come home, maybe we need to think about getting you in to see another specialist, someone who knows what they're doing this time. Maybe we can get you in for another endoscopy and see what's going on down there."

The word "endoscopy" makes my throat seize. The last one they did, the anesthesia didn't work. It's called twilight anesthesia, because it doesn't make you fully unconscious for the procedure, which in this case is a scope being threaded down your throat so the doctor can look at your upper gastrointestinal tract. But you're supposed to be out enough not to know or feel what's happening. The previous six times I'd had it done, I faded away right after they put the plastic tube in my mouth for the scope. But the last time, the seventh time, the tube was in my mouth and I was still awake when the scope went in through the tube. But I wasn't awake enough to really talk or scream or move. The scope kept going down and down my throat. It was going to choke me, kill me right there on the table. I kept looking at the nurse, thinking that if I made my eyes bulge big enough, she would know what I was trying to tell her and stop the procedure. But all she did was stroke my hand and tell me everything was all right.

Afterward, my mother wanted to know why I was crying. I told her that I'd been awake for the whole thing, how I wanted them to stop and they wouldn't. How the doctor never even apologized afterward, just told me I didn't know what I was talking about. I wanted my mother to storm out of the room and rip the doctor up one side and down the other. But she just stroked my hair and told me to stop being silly.

They will have to drag me kicking and screaming to another endoscopy.

"I'm sure I'll be fine, Mom, and we won't need to do any of that," I say. "Besides, when I get home, I've got to pack up my stuff and—"

The phone line crackles with her intensity.

"You know I don't like to talk about that."

"I'm sorry."

"You know I can't stand to think of you moving away from me, leaving me. And you refuse to commute. Here you are, so sick, and you think you're going to be able to live on your own at that stupid academy?"

"Mom—"

"You can't even survive a month without me. If you don't start getting better, we're going to have to rethink your little job and your little apartment away from home."

A thousand knives stab my gut just then and I want to sink to the floor.

"And don't think I don't know what's been going on up there."

"I don't know what you're talking about, Mom."

"You don't, huh?"

"No."

"You think I'm stupid? You think your Grandmother doesn't tell me what you're doing?"

Grandmother is sitting in her chair in the den. The ball of cotton string bounces in its bowl. The thread goes up to her hands, where it wraps around her fingers and is pulled by the tiny metal hook into interconnecting loops that make the web, now the size of a dinner plate. Her hands move so fast I can barely see the hook. She holds the work close to her face. Her ears are bright red.

What exactly has Grandmother told her? Has she seen me at the Grocery, or in the attic? Has she found the things hidden in my room? Has she seen me palm coins and bills from the collection basket that gets passed around at Mass?

"She tells me how rude you are to her, how you go gallivanting all around town when you're supposed to be working."

I'm safe. Grandmother doesn't know anything.

"I'm sorry, Mom. I'll be better, I promise. But I need to go lie down now." I make a little groaning noise. "I gotta go."

"No—please! Don't hang up. Don't be mad at me."

"But, Mom—"

"Say it—say you're not mad at me."

"I'm not mad at you."

"Say you love me."

"I love you."

"No matter what."

"No matter what," I say.

"Because I'm just trying to take care of you. I only want what's best for you."

"I know."

"I'm always trying to take care of you," she says. "I love you that much, you know."

"I know. I love you, too."

This will change when I move away at the end of the summer. We won't have conversations like this anymore. I'll be an adult, and she'll talk to me like an adult. That's what happens when you move out, right? Isn't that when you become an adult?

"Connie?"

"Yes, Mom."

"You still need me, don't you?"

"Yes."

"I know," she says, and I have this strange feeling, like I've just stepped on a landmine. "You'll always need me."

I stand in a big empty room, like the room of a house, but it's not a house. It's too silent to be a house. No sounds of people, feet scuffing on the floor overhead, the hum of water running through the pipes in the walls to a sink where someone is doing the dishes, washing their hands. No voices. The room is dark. There are no windows in the walls of dark brown wood. I stand in the middle of the room, which begins to feel like a giant box.

My mother walks into the room, slowly, looking straight ahead. I call to her, but she doesn't look at me. She keeps walking. I follow her.

She stops in front of a long wooden box, which I don't even see until she's standing in front of it. I am still behind her. She rests her hands on the edge of the box and looks down into it. She does not make a sound. I want to look, but I'm afraid. I start to tremble. I put my hand

*on my mother's shoulder to stop the shaking. I close my eyes and step
up to the box.*

*It's me, but it doesn't look like me. I'm dressed in a white gown. I
have make-up on my face, red cheeks and red lips. But underneath, I
can tell my skin is pasty white, my lips blue. My eyes are shut.
Someone has crossed my hands on my chest.*

It's me. I know I am dead.

*I turn to my mother, but she is already at the door of the room,
still silent, not even crying. I look back at the dead me. A red stain
spreads out from the center of my stomach. When I look down at my
own stomach, on the live me, the stain is there, too, spreading and
burning.*

The moment I wake up, I wish I were back in the dream. I
wish I were dead. Death can't hurt like this.

I desperately want to get up and get a pill, and I desperately
don't want to move. I curl into myself and try to breathe. I listen
to the rain on the roof. Think of it as music. Try to hear a tune.
Make up a story about the rain. Think about anything but this
pain.

Grandmother is up, making breakfast. The smell of butter
melting in the frying pan makes me groan. She assumes I'm out
running, and we don't eat breakfast together anyway, so it takes
her a while to come looking for me—hours, probably. I don't
have my watch on, so I can't say for sure how much time passes
before she begins to wonder about me.

"Oh, my God!" Grandmother says, bursting through the
door just as I was able to doze off a little. Figures.

"I'll take you to the hospital," she says, trying to sit me up.
"Let's go!"

"No!" I push her away. "Don't make me move."

"But you need to go to the hospital."

"It'll pass. Just bring me my pills."

She runs down the hallway to the bathroom and comes
back with my pills and some water. She sits on the bed next to
me and helps me sit up halfway. I put three pills in my mouth
this time, because two don't seem to be enough anymore.
Grandmother holds my hair back while I wash them down with
the water. Then I lie back down, curl into myself again, and

Grandmother covers me with the bed sheet. I close my eyes with the relief of just knowing the pills are fizzing in my stomach.

When I open my eyes later, there's a glass of milk on my nightstand. My stomach churns at the sight of it, so I close my eyes again.

When I open them later still, the milk has been replaced with a glass of water and a metal bowl with a damp washcloth hanging over the side. My face is cool and clean. The water is tempting. I sit up a little, very slowly, so as not to wake the ulcer, and take a sip.

In the evening, when the worst has passed, Grandmother helps me into the shower. She brings me one of her long, white, cotton nightgowns and a robe. She helps me dress, slipping the nightgown over my head, guiding my hands into the armholes of the robe, and then settles me on the couch in the den so I can watch television. The nausea is back, and I wonder if it's from moving around too much or from not having anything in my stomach.

"Could I please have a glass of milk?"

Grandmother jumps up from her chair. "Yes. Certainly. Of course."

She runs to the kitchen to get the milk, which used to be the remedy for an ulcer. Not anymore. Doctors don't even recommend it. They say it doesn't work. But you can't tell me that. Milk's the one thing that makes me feel better after an attack.

Grandmother hands me a glass and then relaxes back in her chair. The ball of cotton thread begins gently knocking the sides of its bowl. I sip my milk and wonder who's taken my Grandmother and replaced her with this woman. My Grandmother wouldn't have tried to get me to a hospital. She wouldn't have brought milk and water up to my room. She wouldn't have wasted a whole afternoon wiping my face with a cool, damp cloth. And she wouldn't have troubled herself to help me into the shower or given me her soft nightgown and robe to wear.

No, this is not my Grandmother, although she watches the same dumb detective show Grandmother does. She loves reruns of that show with the dim-witted, cross-eyed detective. I don't know who's worse—him or the murderers who fall for his stupid act. I'd like to see him catch me committing a crime. He never could. No one can.

Something taps on my shoulder. The remote. Grandmother holds it out to me.

"Change it if you want," she says. "Put on something you like."

I look at the remote, but turn away.

"No," I say. "This is fine."

The ball of cotton thread begins to roll again.

I shouldn't have had the milk. I puke it up in the middle of the night and the ulcer flattens me again the next day.

"We should go to the hospital," Grandmother says, wringing her hands over me.

"No," I say. "It's actually a little bit better."

I'm not lying. I do feel a little bit better—the width of a single human hair better.

The days pass like this. I'm better in the evening, well enough to take some milk and crackers, and worse in the morning, but still better than the previous day. Grandmother won't allow me out of bed.

"I should at least call your mother," Grandmother says the next morning, when I still cannot get out of bed.

"No," I say, sitting up. "There's no need to call. I'll be better soon."

Grandmother looks up and down my body, her nightgown loose on my bony frame.

"All right," she says. "I won't call."

On the third morning of my bed rest, I wake up to find a block of wood and Papa's knife, the small carving knife he loved best, on the nightstand. The knife's wooden handle is the color of fresh-brewed tea with dark grain lines running down to the blade, which is shiny and shaped like a thin triangle, about three inches long. Papa whittled with this knife because he liked the control of the short blade, the sharp point perfect for little details like the pupils of eyes. Papa could whittle anything out of a block of wood: leaves, little troll people, a zoo of animals, an acorn that looks like it just fell from a tree. All of them are on my bureau at home, where I see them every morning and every night.

The wooden handle is smooth with the oil from Papa's skin. Touching it is like touching his hand again.

Grandmother's footsteps are on the stairs. I put the knife down. The door opens a crack.

"You're up," she says, opening the door a little wider.

I nod.

"Any better today?"

I nod again. She looks at my hand, which I hadn't realized is rubbing my stomach.

"Maybe not that much better," she says. She looks at my nightstand and then at me. "I left that for you. Thought you might want something to do."

Who is this woman?

"You remember how he taught you, don't you?" She flashes that tense, scary smile at me.

I nod, wondering how she knows that. Her smile slowly falls.

"Well," she says. "I'm going to the supermarket. You rest."

She closes the door quietly, as if I'm still sleeping, and goes back downstairs. The screen door slams, the car starts and pulls away from the house, down the street.

She checks on me like that every time she leaves for the library, or the grocery store—the real one forty-five minutes away—or the bank, also forty-five minutes away. Every time she leaves, she tells me to stay in bed. I should obey her. My mother would want me to obey her.

When I can't hear the car anymore, I know it's safe to get up.

The attic is almost empty now. Just a few boxes and trash bags still to be hauled away, some to Mable at the Helping Hands and some to the dump. Grandmother decided she didn't have a use for twenty-five years of calendars, thirty years of Christmas cards or ten years of the Green Hill Gazette after all. She'd given up the idea of making a life-size replica of the Statue of Liberty in *papier-mâché*, I suppose, and gave me permission to chuck them.

The trunk is still there, one of those old steamers made of thick wood with metal corners and seams painted black. It was locked, of course, when I found it, but it took me about two seconds to pick it with one of Grandmother's bobby pins. The lid still would not budge. Grandmother probably sprayed water on the hinges periodically to make the rust crust over them. I tried to pry the trunk open with the end of a broom handle, once, but it was too thick to wedge under the lid. I put all my weight into it anyway, and the handle slipped and whacked me in the head.

I tried a more subtle approach—Vaseline, using Q-tips to get the thick oil into the cracks of the hinges to coax the metal cylinders back into motion. I paused at the sound of every car, listening for it to turn into the driveway.

Today, the lid gives a little, just a hair, the space of a breath. I rub gobs of Vaseline into the hinges and try the lid again. It gives a little more, the space of two breaths maybe. I inch the lid open this way until I can see into the trunk and reach my hands inside.

A garden blooms in there. Miles and miles of linens—sheets and pillowcases, cloth napkins and tablecloths, handkerchiefs, placemats and table runners, bedspreads even—unfurl in my lap, each piece touched by a needle and colorful silk threads. Daisies sprout along the edge of the pillowcases. A hedge of pink roses spreads across one tablecloth; orange lilies nod their tiger faces in the corners of another. Tiny violets dot the edge of the handkerchiefs. Matching purple thread forms the letters "CG," all loops and curves, in one corner of each small square edged with lace.

Under the linens are clothes. There's a white cotton nightgown, with daisies around the collar, two plain white blouses and a long navy-blue skirt. A pair of white cotton gloves with pearl buttons at the wrist. The gloves give away the owner of the trunk, but then I find this dress, a long satin thing in a bright sea-foam green. I can tell by the seams that it's meant to fit tightly around the torso. It's sleeveless, with wide straps. The neckline plunges enough to show cleavage. The back scoops low, too low for a bra. That's how I know it doesn't belong to Grandmother. She would never, ever go without a bra. If the house were burning down in the middle of the night, she would stop to strap herself into a bra, right over her nightgown, and pull on her white gloves before rushing out of the house, a ball of flames bursting through the door behind her.

The dress does not belong. Neither do the linens. Grandmother uses only plain white sheets, plain white tablecloths, plain white napkins, and not a stain on any of them. Not even on the napkins, which just confirms that she's some kind of witch. How else can she use white cloth napkins on a regular basis and never get a stain on them? I'd seen her wipe her own mouth with them. I check them after dinner—and nothing. Not even a smear of food. Isn't that kind of like vampires not having any reflection in a mirror?

There's something else wrong with those linens: The flowers. Only a happy person could sew flowers like that, spend hours, days, months painting those petals with a needle and thread. I close my eyes and run my fingertips over the rose-covered tablecloth. The texture of the blossoms tickles my skin. I try to imagine Grandmother young and happy. The only smile I can conjure on her face is that scary, toothy grin she gives with her lips stretched all weird, so I try to just imagine her young. I try to imagine her in the green dress, but she keeps coming up all brown, beige and navy blue.

Less than two hours have passed since Grandmother left for the supermarket. There's plenty of time to slip it on and slip it off.

The dress fits every minor curve of my straight body. That's the downside to running—it keeps your body small, straight, efficient. Minimal. I guess it's a downside. I wouldn't know what to do with curves, anyway.

Still, the dress fits. And from what I see of my reflection in one of the attic windows, I don't look half bad. I wouldn't say pretty. But the dress suits me. The bodice fits snugly around my middle; the straps rest comfortably on my shoulders. It's just the right length, too, the edge of the hem brushing my insteps. The color reminds me of the mossy banks along the river where Papa and I spent so many afternoons fishing. The satin is cool against my skin.

There are two of me in the reflection in the window, the one on the inner pane overlapping the one on the outer pane. One reflection is higher than the other and shifted to the left. There are two sets of hands, two sets of shoulders, two faces, or really no face at all. Instead, there are two gray patches where my eyes belong, a shadow beneath a smudge of a nose, a round spot where my lips meet, nothing more specific than that, nothing more defined. I strain my eyes to bring the two images together into focus.

I realize I could just walk closer to the windows to make the two reflections merge into one. But I don't.

I take the dress off and fold it along the lines that have been pressed into it by the weight of the linens. When I go to put it back into the trunk, I see something else. An envelope pressed against the side of the trunk. The envelope is sealed, but the glue is so old, it just falls open.

The squares of newsprint inside look like they might crumble into dust under my touch. I pull one piece out, carefully, as if it were a paper-thin sheet of glass instead. A man's face stares straight ahead out of the photograph. His skin looks smooth, no wrinkles, and no stubble. A dark ridge of hair, freshly buzzed, stands up at his hairline. His eyes are dark, shadowed by a prominent brow. His mouth is a straight line, no hint of a smile.

According to the paragraph under the picture, he was heading off to war in Korea. Edward Henderson was shipping out with the Marines. Edward Henderson—that's the name under the picture, a name I've never heard before.

Another Edward Henderson, this one wearing one of those little military hats to go with the uniform, is on the other clipping in the envelope, too. This clipping announces Edward Henderson's homecoming, along with calling hours at Pillsbury Brothers Funeral Home and the service the following day at St. Joseph's.

He could have belonged to Grandmother's family, a brother or cousin. I wouldn't know. We don't share that kind of thing in our family. Whenever I had to make a family tree for homework in grade school, my mother and I had great fun making up our whole family. We'd come up with great relatives, like crazy Uncle Snodgrass and Great-Grandmother Hortensia. The wilder the name, the better.

We had to make up my father's side of the tree, because we didn't know anyone from David Hobbs's family. I never met my paternal grandparents. I don't know if I even have paternal grandparents, or if they know about me.

I don't know why we made up my mother's side of the family.

But I do know one thing. Grandmother's maiden name is Pritchard. And the man in the newspaper clippings is not Edward Pritchard. He could have been Papa's friend or relative, but I'm sure Papa would have told me about him. He talked to me about these things, growing up with all his brothers and sisters, getting into trouble when he was a boy. And even if Edward Henderson was part of Papa's family, it doesn't explain why these two clippings were sealed in an envelope and locked in the trunk. Something tells me I was not meant to find Edward Henderson.

I figure it out when I fold all the clothes and the linens and put them back into the trunk—exactly the way I found them.

It's a Hope Chest. The skirt and blouses, the nightgown and green dress are traveling clothes for a honeymoon, the linens for a house after the honeymoon. The flowers look much like the ones my mother had sewn on all those baby clothes she'd made for me. She'd monogrammed the handkerchiefs with my initials. She made the dress in my size. That's some trick, predicting my exact shape and size twenty-two years out. It was bold to hem it before I was even born, because she must have made all of it when she was pregnant with me. That's how it ended up in Grandmother's attic. She left it behind when we moved away and forgot about it.

I run my hand over the tablecloth lying on top of the pile in the chest and smile. I lower the lid and make sure the attic looks like I've never been there.

When I open the door to leave, Grandmother's nose just about touches mine. I jump out of my skin a little. She squeals and slaps a hand on her chest.

"Oh, you startled me!" she says.

"Sorry," I say.

"What are you doing out of bed?"

"I needed to walk. I think I'm getting bed sores."

"You shouldn't be up," she says, taking my arm and leading me back down the hallway to the bedroom. "You're still white as a sheet."

"I only just got up a few minutes ago."

"Will you try to eat something tonight?"

"Maybe." I sit on the bed. She stands in front of me.

"All right, then. I'll boil up some potatoes and call you when it's ready."

When her footsteps go all the way down the stairs and down the hall, and I hear the kitchen door swing, and the fan over the stove starts to hum, I take the envelope and one of the handkerchiefs my mother made for me and hide them under some clothes in a bureau drawer.

11

I am up and dressed, making myself some tea and toast, before Grandmother can come to my room. Every morning since the start of the attack, she'd place a tray of tea and toast on the bureau and then sit on the bed next to me. She'd ask me how I felt and then sit a few minutes more after I'd tell her that I felt a little better. Then she'd leave.

I couldn't take it anymore.

"What are you doing out of bed?" Grandmother says, stopping abruptly in the kitchen doorway. She's dressed in a straight navy-blue skirt, cut just above her thin ankles, and a white short-sleeved blouse. Her hair is already swept up in a high bun, not a strand escaping. Eight a.m. and Grandmother is as polished as her leather pumps, navy to match the skirt.

"What are you doing, Constance?"

"Eating," I say, although what I'm doing may not qualify as such. I sit at the kitchen table, nibbling a piece of dry toast, washing the crumbs down with small sips of lukewarm tea. The kitchen is almost empty. The nails still need to be taken out of the walls where Grandmother's antique plates and kitchen utensils once hung. Even in Grandmother's spotless house, there are dark outlines of each plate and eggbeater on the avocado green walls. She already has a bucket and a big bottle of Murphy's Oil Soap out on the counter, ready to scrub the walls. The white cabinets hold just enough dishes for the two of us—a frying pan, a spaghetti pot and one roasting pan. I tried to pack the roasting pan, but Grandmother pulled it back out of the box. She continues to roast a chicken or turkey or ham just about every Sunday.

"You shouldn't be up," she says, taking a step toward the table. She's moved around me like this since the start of the attack. Carefully, like I'm one of her little porcelain girls on the shelf in the den, which is also, almost, empty of her things. The den's dark wood-paneled walls and the bookshelves are bare. She's even started taking up her plush Oriental rugs and taking down the curtains. Our voices are beginning to echo in the house.

"I'm fine," I say, taking a big bite of toast as proof.

Yesterday, she came to my room, put the breakfast tray on the bureau and sat next to me on the bed. She crossed and uncrossed her legs several times before coming to a rest with her knees together, both feet flat on the floor. A square of sunlight covered her lap.

She didn't know what to do with her hands. They held the edge of the bed, and then she folded them in her lap. She crossed her arms, cupped her hands over her knees, crossed her arms again, and then one of her hands landed on mine. It fell there by accident, like a dying leaf falling from a tree, landing wherever the breeze takes it. I stared at her hand, wondering if that was really where she meant it to be.

My eyes traced an imaginary line from the end of her fingers, across the bony back of her hand to her wrist, her forearm, her elbow, up to her shoulder, her neck, to the bun on the back of her head. The muscles in her neck stood out like thin cords, straining to keep her face turned as far away from me as possible. My eyeballs moved slowly, careful not to disturb one molecule of air surrounding this delicate tableau.

Her hand was a slab of ice against my skin. It was such a contrast to Mable's hands, which were always warm. But as the square of sunlight on her lap moved in immeasurable increments toward her knees, her hand grew warmer. Or maybe it was my hand that grew warmer. Or maybe the warmth started with her, traveled to me, where it became warmer, and went back to her, where it grew warmer still, the exchange continuing, one tiny circle of energy connecting us—finally connecting us. I closed my eyes, pictured a small band of light surging around our joined hands. I drifted back into sleep, and when I opened my eyes again, she was gone.

I'd seen how other families traded in touch, dads hugging their daughters after our track meets, mothers ruffling their sons' hair, siblings, husbands, wives, whole families resting their hands on each other countless times each day in silent gestures of love.

My family does not communicate this way. A hug from my mother is never just a hug. It's a desperate grasp, crushing me into her, bruising me with her fingers, and drowning me until I feel I won't be able to breathe again. A kiss on the cheek, an embrace, a hand on my hand evokes the same feeling as watching a boulder roll uncontrollably toward me. And my feet are always stuck in quicksand.

The only other people who lay their hands on me are doctors and nurses, who come at me with needles and scopes to poke and probe me. At the hospitals, the way they shuffle you from test to test, leaving you in basement hallways until it's your turn with the endoscope or the CAT scan, I feel less and less like a person and more like chattel.

"You should be in bed," Grandmother says. She sits down opposite me at the kitchen table with her own cup of tea, I put my hands in my lap, just in case she gets any big ideas.

"I can get someone to finish the rest of the packing. You're almost done anyway. I can have Ethan—"

"No. I can finish. It's better if I move around anyway, if I have something to do. Keeps my mind off it."

She spoons some sugar into her tea. "Well, I don't like it. But I guess there's nothing I can do about it. You're a big girl. I can't force you to stay in bed, if you don't want to." She takes a sip of tea and then puts her cup back down in its saucer. "I'm not going to tell you what to do."

Who is she trying to kid? Scientists need to develop a nicotine patch for bossiness in order for her to kick that habit. If she ever goes cold turkey, the cravings will kill her. I picture her crouched in a corner, shaking, sweating, her eyes wide and wild, searching for the next fix, the high that comes after bullying me.

I eat my toast. I sip my tea. She sips her tea. I look out the window at the side yard, watching the mist of another cloudy day gather on the grass. She stares into her cup, stirring the tea every now and then. Her spoon clinks against the side of her cup. The tea and toast settle into my raw stomach, which, to my surprise, isn't churning as badly anymore.

"That trunk in the attic," she says.

"Yes."

"There's nothing in it, so just leave it."

"You're sure it's empty? Or do you want me to sort through it?"

"I didn't say it was empty. I said there's nothing in it." Her spoon clinks against her cup. "Just leave it alone."

"Sure," I say. "I won't touch it."

Mable is a ball of sunshine on this gray, drizzly day. "There's my girl," she says, waddling toward me. The pleats in her yellow skirt billow in rippling waves around her heavy legs. She wears a white blouse under a cardigan that matches her skirt. I meet her halfway this time.

"Where have you been?" she says. I lean into her embrace and let the warmth from her body penetrate mine. I'm chilled and wet, but it's still a good day to get back on my feet. A brisk walk is all I need. Tomorrow, maybe I'll run.

Mable lets go and holds me at arms' length, like she does.

"You look pale," she says, then squeezes my arm. "And thin. Are you getting thinner? You're cold as an ice cube, too." She rubs her hands up and down my arms. "What's wrong with my girl?"

"Just a little upset stomach. But I'm fine now."

"Come sit down in back. You can keep me company while you warm up."

It feels good to sit in my mustard-yellow chair. I'd forgotten how cold it could be in the summer here. At the top of Main Street, my legs threatened to buckle beneath me. I feel light-headed, like I'm breathing the thin air at the top of Mount Washington. It must be freezing up there today. But I don't care about the cold or the dizziness. The walk erased the pain. I could pass out now, for all I care.

"Ah-ha!" Mable says, plucking a man's dress shirt from the new pile of clothes at her feet. "Time me on this," she says, whisking the shirt onto the ironing board. "I'm going for under three minutes."

She pushes the iron over the shirt with short, jerky movements, her chubby arms jiggling with the effort. She attacks the body of it first, then the shoulder and sleeves, the cuffs and finally the collar. Clouds of steam puff from the iron as she methodically restores the wrinkled mess back to smooth order. She whips the shirt onto a hanger. I check my watch.

"Two minutes, fifty-five seconds."

"Ha!" Mable shouts triumphantly. "I knew I was under three minutes."

I don't have the heart to tell her I can do my mother's blouses in fewer than two. Instead, I tell her about the Hope Chest, the linens, the clothes, the dress.

"You could frame the napkins and hang them in a museum," I say.

Mable pulls the end of a huge sheet from the pile on the floor. She tugs at it, shaking the clothes off of it.

"I don't know why she doesn't want all those beautiful things," I say, a little louder, in case she can't hear me.

Mable folds the sheet in half, lengthwise, and lays one end over the ironing board.

"Do you think she really knows what's in that trunk?" I shout.

"What's that?"

"The trunk I found, with all those embroidered linens."

"What about it?" she asks, moving the iron over the sheet.

"Do you think she knows what's in it? Do you think she really doesn't want it?"

"If she doesn't want it, then I guess she doesn't want it."

"But how could she not want it? Unless she doesn't remember what's in it."

"Maybe," Mable says. "Maybe you should remind her."

A draft whispers through the room, raising goose bumps on the back of my arms.

"It's not hers to keep, anyway."

"Whose is it, then?"

"Maybe it's mine." Funny how it made perfect sense to me when I was alone in the attic with the Hope Chest. But when I say it out loud, to someone else, the idea doesn't seem to make quite as much sense.

"I just don't see Grandmother making all those frilly, flowery things. I don't think she could make anything beautiful."

"Maybe," Mable says.

"Maybe my mother made them. The flowers on those sheets and tablecloths look just like the baby clothes I found — the baby clothes my mother made for me. And the handkerchiefs have my initials on them. And the dress fits me — which is probably just a coincidence because how could she predict my exact size like that. But you can't deny that it fits, and you can't deny my initials."

I'm on the edge of my chair, breathless after the rush of words.

"You and your grandmother have the same initials, you know," Mable says.

I sit back in my chair. "I know."

My name is the only thing that makes me question just how much my mother loves me. I hate the name itself—Constance. So old fashioned, a throwback to an earlier century when people actually named their kids Independence, Prudence and Increase. The fact that it's also my Grandmother's name makes it that much worse. Every time someone says my name, every time I write it, I'm reminded of this cold presence in my life. I'm reminded of the hate that is always aimed right at me. I don't care if she did give me her nightgown and robe, or offered to let me watch what I wanted on TV. It feels like I have one of those laser-beam targets trained on me all the time, a little red dot marking the spot on my back where the next dart of hatred will hit. *Whap!*

"Your grandmother wasn't always an old woman," Mable says. "It's hard to believe, but she was young once."

"You're right—it is hard to believe."

Mable pushes the iron in slow circles over the sheet. Her feet are hidden under the wrinkled end, and the freshly ironed end hangs only halfway to the floor on the other side of the board. The big, flat rectangle apparently requires greater talent than the folds of a man's dress shirt.

"Have you thought of the possibility that maybe your grandmother made those things for herself?" Mable says.

"Of course, I thought of that," I say. "But she couldn't have made those things. That green dress—she'd never wear anything like that."

"You never know."

"Oh, yes I do," I say. "You don't know her like I know her."

Mable shifts the sheet again and slowly moves the iron over the next section of wrinkles. "You're right. I don't know her like you know her," she says. "But that doesn't mean you know any more about her than I do."

"Do you know who Edward Henderson is?" I say, trying to change the subject.

"No. Who's he?"

"I don't know. That's why I'm asking."

"I never heard that name before," Mable says. The iron picks up more speed. The smooth part of the sheet almost touches the floor on the other side of the board.

"I found some newspaper clippings about him in the attic."

Mable puts the iron down and wipes her forehead with her handkerchief. "I'm sorry I can't help you," she says. The sheet is more than half finished.

"Sure," I say, sulking. "That's O.K."

Mable stops again to wipe her face. She's sweating even in this cool, damp air.

"I can't stand this stuffiness," Mable says. She hobbles over to the door and opens it part way, sticking her face outside. A chill fills the room. Mable's back moves in and out with her breath. She wipes the back of her neck with her handkerchief. The gray curls at her neckline are damp with sweat.

I smell it first, that dry, acrid scent of scorching fiber.

"Mable!" I yell, running to the ironing board. The iron has already branded the sheet.

"Oh, no!" Mable holds both hands to her cheeks as she hobbles back to the ironing board. The faster she tries to move, the slower she seems to go. "How stupid of me!" "I can't believe I did that. I've never ruined anything with an iron in my life."

"I'm sorry," I say.

Mable looks down at the scorched sheet and pats my hand. "Don't be sorry. It's not your fault. And besides, it's just a sheet." She folds it and drops it on the pile of discarded clothes, items Mable deems unfit even for the desperately poor—shirts with mustard stains down the front, pants with holes in the crotches, underwear, of all things. Yuck.

Mable sits down in her chair, and I take my seat next to her.

"I guess I'm getting old," Mable says. It's the scorched sheet that tells her this, not her wrinkled face, gray hair, bad eyesight, or the fact that she can hardly walk anymore. "I guess I need to pay more attention to what I'm doing."

"Like you said, it's just a sheet."

"You're a sweet girl," she says, patting my knee. Even after standing in the cold, Mable's hands are warm, like she's been holding a mug of hot cocoa. "I suppose you're right. I shouldn't be so gloomy." She smiles at me, her cheeks pushing her glasses up off the bridge of her nose. "It's a good lesson, though," she says, resting her hand on my knee again. "Pay attention."

Clouds hide the mountain when I leave Mable and start walking back to the white Victorian on Grove Street. Weather like this, Papa always told me, is what gets people into trouble on Mount Washington. The unrelenting wind, he said, rips the heat right out of a body. The clouds and fog erase the trails, hide, viciously, the path to shelter. People never turned back when they should, Papa said. It's such a simple idea. Turn back and take cover under the trees. Wait for the weather to clear, and then continue to the summit. A little patience made all the difference, he said, sometimes the difference between life and death. And yet it happened again and again.

12

A family of Hassids mills about on the sidewalk outside the Mayflower Theater. The Hassids constantly meander the streets of Green Hill. They walk everywhere, but never appear to have a destination. On my walk to the Helping Hands, I saw this same family walking down the hill, past the Youth Center, away from the center of town. And now here they are near the top of Main Street. The father stands in the middle of the sidewalk, looking straight ahead at nothing, one hand stroking his beard. A boy, maybe eight years old, walks around the father like Frankenstein, arms and legs out straight, his face twisted into a monster's scowl. The mother and her daughters stand off to the side. Don't stare at the mother's wig, although she's probably trying not to stare at me in my shorts and T-shirt. So much skin showing. It's the wrong thing to wear on a day like today—the wrong thing to wear, period. I step off the sidewalk and into the street to pass them.

The air is so heavy with mist it could all turn into a downpour at any second. I start to jog a little, hoping to beat the rain. My arms and legs are filled with sand, heavy and dense. But my stomach doesn't hurt, so I keep up my pace, the mantra pushing and pulling my limbs forward: *Don't – shame – your – mother – Don't – shame – your – mother.*

A wet splotch hits my shoulder. Another splashes on my knee, then my hand. I change the mantra: *Just – one – more – week – Just – one – more – week.* My legs refuse to move any faster. Cold and wet, my body goes on strike.

A truck slows alongside me.

"Hey," Ethan says. "Want a ride?"

I shake my head and wave him off.

"Come on—you'll get drenched."

I take a few more strides, telling myself I don't need a ride. I'm doing it—I'm running. And then I realize that my legs have already stopped. I lean forward, hands on my knees, like Ethan did that time I let him catch up with me at the top of the hill.

Inside my head, I'm screaming at myself, my legs, my feet, my arms, to move, move, move. *Don't be so weak.*

Ethan leans over and opens the passenger door to the truck. "Come on," he says.

Hot air blasts on the windshield to keep it from fogging, warming my face at the same time. The whole cab rumbles with the engine. I wipe water from my forehead with the palm of my hand.

Ethan leans toward me, reaches an arm across me. I pull back, suck in my stomach, flatten myself against the seat, and hold my breath. Why does that beautiful arm need to come so close?

He opens the glove compartment and pulls out a handful of napkins.

"Here," he says.

I stare at him, still holding my breath.

"To dry yourself off a little."

"Oh," I say, pulling my fingernails out of the vinyl seat. I reach a hand out ever so slightly and snatch the napkins from him. "Thanks."

"Haven't seen you on the road much lately," Ethan says.

"I've been a little under the weather." I dab my face with one of the napkins.

"That's too bad. Nothing serious, I hope."

"No."

"Hey, have you had lunch yet?" Ethan says.

I shake my head.

The coffee shop is packed. There are a lot of tourists in the booths and at the tables near the picture windows at the front of the shop. I can tell they're tourists by their T-shirts. They say things like *This T-shirt Climbed Mount Washington* and *I Brake For Moose In North Conway.* The rain is keeping them from the attractions at the National Forest. It's a bad day to see the Flume or the Old Man on the Mountain. The fare for the cog railway to the summit of Mount Washington would be wasted on a day like today. No one here is really dressed for it anyway. It's probably about twenty or thirty degrees up there. On days like this, the tourists comb the antique stores in towns like Green Hill.

Mixed in with the tourists are lesbians, who want a break from the food at the Womyn's Center, and townspeople, young married couples with children who moved to Green Hill since my last visit and old men and women whose families have lived here since the birth of the granite mountains. I recognize some people from church and some from all those summers. One of the old men used to fill Papa's truck at the gas station. Another used to be the mailman.

Ethan and I wait by the door for a table to open up. In a few minutes, two women get up from a booth and head for the door. They are both in their mid-forties. One of them looks like she just stepped out of an L.L. Bean catalog, wearing a long khaki skirt with buttons down the front and a denim button-down shirt. She has short dark hair and glasses. Her friend is in black pants and a pink short-sleeved shirt. A lesbian couple, I bet. They chat as they approach the door. The one from the L.L. Bean catalog stops in front of me.

"You're Constance, aren't you?"

"Connie," I correct her. "Yes."

She holds out her hand. "I'm Maxine," she says, and waits for a flash of recognition from me. "From the library? Your grandmother is one of our best volunteers."

Her hand is still there, waiting for mine to give it a shake.

"Oh. Hi," I say.

"Your grandmother is just so happy to have you this summer. You're all she talks about."

Two teenage boys and a teenage girl push in through the door behind us. Their clothes are wet and water drips from their hair. Rain pounds the sidewalk outside and pours down the coffee shop's windows, blurring the view of the street.

"We better grab your booth," Ethan says to Maxine. She squeezes his wrist.

"Have a nice lunch, Ethan. Nice to meet you, Connie." Maxine and her friend shuffle out the door as Ethan and I wind our way to the booth.

Ethan orders a hamburger and French fries and I have a large vanilla milkshake.

"That's all?" Ethan says, as the little French Canadian guy makes his way back to the grill with our orders. "You're sure? It's my treat."

"Yes," I say. "I can't really put too much on my stomach right now."

"I'm sorry," he says, shaking his head. "You've been sick. Maybe this was a dumb idea."

"No, no—it's fine." I try to think of a way to explain, so he doesn't feel bad. "I'm not that sick. I just can't eat certain foods, a lot of foods. I have allergies, but no one really knows what I'm allergic to, and then this ulcer, my mother keeps taking me to doctors, but..."

Ethan looks at me with his eyebrows pinched together, like I'm speaking in tongues. Why am I telling him all of this?

"Aren't you kind of young for an ulcer?" he says.

Part of me wants to tell him everything. But there is no explaining this, and there are some things no one really wants to know.

"It's nothing," I say. "I just like vanilla milkshakes."

When our food arrives, I let the sweet cream and vanilla melt on my tongue, the cold coating my slowly healing stomach. Between bites of his burger, Ethan tells me about his plans for his father's landscape business. It's really his business now, with his dad too ill to work. He wants to expand and get more into landscape design, not just mowing lawns and mulching. He's taking a landscape course this fall at a nearby college.

"Sounds great," I say.

"What about you? What are your plans?"

I tell him about my job at the academy.

"Teaching," he says, through a bite of French fry. "That's something."

"I get to live there, in my own apartment in one of the dorms. It has a kitchen, a pretty big living room, and a really nice bedroom with a private bathroom. I'll be able to cook my own meals, go food shopping, do my own laundry."

"Laundry," he says. "Fun."

My cheeks burn. I stir my milkshake. "I just meant that I'm looking forward to being on my own."

"I know what you mean," Ethan says, leaning forward on his elbows. "I have my own place, but my parents are right there, you know? Don't get me wrong—I'm really glad I can be there to help out with my dad. But sometimes you just want your own space, to be alone, by yourself. On your own, like you said. I can understand you looking forward to getting away from your mom."

I look up from my milkshake. "I didn't say that. That's not what I meant," I say, a little too forcefully. "I don't want to get away from my mother. We get along really well. She doesn't even want me to move."

"But you are."

"Well…yes," I say. "I have to. It's part of the job."

"Maybe it's just me then," Ethan says. "But sometimes I just wish I had more space."

Ethan works on his French fries while I savor my milkshake and look at the pictures hanging in our booth. One is of skiers careening down the steep side of Tuckerman's Ravine, little black dots against the deep white snow. The other is of the observatory on Mount Washington's summit. Long shelves of snow stretch off the back of the building, the result of the punishing winter winds. Scraggly shrubs near the summit grow this way, too, all their branches on one side.

"You know, I've been thinking," Ethan says.

I hate that phrase—"I've been thinking." It's a sure signal of a bad idea.

"You should come up to the Youth Center tomorrow night. We're having a swing night."

"A what?" I say.

"A swing night. You know, dancing."

And there it is—the bad idea. My being in a social situation is bad enough, but a *dancing* social situation—forget it. This is a very bad idea. This is like that guy who tied a whole bunch of weather balloons to his lawn chair, which launched him into the air so high, so fast, that pilots on planes saw him. Good thing he had his BB gun with him to shoot the balloons and bring the lawn chair back down to earth, getting tangled up in the power lines on the way.

"It'll be fun," Ethan says, and I'm sure floating away in a lawn chair sounded like a lot of fun, too. "You really should come."

"Maybe," I say, and suck down the rest of my milkshake.

After lunch, Ethan gives me a ride back to Grandmother's.

"So, the dance is tomorrow night, if you're interested," Ethan says, as we pull into Grandmother's driveway. Raindrops ping loudly against the roof of the cab. "Just think about it."

"I will," I say. "Thanks for lunch." I slam the door behind me while he says something like "Maybe I'll see you there," and run to the house. The rain chills me all over again. I stop on the porch. The truck still idles in the driveway. He's waiting for me to get all the way inside before leaving. I go inside without looking back.

The problem is, I don't look forward either. I look down at my feet, and before I know it, there is another pair of feet on the floor in front of me. I almost step on them.

"Constance."

And then I want to step on them, grind her long, pointy toes into the floor with my heel. Instead, I look up and say, "Yes?"

"Where were you?"

"I went for a walk."

"You shouldn't be out in the rain. It's not good for you."

"Sorry."

"And who was that just now? I thought I heard a car in the driveway."

I look down at my feet, flexing one ankle, then the other. "Ethan Matthews. He gave me a ride home."

"Oh. Well. That was nice of him."

The sound of rain on the roof fills the space between and all around us. I look up from my feet. She looks at the wall to her left. I adjust my ponytail. Satisfied, that our conversation is over, I move toward the stairs.

"Constance."

"Yes?"

"I need you to do some work in the basement now."

"O.K."

"I need you to go through your grandfather's tools and things down there."

My hand grips the banister. "Fine."

"I need you to—" She stops to clear her throat, raising a hand to cover her mouth as she coughs and then wrapping her arms tighter around her middle. "I need you to pick out what you want...of his."

I turn toward her ever so slightly, like a plant reaching for a pale shaft of sunlight.

"I was going to sell them, put an ad in the paper. They're all in perfect condition. He kept his tools in perfect condition, you know."

"I know."

She turns away, so her back is toward me, clears her throat again.

"Then I thought you may want some of them, having spent so much time in the wood shop with him."

This is another one of those "almost" moments. I am afraid to move, to breathe.

"Well? Do you want them or not?"

"Yeah, I guess," I say, as flatly as possible.

"They're all in the basement," she says, walking away down the hall. "Put on a sweatshirt. It's chilly down there."

I control my legs to walk normally up the stairs. If I run, she'll know how much I want those tools, and then she'll change her mind. She'll take them away.

"That Ethan, he's a nice boy," she says, just as I reach the top step. She says it quietly, as if I'm not meant to hear. But of course I'm meant to hear it. I wait for her to mumble the second half of the comment, that he's too nice for me. But she doesn't say it. The absence of the insult makes me angrier than the dig would have. I can't figure her out anymore. I don't know what she wants from me.

I look up at the ceiling, through the roof of the white Victorian, up to God and beg Him to tell me what my mother and Grandmother want. If I only knew—if they would just tell me, I'd give it to them. Whatever they wanted, I'd give it to them.

13

Parties make me go catatonic, with all those people talking to each other, talking to me, laughing, dancing, and looking to draw me in. At the few parties I've been to, I tried to hang back, hide in the shadows, but there's some unspoken rule at parties that says it's everybody's responsibility to uproot the wallflowers and throw us into the fray. They go after me like an invasive weed.

So, I'm glad I have a full day before the Swing Night at the Youth Center. It gives me plenty of time first to decide whether or not I'm going to go, and second, to work myself up into a good frenzy, tie myself into a pile of knots, make myself sick to my stomach about it if I do decide to go. And that's a big "if."

If I go, what do I tell Grandmother? A walk—no, I'd be out for hours. She'd know something was up. She'd call in the State Police to find me—not because she cared, though. Just so she could tattle on me.

I could say I was going to her beloved library—a very pious and prudish activity, on par with going to church. But I can't because the library, and every other place in Green Hill, closes at five o'clock on the dot. The place turns into a ghost town as soon as the sun starts to dip toward the horizon.

Friends are out, because I have no friends in Green Hill, or anywhere else.

The Youth Center itself emerges as a good cover story. I can tell her I'm going to the Youth Center for one of their activities—I want to get some ideas for things to do with the girls in the dorm at my new job. This is the perfect lie. Not only is it partly true—which is the best kind of lie—it will also appeal to Grandmother's industrious nature. To Grandmother, industriousness is Godliness, the sacrament that fills the years between Baptism and the Last Rites.

It's a good lie, but that doesn't mean I'm going. There are other things to consider—like my wardrobe.

All I have with me are old T-shirts and shorts, half of them torn, the other half stained. There are a couple of pairs of jeans and a sweatshirt with the neck cut out of it. My best article of clothing is my nightgown, but that's probably not appropriate. At least I know that much.

Other than my nightgown, the best option is a black, fitted T-shirt with no stains or holes and a pair of jeans. My running shoes complete the ensemble.

The green dress in the Hope Chest has crossed my mind. It's the kind of dress that's made for dancing, to make a woman look like she's gliding effortlessly across the floor with her dashing partner. It's probably better for waltzing, something breezy like that, than for a swing or jitterbug. I don't know much about dancing, but I've seen some of those old movies with Fred Astaire and Ginger Rogers. Long skirts like the one on the green dress are for sweeping across the dance floor.

The green dress would be too complicated. I'd have to carry it out of the house in a bag and find someplace to change on my way up to the center of town. I have a vision of being caught in someone's headlights on the side of the road wearing just my underwear as I dig the dress out of the bag.

No. The dress may fit, but it's not for me. The black T-shirt and jeans would have to do.

A good lie and a decent outfit don't mean I'll go. What would I do there? Dance? Socialize?

The day of said Swing Night, I keep myself busy. I get up early and run an extra long route, checking the golf course for the moose and then heading out of town to the sign—"You are now leaving Green Hill." In a week, I'll blow by that sign for good. I'll speed past it and yell out the window something like, "Kiss my ass!" Only I don't swear. I'd like to learn, so words like "ass" won't get stuck in my throat. I'd like to have the mouth of a toothless mountain woman.

On my way back to Grove Street, I swing by the Matthews' house. The ruts and holes force me to slow way down, weave through them carefully, or I'll break an ankle.

Ethan's truck is gone. The apartment is quiet, but the barn is open. I stop jogging for a minute, listening for anyone in the house. It's dark and quiet, too. I make a dash for the barn.

The smell of oil hangs thick inside. Tools are strewn everywhere, dirty, caked with grease, rusted. The lawnmower I hit is half taken apart on the floor. Apparently Ethan is trying to fix it. Being in the garage reminds me of working with Papa in his woodshop. Papa could fix anything, and he kept his tools immaculately clean and in order. He labeled little boxes of nails and tacks. He even kept his scrap wood separated in plastic trash barrels. When he needed a square of two-by-four, he knew just where to find it.

There's a workbench next to me. I run my hand along it. The wood is dark and shiny with age. It probably belonged to Ethan's father.

I think of Papa's knife, the one Grandmother gave me, how touching the handle is like touching Papa's hand again.

I think of the dance, and how I probably won't go. I won't wrap my arms around Ethan's neck, like the girls in those bad 1980s movies, and sway with him to some sappy love song.

A case of drill bits lays open on the workbench.

The plastic rectangle fits nicely in my pocket, a sad substitute.

I sweep the attic about a hundred times during the day, my only way to avoid Grandmother. She keeps the Hope Chest locked, and I keep picking it with one of her bobby pins. If she only knew, maybe she'd stop wearing her hair in that tight bun. I go through the chest nightly now. Looking at the flowers and designs on the bed sheets and tablecloths is the same as reading a storybook. My favorite piece is a white rectangle, just big enough for a coffee table, with scenes from Peter Rabbit along all four sides. There is Peter, stealing vegetables from Mr. McGregor. And there is Peter in bed taking a spoonful of chamomile tea and honey from his mother. And in the center of the rectangle, the whole family of rabbits gathered in their earthy lodge, a fire glowing in the fireplace. Mama rabbit sits in her rocking chair sewing, with all her little bunnies playing on the floor in front of her.

It wasn't until I found the little pillowcase, with little brown rabbits hopping along the edge, that I realized the linen rectangle wasn't a tablecloth but a baby blanket, a coverlet for a cradle.

After sweeping the attic, I take a walk to the Grocery and take what I need, another compact of blush. It gets lost in the large shoulder bag I use as a purse. Even if they stop me, they won't find it in there.

I put a pack of gum on the counter in front of the Santa reject. Today, he's wearing a pale blue T-shirt with a white polar bear on it. The polar bear's back shimmers with white glitter. I know I'm showing off, being stupid. The only people who wander a whole store just to buy a pack of gum are shoplifters. But I do it anyway. Santa rings up my gum, a little slower than usual, but he does it. He looks me in the eye the whole time, waiting for me to slip up, to give a sign. He has no idea with whom he's dealing.

Grandmother makes salad and corn on the cob for dinner. I'm supposed to have white rice and more broiled chicken, but I just can't. Grandmother doesn't say a word as I put a steaming ear of corn on my plate and fill the other side with salad.

It's the perfect meal for the two of us. It requires a lot of chewing and for me, actually sticking an ear of corn in my mouth. Grandmother cuts the corn off the cob onto her plate—dentures. Instead of talking, we let the crunch of iceberg lettuce and the corn fill the silence in the bare kitchen. Not even the grimy outlines of her plates and utensils are left on the walls. Last week, Grandmother pulled out all the little nails that held them in place and swabbed down the whole room, floor to ceiling, with Murphy's Oil Soap.

Avoiding Grandmother all day meant no lunch, so I'm starving. I eat three ears of corn and two bowls of salad. And then I remember that lettuce makes me burp and corn makes me fart. I'll be belching and tooting all night. Charming. The Youth Center is definitely out.

Grandmother chews her last bite of salad. She dabs the corners of her mouth with her napkin—not leaving even a smudge on it, I'm sure—and places it next to her plate.

"I'm going out tonight," she says.

Just then a corn kernel gets sucked down my windpipe. I can't breathe, and yet I'm able to make this hacking noise. Grandmother runs over to me and whacks my back with the palm of her hand. I want to ask her if this is supposed to help with the choking or just really hurt my back, but I can't breathe yet. She whacks me until I stop.

"Good God," she says, bringing me a glass of water.

"I'm sorry. I'm fine now."

I take a sip of water.

"I'm going out with some friends."

Some water goes down the wrong way and I spew a mouthful all over the table.

"What is wrong with you?" she says.

"Nothing," I say, wiping up the water with my napkin, which is dotted with oily smudges from the salad dressing and butter. I wipe the water up quickly and shove the balled-up napkin back in my lap. She starts to clear the table.

"The historical society meeting is tonight. With all the work around here, I haven't been all summer," she says. "I thought I'd let you know because I could be home late."

"O.K. Have fun."

She turns on the hot water and squeezes some dish soap into the sink.

"You should have fun, too," she says. Her voice is a little too high. The words come out of her mouth slowly. She puts one of the plates in the sink and starts to scrub. "If you want to go out...somewhere, I don't know. You could. That's all. You could go out tonight if you wanted to."

The woman standing at the sink looks like my Grandmother, a tall spindle tightly wrapped in navy-blue linen. She has white hair like my Grandmother, pulled just as tightly into the bun at the back of her head, creating the same instant facelift. She is scrubbing an already fairly clean plate with too much force just like my Grandmother would. But this is not my Grandmother.

"Sure," I say, scrutinizing her as she rinses the dish and begins scrubbing it again. I scan her back for the hole where the alien entered her body.

"Maybe there's something at the Youth Center tonight," she says. "I thought I saw a sign, that they're having some program tonight. An activity. Something." The plastic scrubber scrapes against the plate on its third pass. "It's just a suggestion. You don't have to go. I just thought I'd mention it."

I look at the spot on her neck just above the collar of her dress.

"Maybe I'll do that," I say.

"It's just a suggestion." She starts scrubbing my plate. Scrub and rinse, scrub and rinse, scrub and rinse, before she puts it in the dish drain.

"It's really up to you," she says, and I am glad I'm done eating, or I would have choked to death for sure.

She rips a sheet of paper towel off the roll and squirts Windex all over the stove. She wipes every corner of it, even though all she did was boil water for the corn tonight. When the stove has been done three times, Grandmother wipes down the counters three times, where all she made was salad.

Grandmother rips a new sheet of paper towel off the roll and comes toward the kitchen table. Convinced I'm next to be cleansed, I jump up and go to the sink. I dry the dishes and put them away in the empty cabinets.

When she's finished, Grandmother puts the Windex under the sink and then washes her hands in water so hot it turns her skin pink. She dries her hands and puts on her rings. She still wears her wedding and engagement rings. Papa's ring has not been seen since he died. When she leaves, maybe I'll go through some of the drawers in her room. Maybe I'll do that instead of going out.

All of a sudden, this is all up to me. Grandmother might as well have shoved a rattlesnake into my hand and said, "Here — take it or leave it." The situation is that unfair.

I'm afraid, too, of what Grandmother really wants from me. It feels like a trap, or a test to see what I'll do, if I'll make the right decision, or if I'll make a mistake. A cup of coffee, a milkshake she doesn't know about, is one thing. But this is something else. Did she want me to stay or go? What would she tell my mother? Did my mother tell her to do this? My mother likes tests. My Grandmother does, too; at least I thought she did. But then she did offer me my pick of Papa's tools.

That could've been a trick, too, although I'm not sure how or why.

It doesn't matter. I just need to know what my mother and Grandmother want me to do. I'll do it, whatever it is, but the guessing kills me. The guessing ignites a little flame in my belly.

It's a cool evening, but I'm hot. I sit on the bed and lean in front of the open window. A breeze sweeps across my face. If I go, my mother will find out and I'll be punished. She'll probably ignore me for a year.

Then again, maybe that's not such a bad punishment.

I won't go. I'll stay in this little room and call myself names all night, maybe write them down, so I don't forget how dumb I am.

This, or something like it—I can't articulate what it is— seems bigger and worse to me than disappointing my mother. The way I turn my back on it, I know it's important to understand what this is, to know who I'm disappointing by not going to this stupid dance.

I could walk there and walk back, stay for just twenty minutes. I'd be home in plenty of time to call myself names for being such a useless idiot about boys—for instance, still referring to them as "boys," like a kindergartener.

And then I think of my mother again. Grandmother will tell her—no doubt about it. Maybe she has been nicer to me lately, but that doesn't mean anything.

I shouldn't go. *Don't go. Stay here. It's safer all around.*

At this point, a certain kind of person would start to wonder about herself, wonder what kind of girl, at age 22, still worries so much about how her mother will punish her. A certain kind of person would wonder why, on the brink of adulthood, she couldn't make a simple decision like this. It's a dance at a Youth Center, after all, not Amateur Night at a strip club.

I pick through all the compacts in the bottom-most drawer of the bureau. I've collected quite a sampling of colors during my stay in Green Hill, all of them compliments of the Green Hill Grocery. I choose Bubble Gum Pink because it's the only one with a mirror. How else could I apply it? I can't very well stand in the kitchen and hold Grandmother's chrome toaster in front of my face to see what I'm doing.

The instructions on the back of the cardboard packaging say I'm supposed to pucker my lips and then apply the blush along the line of my cheekbones. Do I even have cheekbones?

I swipe the brush over the cake of powder a few times. I raise it to my face, tentatively, watching the sliver of my cheek in the mirror. I move my hand slowly and carefully, as if I'm holding a razor blade and not a soft brush dusted with pink powder.

I move the brush back and forth across my cheek, wondering how much to put on. It doesn't look like enough. You're supposed to see it, right? Isn't that the point of make-up? I raise the brush to my face again, but the knocking at the bedroom door stops me. I snap the compact shut and shove it under my pillow.

"Come in."

Grandmother opens the door just enough to stick her head in.

"I'm leaving now," she says.

"O.K."

"I'll be home later."

"O.K."

"If you go out," she says, looking down at her feet, "just leave the door unlocked."

"Fine."

"Well, then," she says, offering another failed attempt at a smile. This time, it's one of those weird anti-smiles, the kind where the mouth actually curves downward. It's the opposite of a smile, and yet not really a scowl either. Other people do this too, mostly mothers who probably don't realize what they look like. Grandmother, I'm sure, knows exactly what she looks like, and she's doing it on purpose to keep me guessing. Is this approval or disapproval?

Her next facial expression is much more clear—a frown. "Are you feeling all right?"

"Yes. Fine. Why?"

"You look flushed. Your cheeks are so pink."

"I'm a little warm," I say, and my heart slowly slides down into the bottom of my sneakers. My first attempt at beauty and I only succeed in making myself look ill.

"You're sure you're all right?"

"I feel fine. Really."

She looks at me long and hard, and I pray she can't see the powder particles on my face. I feel like a teenager about to get caught smoking. My heart pounds. But it's just blush, a little powder with a tint to it. Nothing nearly as sinister as cigarettes or liquor or—God forbid—hair dye.

"I'll see you later tonight then," she says.

"Right. See you later."

I listen to her walk down the hall, count her footsteps on the stairs and wait for the slam of the screen door before I take the compact out from under my pillow. I look at my cheeks in the mirror. I wipe off some of the blush with my fingers. Then I brush more on. Then I wipe some off.

Grandmother's car starts and then fades away up the street. Only then do I go down the stairs and out the front door.

14

I keep looking over my shoulder as I walk to the Youth Center. Even though she's three hours away, I still believe my mother could be following me. Three hours' distance doesn't mean anything. She's still with me. My mother is always with me. Just like that night I went out with some of the girls. That night she marched me out of the ice-cream shop in front of everyone.

A promotion kept her from following me to college, getting an apartment and cooking my meals, but she found other ways to watch me. She demanded I come home every weekend. The cross-country and track seasons allowed me to stay on campus most weekends in the fall, but during the long winters, she insisted I come home every Friday after my last class. And she wouldn't let me leave until Monday morning, even if my first class was at 8 a.m.

I protested, in my own way. I kept my nose in my books. I was slow to help with the dishes after dinner. I left my room a mess, the bed unmade, of course. It was lame, but I didn't have much choice. My mother said as long as she was paying for my education, I lived by her rules. Of course, she wasn't paying that much since all my running trophies had earned me a full scholarship. But still, she was paying something. Room and board, books — that cost money.

A little gift always waited for me on my bed — small things, a new shirt, a box of stationery, a bracelet or a pair of earrings. She'd stand at my bedroom door and watch me open them. I was good at faking my enthusiasm at these gifts. I never wanted them. They were just little treats, and yet far too expensive in their own way.

Every weekend, my mother planned a day of shopping at a different mall. She'd buy me new pajamas and new clothes. With her promotion, my mother didn't have time to sew anymore. She'd come in the dressing room with me and help me try on the girly shirts and designer jeans she'd chosen for me. She'd stand behind me in the mirror sizing up the outfits she'd chosen.

"Those are perfect," she'd say of jeans I thought were too low waisted.

"Adorable!" she'd squeal at the bright pink fitted shirt—a color I wouldn't be caught dead in. "You could use something a little brighter than all those drab greens and grays you always wear."

Then she'd take me to lunch and she'd let me share a dessert with her, a chocolate brownie sundae, or something equally awful and wonderful and so far off my special diet. At home, we'd spread out all my new clothes on the couches in the living room. My mother would hold them up to me and sigh over how cute I looked. She was so relaxed and happy for the rest of the weekend, which meant I was relaxed and happy.

And then Monday morning came. I always had to leave early to make my first class. She'd sit at the kitchen table, hunched over a cup of coffee, sulking. She'd stare at me while I made my breakfast, something fast, plain toast or instant oatmeal. She'd watch me eat and never say a word. She'd just sit there in her bathrobe, her hair falling in her face, her eyes slits.

When I finished eating, she followed me through the house as I gathered my things. She stayed right on my heels, whispering in my ear.

"You think you're so smart."

"You think you're better than me, but you're not."

"You're no good. You were never any good."

The whisperings changed and grew louder the closer I got to leaving.

"You don't love me. You say you do, but you don't."

"After everything I've done for you," she'd say, and then shove me from behind.

"If you really loved me, you wouldn't leave me."

"A good daughter wouldn't do this to her mother."

She'd shove me again, two or three more times.

"But you're not a good daughter. You're stupid and selfish. Worthless!"

"You're nothing!"

"Do you hear me—you're nothing!"

She chased me like an angry dog. You should never run from an angry dog, so I just kept moving forward at a steady pace. Packed my bag, gathered my toothbrush and medications, put on my coat and walked out the door without looking back at her. Saying goodbye, I'd learned, only made things worse. Her anger turned to hysteria. She'd grab me and cry against my neck, holding me so tightly I couldn't breathe.

"I didn't mean it—I take it all back. Just don't leave," she'd cry.

"But I have to."

"Please stay with me. I miss you so much—that's why I say all those things. I miss you so much, it makes me crazy."

"I can't stay."

"Don't you love me?" she'd say. "Don't you even love your own mother?"

"Yes," I'd say. "I love you."

And then she'd shove me away from her, sometimes knocking me to the floor.

In April of my senior year, I tried to spend one weekend on campus. The coaches of the running teams planned a party to honor the graduating seniors. It was stupid. I don't even know why I wanted to go. But for whatever reason, I tried to tell my mother that I would not be coming home that weekend.

"Is there a meet? I don't have a meet on my calendar."

"No."

"If it's exams, you can study for them at home."

"Exams won't be a problem," I said. They never were. I studied as if my life depended on the next pop quiz. By the time finals came around, I could write a dissertation on just about every class I'd taken. While everyone else pulled all-nighters at the end of each semester, I slept.

On the flip side, while everyone else had friends and a life, I was the only loser at the library every single night. People started to think I worked there, asked me how to find the periodical stacks and the Oxford English Dictionary.

"Then I'll see you Friday at home," my mother said.

I paced my dorm room, which was so small I couldn't really walk from one end to the other without bruising myself on something, the corner of my desk, or the end of the bed. It was tiny, but it was a single, and that's all that matters when you're a senior in college—that, and getting a job.

"There's a party for the running teams this Saturday, and I thought I'd go."

"Oh. I see."

"It's just one weekend," I said. "I really would like to go. It's a special thing for the seniors, and since I'm a senior..."

"Then I guess you should go."

My mother is good at this—tricking me into thinking I'm making a decision.

Then, she very calmly said: "I have something to tell you, but it can wait until next weekend."

"What is it?" I said, slowly.

"It's nothing. Besides, if I tell you now, you'll worry. And I don't want you to worry."

I had that feeling again, of stepping on a landmine. "I'm already worried, so you might as well just tell me what's going on."

"I don't really know how to say this," my mother said. "So, I'll just say it: There's a lump."

All of my muscles and blood vessels and organs—all of my insides—pulled away from my skin then. "A what?"

"A lump," she said. "But don't worry. If it's cancer, the doctor said we're catching it early. At worst, I'll have surgery and chemotherapy."

"Cancer?"

"See, I knew I shouldn't have told you over the phone. But you insisted."

I swallowed a few times, just to feel my throat working inside my body. "When did you find out about all this?"

"Just this week. It's been a very hard time for me," she said. Her voice was flat, even. "Now you know why I was looking forward to seeing you, but if you can't come home..."

"I'll be home. I'm leaving right now."

"Don't be silly. You still have classes, and your party this weekend. You should stay. Have fun. I'll be fine."

"I'm coming home now."

"There's nothing you can do."

"I want to be there."

"Well, if you really want to, then I guess you should."

I pulled into the driveway an hour later. I didn't even pack anything, not even my books. I ran to the door, where she waited for me. Before I knew what I was doing, I fell into her arms.

"It's O.K.," my mother crooned, rubbing her hand across my back in large circles. "Everything is O.K."

"Tell me the truth—how sick are you?"

She let go of me and straightened me up in front of her. She smiled at me with that cool, strange smile. She was so calm that it started to make me mad. How could she be so calm?

"Listen to me," she said, running her hands over my shoulders. "There's no lump."

My mouth filled with saliva, and I had to keep swallowing it back, fighting the gag reflex rippling through my throat. At least I knew my insides were still there, working.

"I'm not sick," she said, still smiling. "And you've made me so happy. You chose me, and now I know how much you love me." She folded me back into her arms and held me so tightly I thought for sure I was going to throw up all over her. There was nothing left in me then, and I wondered if I would ever feel the blood pulsing against the back of my skin again. I wondered if running would even bring that feeling back.

When Monday morning rolled around again, I showered, dressed, and ate breakfast. My mother sat at the kitchen table, hunched over her cup of coffee. After missing almost a whole week of school to be with her, I was going to receive the same farewell.

At that moment, a certain kind of person would've wished cancer on her mother, a particularly painful and prolonged cancer. But I'm not that kind of person.

"You'll be sorry when I'm dead," my mother said, dogging me through the house as I collected my things.

"Who's going to take care of you then?"

"You think you can get away from me, you sick little worm?"

Faster and faster, I moved through the house, hopping into my sneakers, grabbing my jacket out of the closet, and opening the front door to leave.

"You'll never get away," she whispered in my ear. "You can't live without me."

By the time I reach Main Street, I'm out of breath and I don't know why. Then I realize that I'm running, fast. I'm running like someone is chasing me. I look over my shoulder. The street is empty. A family of Hassids loiters along the stone wall that extends out on both sides of the Youth Center. A girl in a dark-brown dress looks at me, then down at her foot, which is tracing circles on the sidewalk. Maybe she wants to go to Swing Night. Maybe she could go in my place, one misfit helping another. She's my height, and we have the same color hair. If it were dark enough inside, Ethan would never know the difference.

"Hey, there," a voice booms behind me. "You made it."

Up until tonight, I'd only seen Ethan in his work clothes, shorts smeared with dirt and shirts full of holes and grass stains. Tonight, he has on a clean, white T-shirt that hangs loosely from his shoulders. The shirt is tucked into khaki shorts that stop just above his knees. My eyes land on his scar just for a moment. His hair looks shorter, and I hope he didn't go out special and have his buzz cut trimmed up just for tonight. I can't take that kind of pressure, not on top of my two strongest urges at this moment—checking to see if my nipples are poking through my bra, and sniffing my armpits to be sure I'd put on deodorant.

"You got some sun. Your grandmother must've given you a break and let you out of the house," Ethan says.

I frown at him.

"Your face—looks like you got a little sunburn."

"Right," I say, "Sunburn." I make a mental note—no more blush.

"Come on in. They're just about to start."

I look at the girl in the brown dress one more time, but she's wandering down the sidewalk away from me, trailing behind the rest of her family. Kiss that plan goodbye.

The Hassidic family and their special clothes, special hair cuts, the big fur hats the old men wear, the prayer shawls, the beanies on the boys' heads, the extra thick nylons on the women's legs—all those rules make me think of my mother again.

"There's no turning back now," Ethan says. He holds the door open for me. I look over my shoulder once more and step through.

Inside the Youth Center, all the quaint charm of the exterior of the old train station has been stripped away. What's left is a long rectangle with bare white walls and a pea-green linoleum floor. The windows along the long walls of the rectangle are wide open. Fluorescent lights hum overhead, making the room obnoxiously bright. Switching places with the Hassidic girl never would have worked.

Two rows of people are already lined up. Most of them are unenthused teenagers dressed all in black, right down to their black canvas All Stars. Thank God I decided against the green dress. The girls wear thick black circles of eyeliner around their eyes. It must take a lot of skill to coat the rim of their eyelids. I can't even get blush right. I'd probably lose an eye trying to do that.

Some of the boys painted their fingernails with black nail polish. That always creeps me out—not the black nail polish, the boys who wear it. I glance at Ethan's hands, just to be sure. All clear.

There are spots of color in the group, too—the nerdy kids who cross off the days on the calendar leading up to Saturday swing night. Some of them wear their Boy Scout uniforms and hover around Ethan. The way they yap at him and nip at his heels, I can tell they worship him.

He knows all of their names, of course—Forrest, River, Sky. This is what people name their kids up here.

Ethan and I and a few others are among the oldest in the room, and I pretend that I actually am the oldest. Instead of following my first impulse to sit down in a corner and bang my head into the wall as I rock back and forth on my butt, I pretend I'm perfectly comfortable, that this is something I do all the time. That I enjoy people and crowds and parties.

Ethan and I take a place at the end of the lines, at the back of the room.

"Thank you, God," I say—out loud.

"What?" Ethan says.

"Nothing. Are we chaperones or something?"

"Sort of. They like to have some older people here to keep an eye on things. There's nothing better to do anyway, so why not, right?"

"Right," I say. "Why not?" I think of my mother again, one of a million reasons why not. And then I smile—at myself, the perpetually chaperoned girl keeping an eye on someone else's kids. I don't know if this is poetic justice, just ironic, or merely sad. The chattering stops when a small woman with a bright red crew cut breezes into the center of the two rows: The dance instructor. She wears a yellow dress, circa 1940, with a full skirt that stands out when she twirls around. Her high-heeled shoes are tan, to match her tights. She points to a guy tying his shoes at the front of the room. She says his name and explains that they're from some dance studio in Littleton, but I don't hear it because my ears are ringing with the realization that I am going to have to touch Ethan Matthews.

The woman uses one of the Goth boys—Tree or Grass, I think his name is—to demonstrate how we're supposed to stand with our partners. My mouth goes dry as her right hand grasps the boy's left. I get all light-headed when she takes the boy's other hand and wraps it around her waist.

This is a bad idea.

This is like the time I lied to my mother about going to a boy-girl party when I was in seventh grade. I couldn't help myself—I liked this boy, and he liked me, and we were both invited to this girl's birthday party. I can't even remember their names now, but it was so important to me at the time that I be at that party, even if only to watch it all from a dark corner. My mother followed me there and marched down to the basement that was all decorated with streamers and balloons—helium balloons, no less. She yanked me out of my dark corner, pulling me into the light where she called me a lying slut in front of everyone.

Two months later, my mother ended the silent treatment by saying, "You must think I'm very mean, but I'm only trying to protect you." I was lying down in my bed. She gripped my ankle so hard it bruised. "I can't let you make the same mistake I made," she said. "I can't allow it, Connie. You know I can't allow it."

Dancing with Ethan is that kind of bad idea.

There's a warm hand in mine. Then I see the hand is attached to Ethan's body, and the only thing that stops me from screaming is the big bubble of salad dressing that I belch out right in Ethan's face. I slap my hand over my mouth and take three big steps backward. An invisible cloud of vinegar and garlic vapors hangs in the air between us.

"Sorry," I say, through my hand.

Ethan just laughs—at me, for sure, not with me or near me.

"Forget it." He waves me back toward him. "Come on—we're falling behind."

"Maybe I'll just sit this out. I'm not good at dancing, anyway."

"Oh, come on. I'm no good at it either. Just try it—if you really hate it, you can sit out." He holds a hand out to me and takes a couple of steps toward me. "Come on. We'll look like a couple of klutzes together. It'll be fun."

I step toward Ethan, put my hand in his. The calluses on his fingers and palm are dry and rough. They remind me of Papa's hands.

"Your hands are cold," he says.

"Sorry," I say, instinctively pulling away. He doesn't let go.

"Don't worry about it." His feet are moving already, and I follow his gaze down the line of couples to the instructors. They demonstrate the step—Right, left, back-step. Right, left, back-step.

In order to do this, I need to remember which is my left foot and which is my right, and in order to do that I need to stop thinking about Ethan's hand on the small of my back. My whole body is cold except for that spot underneath Ethan's hand and where our palms meet. Two pools of electricity that make me shiver when they pulse.

Everything inside me starts to pull away from my skin, collapsing into a tight ball that can be buried far away from those two pools of electricity. Only I don't want to disappear this time. I kind of want to stay. Maybe. Just a little. I want to stop looking over my shoulder and look in front of me instead.

My feet move—Right, left, back-step. Right, left, back-step. Only with my feet it comes out *clomp, clomp, clomp-clomp*. I'm a runner, not a ballerina.

"Don't look at your feet," the instructors call out. I obediently raise my chin and I'm face to face with Ethan.

Every now and then, the instructors teach us a move. They stand inside what has become a misshapen circle of awkward couples and demonstrate how the guy spins the girl, how to twist our arms up like pretzels and then magically unravel ourselves, how the guy and the girl can both spin, get twisted up, unravel and twirl out of the whole big move. All of the couples stay connected while they watch the demonstration, but not us. When the instructors clap their hands to get our attention, I let got of Ethan, step away and try to catch my breath.

The woman with the red crew cut spins under her partner's arm to show us how easy it is. When she finally stops—the show-off—one of the girls with the black eyeliner asks how to do that without falling.

"You have to move from your center," the instructor says. "You always move from your center. If you do that, you won't fall."

I repeat the words in my mind—Move—from—your—center. They make a good rhythm, just right for running. Two on the inhale, two on the exhale, one foot hitting the pavement with each word.

Ethan and I try all these moves. I suck in my breath every time Ethan's body passes close to mine. I make myself as thin as possible, so we don't touch. I fear the surge of electricity that would come if more than just the palms of Ethan's hands touch me. I imagine my hair standing on end, charred and smoking from the shock.

After a while, once we really get going, I start to enjoy it a little. All of my muscles move, different ones than when I run, muscles I didn't know I had. My insides expand and fill out the shell again. We pick up speed. Music comes on, loud. The lights go off, saving me from looking at Ethan's face and from seeing him look at me. I start to forget where I am, who I'm with, what I'm doing. I forget who I am.

But that's only while the lights are off. When someone turns them back on again and shuts off the music, my insides start to shrivel away. I let go of Ethan's hand, but he doesn't let go of mine.

"See," he says, smiling at me with that stupid, endearing gap between his front teeth. "I told you it would be fun."

I nod and look down at my feet. The instructors tell everyone to take a break, get some water.

"I'm going to get some air," Ethan says.

"O.K." I watch him until he's out the door. Then I run to the bathroom at the back of the room. I lock myself in one of the stalls, sit down on the toilet and quietly hyperventilate. The teenage girls who come into the bathroom can't hear me over their conversations about which guys they think are the cutest and which girls they think look the best or the worst. They rip apart some girl named Heaven, who has committed the mortal teenage sins of having braces and acne.

I hate kids. But my mother said teaching is a good field. I could major in English as long as I got a teaching certificate. If it doesn't get you a good job, she said, college is just a waste.

The teenage girls all shuffle out of the bathroom together, shredding other girls for being too fat, too thin, or too ugly.

Back in the dance hall, I creep along the wall until I reach the door. Outside, the sun is going down. The sky is turning purple.

Most of the kids are outside, standing around, talking. Some of the chaperones are on the sidewalk, smoking. Ethan's on the sidewalk, too, leaning into a car window. His back is to me as he talks to someone in the car. The car looks a lot like Grandmother's, a tan sedan she's had for years. There's no way to tell how old it is because it looks brand new. Grandmother cleans that car so much it still even smells new.

When Ethan stands up, I can see a little bit of the driver—a blue dress, and white hair glowing in the twilight.

I hop the stone wall and hide there, hoping no one will hear my pounding heart as they filter back inside. When Ethan finishes plotting against me with Grandmother, he laughs. I hear her stupid giggle.

She wants to get me in trouble so I can never, ever have any kind of fun again, any kind of life.

She wants to torture me. This whole night—"Why don't you go out, Connie? Why don't you do something fun?"—has been about torturing me.

How I wish I had a cup of coffee, strong and black, to suck down and really get my stomach churning, because that pain would be better than this pain. Such betrayal—that's what my mother has been trying to protect me from.

When they're done laughing at me, Ethan taps the side of her car and waves to Grandmother as she pulls away down the street.

I want to spit at him before he goes back inside. But I don't. I have something better in mind.

By the time he realizes it, I'll be long gone.

15

His parents' house is dark, and I know for sure he isn't home. I don't even need to sneak. I just march up the stairs to his door, making all the noise I want.

I stand there, unsure of what to do next. Breaking and entering is not my specialty. In fact, this is my first burglary. Desperate times call for desperate measures. And I am desperate to punish Ethan.

The doorknob turns easily. The door gently swings open. People in Green Hill are stupid enough to leave their doors unlocked all the time. He's just getting what he deserves.

I step over the threshold.

The apartment is one big room, half of it set up with one of those old chrome and Formica dinette sets. A futon couch, a television and a coffee table fill the other half. A galley kitchen is cut into the back of the room. The walls are bare. The coffee table is empty. The kitchen counters are clean, the dinette table clear and shiny. When I run my finger over the surface, it squeaks.

I leave the lights off, just in case anyone goes by, and rifle through some of the kitchen drawers and cabinets. He has junky cafeteria silverware and cheap Corelle dishes. All of his glasses are plastic cups from convenience stores and amusement parks. Story Land, Santa's Village, Weirs Beach. Classy. He has a mishmash of pots and pans probably purchased at the Helping Hands.

This is bad. Nothing here is worth anything. Nothing is special. Nothing is significant. The way all the pots and pans are smashed into the cabinets, he doesn't even appear to have a favorite frying pan that I could take. In fact, whatever I take will probably increase the value of everything that's left.

There are two other places to look. A door on one side of the kitchen opens onto the bathroom, which contains a small closet full of ratty towels and a cup full of disposable razors and old toothbrushes.

The door on the other side opens onto another room. Clothes are piled everywhere, covering the floor. It takes me a few minutes to see the bed under all the clothes. All the bureau drawers are open, too crammed to shut. It looks just like his toolbox in the garage downstairs.

Gold trophies are lined up on two shelves. They are carefully arranged, each set on a slight angle. There are a lot of them, so they are close together, but not touching. Even in the darkness, I can see that they shine.

The trophies are for skiing, most of them first prize for slalom racing, whatever that is. One of them is bigger than the rest, and it has the coveted center of the top shelf. It's heavy, the base made of some kind of stone. The gold cup is real metal. It rings when I tap it with my fingernail. There are two skis, crossed like an X, on the front of the cup.

I leave the empty space in the center of the shelf, so he'll see right away that it's gone. The thought of wiping that goofy smile off his face makes me laugh a little. Just a little, though, because only crazy people laugh after they've done something really mean. And I'm not crazy. I'm just mad.

My first break-in is a triumph. All I need to do is leave quietly now. I go out the door, and a car comes down the road. I crouch down in the shadows and wait for it to pass. But it doesn't pass. It pulls into the driveway. It stops there. Someone gets out of the driver's side—Ethan's mother.

Clutching the trophy to my chest, I close my eyes and whisper, "Disappear. Disappear. Disappear."

I don't open my eyes again until after I hear Ethan's mother get his father inside the house and the front door shuts, so it's hard to tell if the trick worked this time or not. Maybe I disappeared. Maybe it's just too dark for them to see me.

I creep down the stairs and down the driveway to the road. I start to run, holding the trophy in one hand. It's much heavier now than when I held it in Ethan's bedroom. Where will I hide it—somewhere in the bedroom closet?

Then there's this sound, like someone ripping the leg off a raw chicken. There's a million knives stabbing me in the ankle and ripping the side of my leg open. A million stars float in front of my eyes. There's a scream, and my mouth is open and I'm the only one out here, so the scream must be coming from me, but I can't feel it coming out of my throat because all I can feel are the knives. And then my body slams against the ground. The trophy falls from my hands and rolls away into the bushes on the side of the road. I try to crawl over to it, but my foot is caught in one of the ruts, the ruts I've been so careful to avoid. Every time my foot snags there the knives dig into my ankle, the stars burst again, and I howl.

It's not long before there are footsteps on the dirt road, hands on my shoulders, someone asking if I'm all right, can I get up.

"My foot," I groan.

Ethan's mother gently moves my foot so I can roll over. I scream as soon as she touches it. Somehow she gets me onto my back, helps me sit up. Then she puts her shoulder under mine and hoists me up.

"I'm sorry," I say.

Mrs. Matthews says my ankle looks bad and that I need to go to the hospital. She's a nurse; she should know. But I refuse.

"No hospitals," I say through gritted teeth as she replaces the ice pack on my ankle with a new cold one. My ankle swelled so much, so fast she had to cut my running shoe off and cut a slit in the leg of my jeans.

"It could be broken. Your tendons could be all torn up." She straps the ice pack to my ankle with an ace bandage to keep it in place. She gives me four ibuprofen pills for the swelling. It'll wreck my stomach, but I take them anyway.

"No hospitals."

Mrs. Matthews looks at my ankle, looks at me and shakes her head. "You rest here, and we'll see how it goes. When you feel up to it, maybe we can get you home at least." She pats my knee and goes.

"No hospitals," I say again after she's gone.

All together, I've probably spent half my life in hospitals, and they've never helped me. After the ulcer first flared when I was ten, I had these terrible attacks two or three times a week. My mother rushed me to the emergency room, where they shot me up with pain medication. My mother cried more than me at the emergency room, and the doctors and nurses comforted her.

We'd go to one hospital for a while. They'd give me the pain medication and a prescription that was supposed to help the ulcer, stop the attacks. My mother would give me the pills or the syrup, watch me swallow it down, and I'd be all right for a week or so. Then I'd have another string of attacks and another string of visits to the emergency room. This went on for a few months. I couldn't eat, got thinner and thinner, and they finally carved into my abdomen and gave me a feeding tube.

The feeding tube kept getting infected, which made me even sicker. My mother, she tried everything to keep the tube and the incision clear. I remember her constantly fiddling with it, adjusting it, trying to keep it clean.

"Don't shame your mother, now," she'd whisper as she swabbed some new astringent around the tube. "Be a good girl and don't shame your mother."

Specialists were brought in to examine me. Teams of doctors were put on my case.

"We've got to find out what's going on with her lower GI," my mother would tell the doctors. "She shouldn't be this sick for a little kid. There's got to be something serious going on down there."

The doctors and nurses came at me with their scopes and needles, CAT scans, and ultrasounds, and they all came back negative or normal. There was nothing out of the ordinary. Maybe it was just acid reflux, one doctor suggested.

"Acid reflux!" my mother screamed at him. "Look at her— does that look like acid reflux to you? When she dies of cancer, I'll sue your ass."

Then we switched hospitals.

"They didn't know what they were doing at the other hospital," my mother would say to me, as I lay on a bed in a new emergency room. "The doctors are much better here. They'll be able to help you."

But they didn't. It was the same thing all over again, and again, and again—more feeding tubes, more infections—until we were running out of hospitals. By the time I graduated high school, my mother drove me to an emergency room two hours away.

It's amazing that I was ever able to become such a powerful runner. But every time the cross-country season came around each fall, just before the start of the track season in the spring, the infections cleared up and the ulcer calmed down. The running made me well; at least, that's what the doctors told my mother.

There were so many doctors. My records must read like a regular United Nations of medicine, with at least one doctor representing each country in the world. I've had men doctors, women doctors, young ones in teaching hospitals, and old, gray-haired ones who are experts in their field. You think one of them could do something for me? No.

But my mother wouldn't give up. She kept trying to find a doctor who could help me. The last guy looked like he was about twelve, but he was supposed to be the best in the field. We drove to Boston to see him. Waited two hours for my appointment, which only took about five minutes. He scanned my file and said he was going to give me antibiotics. He said the latest research showed ulcers like mine were just festering bacterial infections that can be pretty much cured with a combination of antibiotics and antacids. If I watched my diet, he said I'd be pain free except for the occasional attack here and there. For that, he'd give me a prescription.

Pain free.

If my mother hadn't been sitting right next to me, I would've cried.

My mother thanked the doctor and sent me to the waiting room so she could talk to him alone.

Pain free.

I don't remember what that's like anymore.

In the car on the way home, she told me we'd have to find another doctor.

"Why? He's going to fix it. He knows what to do."

"No, he doesn't."

"But the antibiotics—"

"They won't work in your case."

"What? Why?"

"He changed his diagnosis."

"I don't understand."

"The ulcer that can be cured—that's not your kind of ulcer after all."

"But that's not fair."

My mother swerved the car to the side of the road. She could have killed us, doing that on those highways in Boston. She turned to face me.

"Listen," she spat, "I'm trying to help you, so don't you yell at me when things don't work out your way. I drive you all over this state, all over New England, trying to find a decent doctor — I'd drive to the ends of the earth to help you. All I do is help you, take care of you. And you have the nerve to yell at me!"

She kept leaning closer to me, jabbing her finger into my chest, until I was pressed against the door.

"I suffer for you. How I suffer," she whispered hoarsely in my face. "And you will show me some gratitude."

That was the spring before I went to college, where the nurse practitioners at the health center refilled my prescriptions. I haven't seen a doctor or the inside of an emergency room since. I haven't needed to, with the amount of running I do. And I don't plan to go to a hospital now because of a little sprained ankle.

A sharp pain in my neck wakes me up. I slowly roll my head upright and then lean it all the way to the right, trying to unknot my muscles.

Nothing is familiar. No yellow bedroom. No stupid little figurine staring at me from the bureau.

Instead, I'm on a scratchy wool couch in the Matthews' living room. I'm covered by an afghan with brown, beige and maroon granny-squares. The maroon in the afghan matches the maroon walls. A ripple afghan in the same colors is folded over the back of a brown leather easy chair in the corner. Paintings of various sizes, winter scenes and spring landscapes of pink and purple lupine fields, cover the wall across from the couch where I lie. The images are rough and unsophisticated, which means they are either folk art or just someone's hobby. Sunlight filters through long, plain muslin curtains on the windows, which look out onto the porch.

This is the room where Ethan and his parents talked and watched TV that night I sat on the ground, crouched beside the juniper bush in front of the porch.

I slowly pull the afghan up to reveal my injured foot. My ankle is dark purple all the way around. A lighter shade of purple bleeds down onto my instep. The skin around my ankle, my whole foot, is shiny; it's stretched so much to accommodate the swelling.

My ankle doesn't hurt so badly now with all that natural padding my body has created around the injury. But I can't look at it without cringing. I can see more and more blood seeping into the bruise. Watching it turn slowly darker makes me gag. Or maybe it's the nagging thought that I may have totaled it, that I may never be able to run again, that's made me so sick to my stomach.

And here's the kicker—as sickening as that thought is, as bad as my ankle looks, these are the least of my worries right now. I don't know where that trophy is. If Mrs. Matthews found it, if Ethan has it, they'll know what I did. What if they called the police? The cops could be coming for me right now. What if they called Grandmother? What if my mother already knows?

When I think of my mother, the pain in my stomach surpasses my ankle. She would be so disappointed and angry to know how stupidly I hurt myself, how I stayed out all night. That's not allowed. The fact that I'd passed out in pain wouldn't matter to her. She'd trace the whole calamity back to some fundamental flaw in me.

It seems a little stupid to let her reaction worry me so much. Accidents happen, right? People make mistakes all the time and seem to survive. But I don't know anyone who wants to disappoint her mother. That's just about the worst feeling in the world, almost worse than killing someone. In a way, when I disappoint her, I do kill her. "Why don't you just put a gun to my head and pull the trigger?" she'd say whenever I brought home a less-than-perfect test or lost a race.

"Good morning," Mrs. Matthews says. She stands in the doorway to the den, where I've spent the night. "How's the ankle?"

"It's fine. Much better." I turn a cringe into a smile as I wiggle my toes.

"It doesn't look better," she says. "You should go to the hospital."

"It looks worse than it feels. It doesn't even hurt that much. I'll be fine."

"What brought you down this way last night anyway? Ethan said you were at the Youth Center one minute, and then you were gone."

"I went for a walk."

"He was worried," she says, as if her son is so noble. I wanted to tell her that he's a traitor. "In any case, you could've just come by and knocked on the door if you wanted to say hello." She smiles and winks at me.

Where's the trophy? Does she know about it or not?

I smile back. "Thanks for your help. I should get going now."

"I just started breakfast. You'll stay and eat with us and then I'll drive you back to your grandmother's. I tried to call her, but the line was busy."

I can still lie my way out of this.

"I'll go try her again."

"No!" I say. Mrs. Matthews looks at me like I have eight heads. "I mean I'll be home soon anyway. I'm sure she's not worried."

"Oh, she must be worried sick. We need to call her."

"I called her last night, actually, after you all went to bed. I called and told her where I was and that I'd be home in the morning."

Mrs. Matthews pauses for a moment before answering. "Well, as long as you've spoken to her, then there's no need to call her again, I guess."

"Right. There's no need to call her again."

"All right, then," she says, and turns to leave the room. She stops and turns back. "It was such a strange night. First, I find you lying in the road. Then, Ethan comes home and says someone's been in his apartment."

My mouth is dry as sand. "Really?"

"Yes. And the funny thing is, all they took was his favorite skiing trophy. So strange."

"Yeah, strange."

"Luckily, I found his trophy on the side of the road this morning when I went out for the newspaper. I don't understand it—whoever it was went through all that trouble to steal it and then dropped it in the road."

"Do you have any idea who it was?"

"No," Mrs. Matthews says. "Ethan's at the police station now, reporting it. I wonder if they'll come by and look at his apartment. The excitement continues," she says, backing out of the room. She goes down a short hallway and disappears into another room. The fan on the stove starts up.

I've got to get out of here before the police arrive.

The scissors she used to cut my shoe off are still on the coffee table. The sight of my cut up shoe, my beloved running shoe, hurts me more than my ankle and stomach combined. I almost can't cut it open wider to accommodate my new fat foot. My poor shoe.

I hobble across the den to the side door. My left foot is a big ball of cotton with a tiny pin poking the very center of my anklebone with each step. It's not so bad. In the woods along the driveway, I find a long, thick stick to use as a cane. I feel O.K. I'm good. I'm golden.

The Hassids stare at me as we pass each other on the sidewalk in town. The girl who was outside the Youth Center last night is meandering the sidewalk with her family again.

"Thanks for nothing," I mumble as she passes me. "Way to be a team player."

I'll tell Grandmother that I was walking home last night when I twisted my ankle and fell in a ditch on the side of the road. I'll tell her it was dark and I was scared to walk alone in the dark, and my ankle hurt so badly I couldn't really walk, so I just stayed in the ditch. I'll tell her how awful it was, how scared I was, and that it was my own fault for staying out so late. And if that trophy comes up, I'll play dumb.

Sleeping in a ditch would be much more palatable to my mother than sleeping at Ethan Matthews's house. My injury, my just punishment, will be very palatable to my mother.

It is my just punishment. That part's not a lie.

This is what I get for being me.

I can't feel my foot anymore when I reach the white Victorian on Grove Street. I lean heavily on my cane, hoping this will elicit some sympathy. When I limp in the front door, Grandmother comes through the kitchen doorway, her purse hanging from her wrist and her car keys jingling in her hand.

"I fell in a ditch and slept there all night, it's my own stupid fault and I'm sorry, it'll never happen again."

"Oh my god!" She stays at the far end of the hallway. "Are you all right? Mrs. Matthews just called. I was on my way."

"I fell in a ditch. It was dark. I was scared. I deserve it. I'm stupid. I'm sorry."

She knows what really happened, and yet the lie keeps flowing out of my mouth. I'm a runaway freight train. I'm a herd of buffalo stampeding over a cliff.

I'll offer to stay another week, help her move into the new place. I'll gather up whatever shreds of love I still have for her and shower her with it in some sort of sorry display of fake sweetness. Ours is a relationship fueled by saccharine.

But before I can say anything, her embrace pins my arms to my sides, saving me the embarrassment of not knowing what to do in such a situation. Returning an embrace is a natural reflex for pretty much everyone but sociopaths, and me.

"I'm so sorry," Grandmother says. "I was so worried when you weren't in bed this morning. I didn't know what to do. I called the hospital, the police, and then—" Her heart beats faster and faster against my chest. Or is that my heart against my own chest?

She slowly brings her hands to my shoulders and steps away from me. She looks me right in the eyes.

"You were missing," she says. "I had to call her."

Her eyes are wide and her pupils are large and dark, encircled by a thin rim of blue. My mother had a cat once, whose pupils became big and black like that whenever he was over stimulated, scared of all the noise and motion around him.

The phone rings.

We both look toward the kitchen, where the only phone in the house hangs on the wall just inside the door. Grandmother drops her hands from my shoulders and walks down the hall with slow, quiet steps, as if she's sneaking up on a sleeping giant. She pauses with her hand on the receiver before finally picking it up.

Grandmother turns her back to me, hunching over the phone the way people do when they don't want you to hear a conversation. Her voice is weak and tinny. If they were dueling pianos, Grandmother is a toy plinking out "Chopsticks" against the grand and furious pipe organ that is my mother, belting out the ominous tones of a fugue.

Funny—I'd always imagined it the other way around.

I should creep closer, so I can hear what Grandmother is saying. But I don't want to.

"All right!" she finally shouts.

I close my eyes and whisper, "Disappear. Disappear. Disappear."

When I open them again, Grandmother waves me over to her.

I lean on the wall and my stick and make my way to the phone. Grandmother shakes her head at me, bites her lower lip, thinking about how pathetic I am.

I take the phone from Grandmother, whose hands then cover her mouth. I bring it to my ear, slowly. My mother's breath floods my ear in waves of white noise.

"Mom?" My throat is dry and scratchy from the struggle back to Grandmother's house.

"Mom?" I say again. My mother loves suspense, and she knows how to use it. "I had an attack, Mom. My stomach hurt so bad, I couldn't make it home."

"Don't you lie to me." Her voice is low and thick.

"I'm not lying. My stomach was really bad, and I didn't have my pills with me."

"Do you have any idea how I feel when your Grandmother calls me and tells me you're missing?"

"I'm sorry."

"You embarrass me by making your Grandmother frantic, and you have me worried sick."

"I didn't mean to."

"Oh, yes you did," she spits. "You do these things on purpose to hurt me, to make me look bad, to humiliate me in front of my own mother."

"No, mom, I didn't do it on purpose," I say. "I'm hurt, badly."

There's a pause. I cringe, waiting for her response.

"What's wrong?" she says. "What's hurt?"

"My ankle. I twisted it running last night and now it's all swelled up and purple." I clear my throat. Some part of me does not want to say what I have to say next. "What should I do?"

The medical Rolodex in my mother's mind almost makes an audible sound as she searches her memory for the best care for a sprained ankle.

"Elevate it. Get ice on it. Have you done that yet?"

"No, Mom," I say. "I'll do that."

"When I get up there tomorrow, I'll take you to the hospital."

My heart pounds. "You don't have to do that. You don't have to come up."

"We'll need X-rays, obviously," she says, her voice calm and cool. "Probably an MRI to check the tendons, maybe even arthroscopic surgery. But don't do a thing until I get there. You don't know how to handle those doctors. They'll push you around, if I'm not there."

"You don't need to come, Mom. I can take care of it," I plead.

"Oh, Connie," my mother sighs. "You can't take care of yourself. You never could, and you can't now. And that's why, when I get up there tomorrow, the first thing we're going to do is call your precious academy and tell them that you will not be working there."

My whole body sags, and I lean my forehead against the wall. My hands tremble. "Please don't do this," I whisper. "Please."

"You think it's fun for me, taking care of a sick little worm my whole life?" she yells. "You're nothing but garbage—you're worse than garbage. I should've thrown you in the trash when I had you. I would've been so much happier. My life would've been so much better. But did I? No. And now you push me away, toss me aside like I'm nothing."

"I'm sorry," I say, lightly banging my forehead against the wall. "I'm sorry."

"Why do you do this to me? Why do you hate me?"

"I don't."

"Am I a terrible mother? Is that it?"

"No."

"Am I really so horrible that you need to hurt me like this, after everything I've done for you?"

"No."

"Do you really hate me that much?"

"I don't hate you," I say, for about the millionth time in my life. Then, I gather the next phrase in my mind and begin to push it toward my mouth. The words are heavy, a stack of cinder blocks. "I love you."

She doesn't say anything for a while; her breath comes in short blasts of static in my ear. This is when I'm most afraid of her. Even when I'm in the same room with her, I never know if she's getting control of herself or preparing for a new attack. I never know if I'm going to be gripped in that terrifying cyclone or flung aside. I use the same defense for both. I ball up like a rodent, curl up inside myself as far away from her as I can get. I'd liken myself to a turtle here, except with turtles there's substance under that shell.

"You are not leaving me. Do you understand?" she says. "You will never leave me."

Click.

She's gone.

Grandmother's pointy fingers dig into my shoulders. Her body, all knobby and hard and cold, presses against my back. She's about as comforting as a porcupine.

She rests the side of her face against my neck.

"I'm sorry," she whispers.

"Don't touch me," I say, flinging her off me. She falls backward, catching herself on the corner of the kitchen table. Her eyes are wide, and she's shrunk about a foot in that one instant.

I back away from her out of the kitchen. I lean on the wall and hold my stick out in front of me, like a lion tamer. "Don't even come near me."

Something shimmers on her cheek, a thin, glistening trail from the corner of her eye to her chin.

I back down the entire hallway like this. She doesn't move from the kitchen table.

"Where are you going?" she calls.

"For a walk!" I scream. "And if you try to follow me, I swear to God I will beat you with this stick."

16

I follow my regular route, down Grove to Maple, along a few side streets, and then up the long hill. I can't feel anything in my left ankle and foot anymore. Not even the dagger, not even the little needle. Nothing. I walk normally. I don't even need the stick, but I keep it just in case Grandmother tries to follow me. Walking through the center of town like this is probably a bad idea, with the police possibly after me, and all. But it's worth the risk to get away from Grandmother.

A new mantra beats in my head: *Worse than garbage, worse than garbage.* It's not the worst she's ever called me. My mother must've looked up the word "garbage" in the thesaurus and memorized the entry. Among her favorites are "scum", "swill" and "filth". If she's feeling particularly literary, she goes with "abomination." She prefers such highbrow terms to swearing, which isn't allowed in our house. Although "slut" is another favorite, and that's sort of on the edge of being a swear. I'm not allowed to say it, anyway.

All of these words seem pretty tame when I think of them now, all by themselves. Their power comes from their momentum. Twenty-two years of it.

But rather than take the whole laundry list with me on this walk, I choose "Worse than garbage," a compact phrase, easily repeated — as my mother has proven many, many times — that breaks down into four beats, four steps. Two on the inhale, two on the exhale. In my own weak defense, I don't actually choose to repeat these words to myself. It's a lot like listening to a bad song on the radio. Before you know it, you're singing along.

The words push me all the way down the other side of the hill to the sign that tells me I'm leaving Green Hill. The day I leave for good, I'll yell, "Go to Hell," or "Bite me!" My own Number One hit.

I want to scream or break something so badly my skin shakes with it. I'm afraid, too, of what my mother said about never leaving her.

Why did I tell Grandmother I was going to beat her with a stick?

I toss the stick aside.

Ethan will figure out I was the one in his apartment last night.

Why did I take that trophy?

I'll go to jail for robbery and attempted assault, since Grandmother will also call the police on me for threatening her.

She'll definitely tell my mother.

My shoe is getting tighter. I'll have to cut the whole thing off.

My poor shoe.

I'll never run again. I know that.

Without the running, I'll never have that feeling again, muscles and blood and tissue underneath my skin.

I may as well be standing on the edge of a cliff. In front of me is a long drop into darkness with no bottom in sight. And behind me, the earth rumbles with a stampede of bulls. They're all after me—Ethan, Grandmother, the police, and something else I cannot identify because I won't look at it long enough. If I stay on the edge, I know I'll get trampled, flattened forever. Jumping has its possibilities, but you have to have guts to take a flying leap.

The cicadas hum in the trees. Sweat dries on my face, making my skin itch.

"You are now leaving Green Hill." I read the sign over and over again.

I can leave.

I have a car, and the money I've been pilfering all summer from the church collection. I can stay in a motel somewhere, as long as I don't have to stay here or go home to my mother. I'm moving in another week anyway. My mother didn't really mean that, what she said about not taking that job at the academy. She couldn't have meant it.

All I need is one week away to let the stampede pass, let the dust settle.

Total avoidance isn't just a good survival tip for life with Grandmother. It's a great tactic for surviving life in general.

Later, after it's all over, I'll see my mother, smooth over the trampled ground so it lies flat and neat once more. I'll get my things at home and bring them to my little dorm apartment at the academy. My mother will come with me. She'll help me hang curtains and decorate my bedroom.

I smile at the sign, slap it twice and begin walking toward town. At the top of Main Street, the mountain stops me. It's etched into the blue sky, every curve, every peak, every bald dome perfectly outlined. The trees stand out like stubble on an old man's chin, and I wonder which deep cut into the mountain is Tuckerman's Ravine. A white speck, the observatory, winks on the summit. I've never seen the mountain so clearly, in all its danger and glory.

As I make my way down the hill, people are filing into the Catholic Church for Mass. A tall sliver of navy blue stops on the steps. Her white hair is swept on top of her head and a white purse dangles from her wrist, just beyond the cuff of her white cotton gloves. Grandmother takes a step toward the street. A white glove goes to her face. Then she turns and scurries inside.

By the time I reach Grove Street, my jeans are sticking to my legs and my shirt is soaked through with sweat. Good thing it's black and not white. It's bad enough that I'm not wearing a sports bra.

I sit on the porch to catch my breath. My muscles stiffen with the sudden stillness. The numbness in my foot and ankle has spread halfway up my shin. I can't wait for it to seep through my entire body. Then I'll really disappear.

My shoe is on good and tight now, and I've got to cut it off before it's too tight to get the scissors under it. All I can find are the kitchen scissors. They're so dull; my poor shoe is in shreds by the time I get it off. I throw it away quickly, before it can make me cry. My ankle is black all the way around now, and half my foot is turning a deep, deep purple. I poke at my foot. It feels squishy, like a water balloon.

After a cool shower, I'm revived, like someone from one of those soap commercials in which the zippy smell of the soap wakes you up in the morning, getting you to work on time and smelling great, which leads to a raise, a new car, a bigger house. Only when I get out of the shower, the stampede rumbles behind me. The gaping hole off the edge of the cliff yawns before me.

I take my suitcase and duffle bag from the closet, throw them on the bed and start emptying the bureau drawers. That stupid little porcelain girl smiles her dumb smile at me while I pack. I hate that thing. She's so creepy, smiling all the time, smiling at me in the dark, while I sleep. What's she have to smile about, anyway? She's just a frozen statue who can't do anything. I want to smash her on the windowsill, throw her against the wall, and grind that smile off her face under my fat foot. But she's probably worth something, like all the rest of those porcelain children I'd packed away already. If I break her, I'll have to pay Grandmother for her, and that bothers me even more than that evil little girl.

I want to leave before Grandmother comes home from Mass. If this looks suspiciously like running away, I'm not. Running away implies striking out on your own, taking a stand—much too bold a move for me. I'm going to hide.

My treasures are hidden throughout the yellow bedroom. Half a dozen shoeboxes are lined up on the top shelf of the closet, each one of them a hiding place. There are four pair of sunglasses in one, a couple of bottles of perfume in another, all those blushes, some scarves from one of the antique shops, candy bars and some costume jewelry from the Helping Hands. I took a pair of jeans from the Helping Hands, too, which were so easy to hide among all my other jeans. The Helping Hands gave me an old teddy bear, a pair of knitted mittens and a tiny teapot from a toy tea set.

A normal girl would've just snuggled up against Mable while she sat in her chair in her workroom, would've rested in her embrace.

It looks bad, stealing from the church thrift store. Stealing from the church collection looks even worse. But it's all for charity—for the lowly, the pathetic—right? As long as it's going to the right cause, what difference does it make?

I throw my stolen treasures into my duffle bag. The photos go first, but miss the bag and scatter all over the floor. All it takes is one of my mother's eyes looking out at me from a buried snapshot.

Police sirens go off in the distance.

I pause, kneeling by the bed, clutching the clump of unwanted memories.

The sirens fade away.

I look to the door, the photos, my watch, back to the photos. The need to torture myself wins out, and I begin laying the photos out on the bed.

There are all kinds of addictions.

Looking at the images of my discarded mother makes me feel closer to her somehow. I see how she was pushed to the outer edge of all the family photos, made purposely different from her twin sisters so she would not fit in. The pictures help me see that my mother and I are the same. We have suffered together. Maybe, if I were the kind of person to think such things, I would say seeing my mother in pain also gave me a small measure of satisfaction.

But I'm not that kind of person.

I pull it all out, the whole collection I've stolen from the archives of Grandmother's museum. It doesn't look like much — the wrinkled gingham baby dress with the stained collar, the ratty old doll, the charm bracelet, the handkerchief, the lighter, the newspaper clippings about Edward Henderson and the blue box that contains Papa's Bronze Star. I took the Peter Rabbit baby blanket, too, just because I like it so much. The bracelet I could pawn for some extra money, maybe. But the rest has that other kind of value. I know they mean something to Grandmother, because she'd hidden them so well herself.

I pick up the Connie doll and smooth her rumpled hair, combing my fingers through the strands of brown yarn. She has a round face, like a plate, like mine. I take the compact of blush I opened yesterday and brush some onto her cheeks. Since she can't pucker her lips, I guess where her cheekbones would be. She looks better, less gray and tired. Her dress is terrible, though, stained all down the front probably from me drooling on her in my sleep when I was little.

I'm beginning to think that Mrs. Matthews was right, that I need a doctor to look at my ankle. My leg is numb up to my knee now, and the bruise is spreading not only down my foot, but also up my shin.

I slip the Connie doll out of her dress. There's a red heart embroidered on her chest, just like Raggedy Ann. It's the same red heart as on the tag with my initials that marks her as mine. I take the red gingham dress, which has the same tag, and pull it over the Connie doll's head. I push her arms through the short sleeves and button the three pearl buttons in the back.

"There," I say, "Much better." I smooth her hair one more time and prop her up against a pillow. The charm bracelet, wrapped twice, fits nicely on her wrist.

A sharp pain in my ankle stops my reverie, but after a moment, I go back to packing. As I shove some clothes into my suitcase, Edward Henderson catches my eye. I know I've seen him before, but I don't know where. He reminds me of someone.

The clipping is right next to the picture of my mother and Papa at her high school graduation. She stands close to Papa, who has his arm around her shoulders. His smile takes up his entire face, and he's pulling her close to him in his excitement. She was his first daughter to graduate from high school, the first in his family to go to college.

My mother has the faintest smile. Her shoulders cave toward her chest, as if she were cowering. She looks embarrassed by all the attention. She's shy. She isn't used to it, after being shoved aside by her mother for so long. Or maybe she somehow knew she would fail him.

The way I'm holding the picture, I can see Edward Henderson's face just above it. Something about his face nags at me. I pick up the clipping and hold them side-by-side. Then I slide the clipping over the photo, so Edward Henderson's face lays right on top of my mother's.

The newspaper is so thin, I can almost see through it a little bit, how their noses end in the same round nub, how their eyebrows have the same shape, how their mouths have the same rounded upper lip and thin lower lip, how their eyes are wide set. When I hold it up to the window, I see how their two faces match, the features resting in the exact same place on each.

The clipping is his obituary. Corporal Edward Henderson of the United States Marine Corps was killed in action at Chosin Reservoir, Korea, on November 25, 1950.

Korea.

Papa was never in Korea.

The lighter is on the bed. *Semper Fi,* which is the motto for the Marines.

The obituary says something about Edward Henderson's Bronze Star.

I need that box, the one that held the lighter and Bronze Star. It's under a pile of magazines in the cabinet part of Grandmother's nightstand. The cabinet is locked, of course, but a silver bobby pin opens it easily. I bring it back to the yellow bedroom, dragging my left foot along as I go. I don't even bother to lift it anymore, or put too much weight on it. My leg is numb from the knee down, so when I do step on it, I feel like I'm going to fall.

I listen for more sirens, but all is quiet.

I toss the box onto the bed, in the middle of the photos and the other spoils from Grandmother's attic. Some of the pictures fall on the floor, and the Connie doll flops over. The charm bracelet makes a little tinkling noise as it slips off her wrist. I wrap it around her muslin skin two, three, four times, pulling it tighter and tighter so it won't fall off again. The bracelet pinches the cloth and stuffing, making a puffy little hand at the end of the arm. I pull it even tighter, five, six times around. The Connie doll won't lose that bracelet now.

One of the charms pops off and skitters across the floor under the bureau. I close my eyes and reach under, feeling around the dust bunnies until my finger hits something small and metal. I place the charm in the palm of my hand, blow on it lightly, and brush the dust off with my fingertips. The end where it hangs from the bracelet is a clover shape. I bring it back to the bed. In front of me is the box, the clover shape carved around its keyhole.

The key slides right into the lock. It turns easily. There's that satisfying "click," and the lid pops open.

The varsity "S" filled with football pins is still on top. I read Edward Henderson's obituary again.

He played football in high school. It says he was the fastest wide receiver/corner back in the county.

The silver locket is engraved with scrolls. It looks random, but when I hold it in my palm again and really look at it, I see the letters. E.H.

I put the locket and the obituary down carefully. I look at my mother's face, Edward Henderson, the lighter. I look at the football letter, the locket, the Bronze Star.

What I've stolen from Grandmother is more than I'm willing to accept at the moment.

I sweep it all into my duffle bag and leave.

17

Mable leaves the Helping Hands unlocked on Sunday mornings, so the desperately poor can take what they need without the humiliation of facing a neighbor or coworker at the cash register. There are a lot of poor people in Green Hill, in the whole area, really. It can be tough to find a job at the edge of the planet.

Mable waddles in around one o'clock, after she's helped clean up from the coffee social after Mass. She's humming some hymn, and goes through it several times before reaching the back room where I sit in my usual chair. The duffle bag is in my lap.

"There's my girl," she says. "I missed you this morning."

"You have to help me."

"Sure I'll help you," she says, easing herself into her own chair. She leans back a little, away from me. "You don't look so good, dear."

She spots my ankle.

"Oh, good gracious — look at your foot! What happened?"

I hug the duffle bag to my stomach. "I found things."

"We have to get you to a doctor."

"A doctor isn't going to help me. Only you can help me."

"O.K.," she says. "Let me get you a drink of water first, and then I'll help you."

She brings me a glass from the bathroom, one of those jelly-jar glasses with the cartoons painted on them. There's a whole shelf of them out in the store. They were the targets of my next theft, but it's probably not a good idea to keep stealing when the police may be after you.

I haven't heard any more sirens. Maybe it was just in my head.

Mable pulls her chair opposite me and sits down with a little thud. She's all in red today, like a cherry, with little plastic cherries dangling from her ears.

"Now, what is it?" she asks, as I gulp the water down. I put the glass on the floor, unzip the duffle bag and pull out the box. I open it with the key from the bracelet and hold it out to her.

"Help me understand this. Please."

She leans back in her chair, as far away from the box as she can get. "What is it? I don't even know. I've never seen it before."

I snap the lid shut and take out Edward Henderson's obituary. "Then who's this? Why would my Grandmother keep this?"

Mable shakes her head. "I don't know who that is. How would I know why she kept it?"

Then I take out the photo of my mother and Papa and hold it out to her with the obituary. "Can you explain this to me, then?"

Mable takes the obituary and the picture from me and slumps down in her chair. "Oh, my."

"Why does my mother look like him?" I say, leaning toward her. "Why does my mother look exactly like this man?"

Mable's eyes scan the clipping. She sighs and shakes her head.

"Tell me."

"I can't."

"Why?"

"Because I shouldn't be the one to tell you this," Mable says, handing the picture and obituary back to me. "It should be her."

"Who?"

"Your grandmother."

I stand up, the box and the bag and everything in them landing in a heap on the floor. The Connie doll looks like a murdered infant face down on the linoleum. It won't do any good to get angry. That's what my mother would say. Just be nice, be pleasant. Smile and let it roll off your back.

"Why?" I yell.

The last time I yelled like that I was maybe five years old, screaming, I wanted something, a cookie or a doll. Or didn't want something, like a nap. I remember how my mother slammed me down on my bed, pressed her hand over my mouth to stop my crying. I remember breathing hard, struggling for air, arms and legs flailing until the world went black. And then the bright white of the hospital, my mother crying over me as I came to.

After I yell at Mable, I wait for the world to go black again, or for it to crash down around me like colossal mirrors. The sky is supposed to fall, isn't it?

"If you only knew what your grandmother's been through."

"I'd like to know. I'm trying to know."

"It's her way, her stupid, stupid way," Mable says to herself.

"I don't understand. Please just tell me what's going on."

She takes my hand, her palm against mine, and lays her other hand on top. The warmth from her hands slowly seeps into my body, creeping up my arm and spreading through my torso.

"You don't need me to tell you," she says. "You have all the answers already. You know why your grandmother has his things in that box, things his mother wanted your grandmother to have."

Mable's warmth spreads through my legs, down to my toes. I can even feel it through the numbness in my left leg.

"You know why your mother looks just like the man in that picture, and I bet you can imagine what it did to your grandmother, to have such a vivid reminder of what she lost."

I slowly sit down.

"And I bet you can imagine how a little bit of her always felt unworthy of a husband like your grandfather, who knew the whole story, but loved her anyway and married her just the same." Mable says. "But you listen to me, now — It doesn't change anything. People make too much of blood. It isn't any thicker than water. It just stains a lot worse."

Mable rubs my hand between hers. Anyone who walks in on this scene will think I've just slammed my hand in a car door, and Mable is rubbing the pain away.

The difference is, if I slammed my hand in a car door, I'd probably cry.

The whole thing is a jigsaw puzzle to me — a million tiny pieces and no picture to go by. The pieces are little bits of my life, facts, things I know, that are firm, unchangeable. For instance, I know my Grandmother is a mean old woman who hates me. I know she hates my mother, and that my mother loves me. Papa is my grandfather—that was a fact, too, until this afternoon. It makes me wonder what other fixed points in my life could shift and change.

The pieces of this puzzle fit together many different ways. I put them together one way and get a picture of Grandmother so sad when Edward Henderson died before they could get married. In the next picture, she's pregnant and alone, trying to make me put my hand over my heart and whimper for her. Then there's a picture of her terrified to tell her mother—and I'm supposed to feel some bond with her. Then a picture of her looking at my mother, who reminds her every day of the life she could've had, the one that was so cruelly snatched away from her.

Boo hoo.

Finally, there's the image of Grandmother, watching my mother suffer the same pain, having me with a man who died on her.

The afternoon passes as I sit in Mable's work room and take the puzzle apart, then put it back together, hoping to recreate the picture I know and understand, the one of my mother and I cowering under Grandmother's sinister glare. But every time I try for that picture, it won't work. Instead of missing a piece, I have one too many.

Mable irons, humming the same tune over and over again. "Amazing Grace." I hate that song. You're supposed to feel great about bad things happening to you. You're supposed to be happy that God is piling all kinds of crap on you. And people believe it. "I once was lost, but now am found/Was blind but now I see."

I'll take blindness any day.

At the end of the day, Mable sits down next to me. She wipes her brow with her handkerchief and sighs. My duffle bag and all of its contents are still strewn over the floor in front of me.

"Hand me that dolly," Mable says.

"The floor is no place for a little girl like this," Mable says to the doll. There is something so comforting about adults who talk to dolls like they're real. It hints at the magic that may still exist in the world. I wonder if Grandmother ever talks to the dolls in her bedroom.

Mable brushes dust from the Connie doll's dress and smoothes her yarn hair back down over the doll's muslin forehead.

"I remember when your grandmother made this dolly for you – the dress, too. All those beautiful dresses."

"My mother, you mean."

"Oh, no – your grandmother. She sewed all winter long that year, getting that wardrobe ready for your visit."

"My mother made me that doll, and the dresses."

"No, it was your grandmother. I should know – I cut half those clothes myself. When we were still friends. Before I tried telling her what to do. As you grew older, I pushed and pushed her to tell you the truth, but she wouldn't. I pushed so hard that one day she told me I wasn't welcome anymore." Mable sighs and shakes her head. "She was so afraid."

"But my initials." I tug at the little tag in the dress, showing it to Mable.

"Those are your initials," she says. "But they're hers, too. She puts her initials on everything she sews."

It's amazing how you can get so wrapped up in your own universe. Like one of those girls in those stupid scary movies, the kind where the maniac killer is hiding in the girl's own house and she walks right by him in the shadows. I always scream at the television when that happens – "He's right there, you idiot!" How could she walk right by and not see him standing there, clutching that big meat cleaver?

I've seen Grandmother's initials sewn into a million things this summer. They're on everything Grandmother touched with a needle and thread – the embroidered table linens I'd folded and packed into boxes, the embroidered pillow cases we slept on, the hand-hemmed linen napkins we used every Sunday at dinner, the quilt on the bed I'd slept on all those years, the baby clothes she'd made for me, and the Connie doll. They were on everything in that Hope Chest, all of the things she'd made for her life with Edward Henderson, including the baby blanket decorated with scenes from *Peter Rabbit*.

"My mother made those things."

"I'm telling you, your grandmother made all of it."

I stand up. A sharp pain shoots from my ankle all the way up to my hip. "You're lying."

Mable looks up at me. "Well, I didn't mean to upset you."

"I'm not upset," I grunt through gritted teeth. The pain in my leg recedes to a dull, throbbing ache. Sweat drips down the side of my face along my jawbone. "But you're wrong. My Grandmother never would've made me a doll or a dress or anything like that. I should know."

"You can always ask your grandmother. She'll tell you."

"Maybe I will." I sit back down—because in another second I'll pass out from the pain shooting up my leg again. I lay one arm over my belly and press down. I rub the side of my calf with my other hand.

"What difference does it make anyway, if she did make them?"

"None. It doesn't matter."

The sun has sunk behind the trees by the time Mable and I leave the Helping Hands. I walk her to her car. She faces me with her arms wide open. I lean closer, so she can fold them around me, but I don't fully give in. The tighter she squeezes, the more I stiffen, and the harder I pull away.

"You'll be all right now," she whispers, rubbing her hands up and down my back. "The hard part is over."

I want to press my face into her neck and breathe in her sweet baby-powder scent, but I can't.

Her arms fall away from my body, and then she grabs my shoulders, like she always does. "Now, I'll take you to the emergency room."

"That's all right."

"You need to get that foot looked at."

"It's fine. Everything's fine." It's getting harder and harder to believe that, though.

Mable gives me one of her sidelong glances.

"I'll go," I say. "But I can drive myself."

Mable pulls out of the parking lot, and I'm left holding the bag—literally. I stand outside my car with it, trying to decide what to do with what I know. I remember the day I held a baby for the first time. My mother volunteered me to help Elizabeth after she had Heather, the first of the Two Flowers. She was the first baby I'd ever seen up close, the first baby I ever had in my family. She was so small and fragile, with her tiny, tiny fingers and thin, pink skin. I wouldn't touch her. I cleaned and did the laundry and helped with the cooking, but I wouldn't do anything with Heather. I was afraid to even go near her until after a few months, when she started to look sturdy, like she had some solid bones hidden inside that pudgy baby fat. The first time I held her, she'd been screaming all night, shrieking louder every time Elizabeth tried to put her down for a second. Elizabeth couldn't take it anymore. When I walked in the front door, she shoved baby Heather at me.

The baby dangled in front of me. I held her at arms' length and stared at her, wriggling and fighting against me, howling for her mother.

"What do I do?" I said.

"Just hold her for God's sake, so I can go to the bathroom in peace!"

So, I held her, just like that. At a distance, wondering what to do with her.

That's how I feel about my new understanding of the contents of the bag. I hold it at arms' length, wondering what in the world I'm supposed to do with it.

The police are probably looking for me, although it will take them a while since Green Hill only has one part-time police officer. Or maybe it's a volunteer police department. In any case, it doesn't hurt to be careful, both hands on the steering wheel, ten o'clock and two o'clock. Stop at the end of the church parking lot and count to three.

At the bottom of the hill, a blanket of haze hides the mountain. A low rumble ripples through the clouds from miles away. Not a good day for the summit. Snow isn't a threat, but the bald domes of the mountain aren't the best place to be during a thunderstorm. *Zap.*

Papa would say this is a time to get below the tree line. Take cover and ride out the storm with whatever protection you can muster.

18

At the sound of the front door, Grandmother gets up from her chair in the den and scurries down the hall toward the kitchen. She looks over her shoulder at me, scared, I'm sure, because of what I said about the stick. When she sees I don't have it anymore, she slows down, but keeps going.

In the kitchen, she turns on the oven to heat the platter of sliced turkey she's already carved from the roast. She puts the string bean casserole and mashed sweet potatoes in the oven with the turkey. She stirs the goopy yellow hollandaise sauce for the broccoli, which by now has turned a grayish green in its covered dish. Yum.

This is what she's done at four o'clock every Sunday of her life.

Up in the yellow bedroom, I take Edward Henderson's obituary from the bag and put it in my pocket. I take the Connie doll, the charm bracelet and the box and go back downstairs. I hover in the hallway outside the dining room. Part of me wants to run back upstairs and put everything back in my bag and shove it under the bed, behind the dust ruffle, all the way into the corner where Grandmother can't see it, where no one but me can get to it. My whole body is itching to hide it all. I need to hide it, or Grandmother will take everything back. Or she'll tell my mother, and my mother will take it from me. Yeah, that's what I'm afraid of. That's why I keep creeping back up the stairs, and then slinking back down again.

Or maybe I'm just afraid to tell her the truth. It's a hereditary defect in my family. We are all afraid of the truth.

Grandmother sits at the dining room table with a full New England roasted dinner in front of her, ribbons of steam rising from the platters and casseroles. It looks like Thanksgiving, except for the cheap-looking Corelle and plain flatware, the paper napkins instead of linen. Not even paper napkins, though — paper towels. Oh, the horror.

She pretends she doesn't see me when I finally step into the dining room. The room spins a little, and I lean against the doorjamb to steady myself.

Grandmother folds and unfolds her paper-towel napkin, arranging and rearranging her silverware on top of it.

I approach the table slowly and quietly. Instead of sitting down, I lean on the back of my chair. Grandmother immediately takes my plate.

"White meat or dark?" she says, holding a serving fork over the platter of turkey.

"White, please."

She places the turkey on my plate and adds two more slices, which she knows I won't eat.

"I want to talk to you about something." The words feel funny, unnatural in my mouth, like a foreign language or a food I've never tasted before, octopus or chocolate covered mealworms. And I can't tell if I like it or not.

"And string bean casserole?" she asks. All the packing has reduced her to using plastic serving utensils. The serving spoon trembles in her hand.

"I want to talk to you." I try to sound firm, but it comes out soft and timid. My insides are already peeling away from my skin. Soon, all that will be left is a thin, weak eggshell form of me, so easy to crush.

"All right, then. Just a little." She spoons some of the casserole onto my plate. She smiles, but it doesn't look right, like that creepy painted-on smile on the little figurine in the yellow bedroom. Drops of sweat gather at her hairline and start to cut trails in the powder she wears to help hide her wrinkles.

"And sweet potatoes?" she says.

"Grandmother." My voice echoes in my ears. I'm already in a cave somewhere far away from this.

"Sweet potatoes it is." She digs a different spoon into the orange mush. "And broccoli, too, then." She takes a chunk out of this Sunday's steaming green brain and puts it on my plate next to the sweet potatoes.

I pull my chair out.

It'll be easier to just forget everything.

I can forget.

And then, Grandmother drips Hollandaise on top of my broccoli.

Hollandaise, that thick, gelatinous sauce—just looking at it makes me gag.

She puts Hollandaise on my broccoli. I hate Hollandaise, always hated it. My whole life, she's put it on my food and watched me scrape it off.

"Enough with the Hollandaise!" I yell, sending dangerous vibrations through my thin shell.

Grandmother looks at me, startled but still smiling. "Fine," she says, putting the spoon back in the bowl of sauce and sets my plate down in front of my seat. She picks up her own plate and begins putting some turkey slices on it. She starts humming as she moves on to the casserole.

I plant the doll, the box and the charm bracelet in the center of the table. "I want to talk to you."

Grandmother digs into the sweet potatoes and puts some on her plate.

"Do you hear me? I want to talk to you!"

Grandmother slams the serving spoon down on the table like a gavel. The smile has vanished.

"I will not talk to you about those things."

"I knew it," I say with contempt so thick I can taste it. "You're a liar and a coward."

She replaces the spoon in the sweet potatoes and moves on to the broccoli. "When you're older, you'll understand that some things are better left in the past. Now sit and eat."

Grandmother bores into me with her eyes, a look that would send Satan running back to Hell with his tail between his legs. I remember how my mother described Grandmother's eyes the night she told her and Papa about me. I should sit and eat. Just do what she says.

Sit and eat, and forget.

The doll, the box and the charm bracelet are still in the center of the table. Grandmother is cutting her meat into dainty little pieces. She puts one in her mouth and chews.

It's like jumping into the frigid pools of river water along the roadsides up here. I close my eyes, take a deep breath and sweep my arms across the table, shoving the platter of meat, the gravy boat and all the casserole dishes off the side of the table.

The turkey goes first, making a good splat on the bare floor. I immediately regret taking up the area rugs — what stains this would've left. The broccoli crashes on top of the turkey, followed by the sweet potatoes and that bowl of yellow goop. The string-bean casserole stays half on the table, my arms too short to finish the job. I walk around to the other side of the table, dragging my foot. The numbness seeps into my hip.

The casserole is in a white dish with a clear glass cover. I pick it up by the handles and drop it on top of the pile of food and broken glass.

Grandmother looks at me. So many drops of sweat have drawn lines down her face that she looks like she's behind bars, caged. She dabs at her face with her square of paper towel, removing more and more powder from her skin. She lays the paper towel back in her lap and picks up her knife and fork. She goes to spear a piece of meat with her fork.

I take her plate and smash it on top of the others.

She'll yell at me now. She'll turn into the evil witch and punish me good. She has to, because that's my Grandmother — mean, cold, calculating. That's how I've always known her, so that must be who she is, right? Not the nice Grandmother I've glimpsed this summer, the one who took care of me when I was sick, gave me her nightgown and robe, the one who was afraid to tell me she'd called my mother. All that was just to confuse me, wasn't it?

I brace myself for her fury, but her only reaction is the way her eyelids disappear behind her bulging eyes. She looks at the table where her plate should be. She takes the napkin from her lap, dabs her mouth, folds it and places it on the table where it would normally be next to her plate. She runs her hand over it a few times, pressing it flat, and then arranges her spoon and knife on it, knife on the inside, blade toward the imaginary plate. She places her fork on her left and lines up the bottoms of all three. She folds her hands in her lap.

"Fine," Grandmother says. "What do you want to know?"

I throw the obituary down in front of her where her plate should be. She looks down at it, but doesn't touch it. She seems to be reading it. Then she lifts her head and stares at the wall on the opposite side of the room.

"Well?" I finally say. "Who is this?" She keeps staring at the wall. "Tell me who this is!"

She slowly turns her face toward me. Her cheeks are wet, but it has to be sweat. It can't be tears, can it?

"Edward Henderson," she says.

"You know what I'm asking." She blinks at me. "Is he my mother's father? Is he my grandfather?"

"Yes."

I put the box in front of her and pick up the charm bracelet. Before I open the box, I hold the key up, so she can see I've figured it out.

"Are these his things?"

Grandmother removes each item and places it on the table. She handles them carefully. The silver cross is last. She lays it in her palm, the chain dangling over the back of her hand. She touches the cross with her fingertips and then closes her fist around it.

"Yes," she says, from far away. "These belonged to him."

"Does my mother know?"

"She knows. She's always known."

"No—she would've told me."

Grandmother opens her fist again so she can see the cross. "The truth is, your mother didn't want you to know."

There is almost an audible thud when the words hit my chest, knocking the wind out of me.

"My mother wouldn't lie to me like this, about something so important."

I try to sound confident, like I believe what I'm saying. It requires that I ignore all the other times my mother has lied to me, especially about the lump. She lied to me about that lump, and was so cool about it.

"You're the one," I say, my feeble voice betraying my crumbling resolve. "You hate me."

Grandmother looks at me then, and there's something different about her face. There's something different about the way her eyebrows are pinched together, about the shape of her mouth, the lines around her eyes.

"Is that what you think?" She looks down for a moment, shakes her head. "I don't hate you. I never hated you."

Something breaks in me then.

"Don't think for a minute that I don't know what I am," she says, her voice nice and even. Composure has always been her greatest strength. "I've known for a long time that I'm a terrible mother, a terrible person. I've known for a long time that I do not deserve the life I've had." She slowly puts each item back in the box.

"I've never given you any reason to believe this," she says, "but I have always loved you."

My legs give way. I land hard on my chair.

"Why?"

"You're my granddaughter—"

"No—The lies? She had a different father—so what? How is that any different than me, how I was born?"

She shuts the box of Edward Henderson's things and runs her hands over the smooth lid. "We thought we were protecting you, that if we kept it from you, then you'd be spared. What happened to me, what happened to your mother wouldn't happen to you. You'd be safe. We promised each other that you would be safe."

"Safe?"

"It seemed like such a good idea. And then I saw this control, this...anger, I don't know. And I wanted to stop it. I tried to stop it, but she wouldn't let me. She said she'd take you away, we'd never see you again." She puts her hand to her face. She sighs and shakes her head.

"My mother...she's not like that. You just don't understand her. She tries to protect me, not you. She loves me, not you."

A few strands of hair fall from Grandmother's bun and rest on her shoulder, trailing a little down her back. It stays there, for once, without her hands flying to pin it back up.

"I've tried in my own way, and I'd take it all back if I could, start over. How I've longed to just start over, with everyone."

My fingertips tingle with the urge to pin that hair back up. It needs to be put back in place, in order.

"Who made this doll?"

Grandmother takes a deep breath. Her chin quivers for just a moment.

"Your mother never brought any toys, not even a doll. Never packed enough clothes, never enough dresses." She brings her hand to her mouth. Her eyes are all red, like she's about to cry. She folds her hands on the table and looks down at them. "A little girl should always have a doll and lots of pretty dresses."

The only option now is that she doesn't hate me. You don't make things like that for people you hate.

"But you gave me underwear for Christmas."

"You never got the doll clothes and teddy bears I made for you, did you?" Grandmother says. I blink at her. She shakes her head. "I should have known."

I make one last attempt to turn her back into the Grandmother I've always known. "What about that day at the coffee shop, when you saw me with Ethan? What about last night? I saw you there, talking with him. I know you were spying on me."

Grandmother sighs, smiles a little. "I was just...I wanted you to have a nice time. I was on my way home; he was outside. I stopped and asked if you'd shown up. I was so glad when he told me you did."

Her hands are closed around each other in a ball, fingers rubbing against palms.

"I thought maybe this summer, now that you're grown," she says. "I thought if I asked you to come, maybe things could be different."

Her hands work harder and harder, wrestling with some invisible knot. I put my hand on the edge of the table. I move it toward her a little, and then a little more. I've seen other people do this, so easily. It can't be that hard. And they do it all the time, so it can't be so awful.

I rest my hand over hers, tentatively at first, giving her room to snatch her hands away. But she doesn't. Her hands stop writhing under my touch. I slowly rest my arm on the table, letting the full weight of my hand come down onto hers. Both of our hands are cold, but they slowly warm to each other.

This smell and a weird moaning sound wake me early the next morning. The smell is Sunday dinner still piled up on the dining room floor. It's not so much the stink that wakes me as the fact that the stink exists. I wanted to clean up the mess I'd made, but Grandmother wouldn't let me. She made me lay down on the couch and kept my ankle packed in ice. I fell asleep there, before I could help her clean. It's not like her to leave a mess like that over night. It should smell like ammonia, not garbage.

The moaning sounds like someone trying to hum a tune without knowing the melody. It comes from down the hall, sounding like an animal in distress, a dying cow in Grandmother's bedroom.

I get up and searing pain shoots up my left leg, sending me right down to the floor. I make my own weird moaning sound and hold my ankle. It's just a sprain—a bad sprain. That's why it's so black.

I crawl toward the moaning.

"Grandmother?"

The sound grows louder, more urgent. I push her bedroom door open. She sits on the edge of her bed, rubbing her arm. Her hair is puffy and wild, standing up in every direction. I've never seen her with her hair down, and it takes me a minute to get over the shock. She looks half dead. Half her body has given up living. One cheek sags, sags until her skin folds over itself. Her eye droops, and her mouth is about to slide off the side of her face. She keeps rubbing her arm, which hangs loosely from her shoulder.

"Grandmother?" I say, crawling closer to her. "What's wrong?"

She opens her mouth. Her tongue rolls around, but nothing comes out.

My heart pounds. There's that sinking in my chest again, the same as when we went to the hospital to visit Papa.

"What is it?"

She opens her mouth again and moans.

I use her bed to pull myself up onto my good leg. "You're O.K.," I tell her. I swing her legs back onto the bed and lower her head back down to her pillow. "You're fine, Grandmother. I'll get help, and we'll be fine."

She won't let me go. She grips my upper arm with her good hand, pinching my skin between her fingers. I pull away, but she squeezes harder.

"I have to call the ambulance." I shake my arm, pry at her fingers. Her hand closes tighter and tighter. Her good eye is bugging out of her head. She's trying to tell me something with that eye. She makes a long "mmmm" sound, and grips my arm so hard I yelp.

And then I know what she's trying to tell me.

I make two calls, one for the ambulance and one to my mother.

Then I crawl back to the bedroom and check on Grandmother. Her eyes are closed and her chest is moving. It'll take the ambulance twenty minutes to get here from the hospital in Littleton.

When the paramedics burst through the front door, the mess from the night before is gone. I've mopped the floor three times.

The paramedics stick needles into Grandmother's veins, tethering her to bags of clear liquid. They hook her up to machines that start beeping with the rhythm of whatever life is left in her. They shine bright lights into her good eye, then her droopy one. They listen to her heart, her lungs, her breathing. Is she still breathing? I can't tell. I move to get a better view of her chest, to see if it's rising and falling. One of the paramedics kicks my ankle and I scream louder than the blaring sirens.

He turns and looks to where my hands are gripping my leg. I couldn't even get a sock on my foot this morning, let alone a shoe.

"Jesus Christ!" the guy shouts. "What happened here?"

"Nothing," I say, pulling my foot away, trying to hide it. He reaches slowly toward it.

"Just let me have a look," he says, coaxingly. "Come on, let's see what's going on there."

I hesitate and then slowly take my hands off my ankle. He goes to touch it and I flinch.

"I won't hurt you," he says, moving still closer. "Can you wiggle your toes?" I move them slightly. "Good," he says, and I want to tell him that I'm not a kindergartener. He presses his fingers into my ankle then, past the numbness on the surface, and I see stars from the pain. But I don't cry. I'm stronger than that. I can take it.

At the hospital, the paramedics jump out of the back of the ambulance and pull Grandmother out on her gurney. Doctors and nurses swarm around her, shouting in that secret medical code you hear on those hospital TV dramas. The paramedic who thinks there's something wrong with my ankle helps me down, right into a wheel chair. I try to get out, but the chair is already moving.

Grandmother is rolling away from me down a white corridor toward green double doors.

I'm following her in the wheelchair, but then we turn down another hallway.

"Stop!" I yell, struggling to get up.

"Calm down, or I'll strap you in," says a voice behind me.

I turn around and scowl at the woman pushing my chair. She's wearing pink scrubs and has a stethoscope around her neck. She looks straight ahead as she pushes me down another hallway.

She's small. I could take her.

"I mean it," she says, as if reading my mind. I turn back around and pout. "The best thing you can do is relax, and we'll fix you up."

She has no idea what a tall order that is — the relaxing part and the fixing part.

19

Surgery sucks.

It takes the doctors all day to figure out that's what I need. First, they took a million X-rays.

I asked about Grandmother while the doctors waited for the films. No one could tell me anything.

Then they did ultrasounds.

I asked about Grandmother while the doctors read the scans. Still nothing.

Then they stuffed me into that coffin better known as an MRI tube—twice, once plain, and once after they shot dye into my ankle. At least I didn't have to drink the dye, like with the CAT scans. The memory of that sickeningly sweet, thick chalk on my tongue, filling my throat, my stomach, my intestines, making my insides glow for the radiologists, still makes my toes curl.

I asked about Grandmother while the doctors analyzed the images. They'd tell me as soon as they had any information.

The MRI with the dye revealed all the rips and tears. And I forgot about Grandmother for a little while.

My choices were surgery or never walk normally again—let alone run—and a life of pain. The pain didn't frighten me. It was losing the ability to run that scared me into the operating room.

But that wasn't the worst of it.

After discussing the surgery with me, the doctor started talking about antibiotics and antacids to take care of my ulcer.

"No. That won't work on me."

He flipped through his chart. "Are you allergic to antibiotics or other medication?"

"No."

"Then this treatment should work just fine."

"No, not with me, not this kind of ulcer."

The doctor looked at his chart again. "Yes, this will heal it."

"That's not what the other doctors said—that's not what my mother told me."

"Let's just try, O.K.?"

He patted my hand and then said something more about the surgery. It didn't matter anymore. They could carve me up into a million pieces for all I cared.

I went under scared, confused and angry and came out hysterical. All the tears I'd swallowed back my whole life came crashing through the dam of my reserve. I cried for hours. A nurse kept checking on me. She was a heavyset woman with curly brown hair that hung in spirals around her face. She'd check my IV, make sure I hadn't ripped it out, and then try to calm me down. She'd wipe my face with a cold cloth and tell me I was all right, the surgery went well, a success, I'd be good as new soon.

But that's not true. My ankle will be all right maybe, but not me. Not with what I'm left to ponder now. How my mother cooked every meal for me, made me eat every last bite. How she doled out my medications, watching me swallow down all the pills and syrups. How I took them anyway, even when I told her they made me feel worse. Side effects, she'd said, they'll pass. And I believed her. Every time, I believed her, even when I was older and could've questioned her. But why would I, after she'd taken care of me all those years? She took such good care of me. And I was sick, really sick.

I believed her when she told me that doctor, the one who said he could fix my ulcer, was wrong. I believed her when she told me antibiotics wouldn't work. I never would've doubted her then. But now...

What else has she lied to me about? My father? Maybe he isn't David Hobbs. For all I know, he could be the town librarian, my high school math teacher, some guy I've never seen or heard of before, a one-night stand gone all wrong.

But I have the rubbing of David Hobbs' name from the memorial. He did exist; he did die in Vietnam. I have evidence. It must be true. And anyway, how could a mother love her child and lie to her like that?

The nurse was very nice, but I still wonder where my mother was when I came out of the operation. It's been another day, and she still hasn't come around.

I tell the nurses I don't want to get out of bed. I don't feel well. All the numbness is gone and my ankle hurts worse than it ever did before the surgery. The pain makes me sick to my stomach. Or maybe it's the antibiotics.

If this is what it's like to be fixed up, I'd rather stay broken.

But they get me up, shove the crutches under my arms and make me move. I can't put any weight on my foot yet, they tell me, but I have to get up and move.

I didn't realize torture would be part of my recovery.

They won't let me back in bed for twenty minutes, so I roam, looking for Grandmother.

My mother leans over the bed, putting her face close to Grandmother's. She runs her hand over Grandmother's forehead, smoothing her long, white hair back, tucking strands behind Grandmother's ears. The hair falls well past her shoulders, tickling her elbows, which rest on the metal bed rails. Grandmother grips the rail with her good hand. My mother coos to her, and Grandmother's hand grips even tighter.

I watch all this from the door, peeking through the window, so my mother can't see me. I don't want to disturb them. Or maybe I'm afraid of what she'll do when she finally sees me. Or maybe I'm not ready to see her, afraid of what I'll do.

I don't know anymore.

I'm sure my mother would've come to see me by now, if Grandmother wasn't in such bad shape. When I asked the nurses about Grandmother, they gave me this long, technical answer. I latched onto the three terms I understood — "stroke", "paralysis", and "brain damage".

My mother probably doesn't even know I'm here, that I've had surgery. Although, it seems like the hospital would've told her that, right? Still, maybe she doesn't know I'm here. Otherwise, I'm sure she would've come to see me. A good mother would. And she's a good mother. She has to be. If she's not — if she's been keeping me sick, making me sick all these years — why have I been working so hard to make sure she loves me? What have I been doing all this time, my entire life?

All of a sudden, I am very nauseous. My ears start to ring. The floor shifts under my feet. The crutches fall away from me, and the floor tilts and slams against my body.

Then there are nurses all around me. They take my pulse, check my eyes. When they're sure I'm O.K., they get me into a wheel chair. One of them sees from my wristband that I'm on the wrong floor and wheels me back to my room.

I can't stop thinking about my mother. She must've heard all my doctors wrong. Or it could be that she didn't have all the information. I'm sure she thought she was doing the right thing, that she was helping me. There must've been some other danger I don't know about.

I'm sure there's a logical reason she hasn't been to see me yet.

After a few days, the doctors send me home. I try to ask my mother for a ride. I stand outside the door to Grandmother's room, gripping my crutches until my palms ache. The thought of the two of us locked inside the car together makes me tremble with fear. The same fear that has kept me from approaching my mother all this time in the hospital. Not of what she might do to me, but of what I might do to her. I decide to take a cab back to Grandmother's instead.

Fortunately, I wrecked my left ankle and not my right, which means I can still drive. And fortunately, my mother hasn't been to Grandmother's house yet, which means she hasn't seen the dent in my car. The auto body shop in Littleton makes it look good as new, matches the paint perfectly.

I go to the hospital every day and watch them. My mother doesn't let a nurse near Grandmother until after she's been told all the details of the procedure they have to perform. Most of the time, the nurses just want to change Grandmother's IV and take her pulse, her blood pressure. It doesn't matter. My mother demands a full briefing before a nurse can even set foot in the room. And then she breaks down, weeping on the nurse's shoulder while the nurse coos to her that everything will be all right.

Every time my mother cries like this, my stomach grows warm and queasy and I end up rushing to the bathroom to puke. Her control is such a part of me.

My mother bathes Grandmother, changes the sheets on the bed, and massages her arms and legs. They moved a cot into the room, so my mother has a place to sleep at night. She only leaves Grandmother to go to the bathroom or get food from the cafeteria. I've thought about leaving a bag of clean clothes by her cot, packing up some sandwiches and snacks for her. I haven't done it yet, though.

Watching my mother is like watching one of my favorite 1980s movies over and over again. I've seen it all before. I can predict her next move and mouth her next line before she says it. It's the same scene that was played out in all those hospital rooms and doctors' offices − my mother begging the doctors and nurses to help her with the burden of her sick daughter, the way she became a regular Florence Nightingale catering to my every need. She changed my sheets, brushed my hair and bathed me. She could never do enough to keep those feeding tubes clean. And how the nurses and doctors praised her for her unyielding dedication to my care. Sitting in my front row seat of introspection, I now wonder for whom she did these things.

Whenever my mother leaves the room and gets on the elevator, I know she's going to the cafeteria, which gives me enough time to check on Grandmother. Maybe I'm just not used to seeing her with all her hair down, or without the powder on her face, but every time I check on her, she looks another few years older. I've never seen her still, either. She's always moving, cleaning, working with her hands at least. I've never seen her hands so still before. I've never seen her in bed.

Today, she opens her eyes when I'm at her side. She grabs my wrist with her good hand and pulls me toward her. I resist by reflex−no one ever wants to get too close to the sick. She yanks my arm with such strength for a half dead person. I lean in, and she moves her hand to the back of my neck, pulling my face toward hers. Her eyes are wide.

"Do you need a nurse?" I whisper.

She shakes her head and scowls at me. She can still muster a scowl. She pulls my face closer and closer until our foreheads touch. She closes her eyes. Her hand relaxes on my neck. I'm afraid to move. What if she's dead?

Just when I'm about to press the button for the nurse, she lifts her chin and puts her rough, dry lips to my forehead.

She relaxes back into the bed, her head sinking into the cloud of her hair, her eyes closed.

"Are you afraid of her?" I whisper.

The corner of Grandmother's mouth twitches and twists into what looks like a nearly half smile. She keeps her eyes closed and slowly moves her head from side to side.

"Not anymore?" I ask.

The corner of her mouth relaxes. Her eyelids tremble as a thin layer of moisture gathers on her sparse eyelashes. She slowly rolls her head back and forth again.

Her hand slides down my shoulder and falls to the outside of the metal handrails. I take her hand—it's so cold—and lay it across her stomach. I take the bracelet out of my pocket and fasten it around her wrist. It's so loose; I probably could've slipped it right over her hand instead. The key, which I put back on the bracelet with a piece of wire, shines against the bones running up the back of her hand. All of her bones seem to be right beneath the surface of her skin, sharp and pointy. And yet, she looks so much softer to me now than she ever did before.

I'm down the hall when my mother returns with her lunch. She takes two bites of a sandwich and then adds it to the line up of half-eaten food on the windowsill. She starts brushing Grandmother's hair, humming softly as she runs the brush from the top of Grandmother's head all the way down to the ends of the white strands. She lifts Grandmother's head off the pillow to get at the hair at the back. Every now and then she hits a knot and works at it slowly, gently, so it won't hurt. Then she twists the hair into two braids, one on each side of Grandmother's face.

When she's finished, my mother leans in toward Grandmother and strokes her cheek, says something softly to her.

All the pieces of that million-piece jigsaw puzzle come together then. To get them to fit, all I have to do is make the picture much larger and move myself away from the center of it. The center is between the two of them, my mother and Grandmother, and I am not there in that space. I am at the door, on the outside, looking in.

I watch my mother take the bracelet from Grandmother's wrist and slip it into her pocket, and the final piece of the puzzle falls into place.

Standing in the center of the picture is my mother, alone. The very picture of a compliant martyr.

When I get back to Grandmother's that afternoon, I search the pile of Papa's tools. The ones I want have been in my trunk ever since Grandmother offered them to me. The table saw, his box full of carving knives, the drill, the belt sander, a hammer and a bunch of screwdrivers. His leatherman. I took most of it. I don't know where I'll keep it, but I know I want it. Maybe I could be a carpenter someday.

I'm not looking for anything so precise as a carving knife or a drill. I want the sledgehammer, which stands on its heavy head with its handle leaning against the garage. It's awkward getting the sledgehammer over to my car. I have to drop one of my crutches to do it. I'm still not allowed to put weight on my ankle. The new connections in my tendons and ligaments are still tender. They could still tear.

I'm conscious of this as I heave the hammer over my shoulder. I lean heavily on the crutch under my left arm and hold my foot as far away from the car and me as possible, to keep it from getting whacked by accident. The sun glints off the shiny new fender, the secret my Grandmother kept for me. I've been over and over every conversation with my mother this summer, and not once did she mention the damage to my car, because she didn't know.

I bring the hammer down onto my car's new fender as hard as possible under the circumstances.

Boom!

It's a nice dent, a fine dent, but too small. I bring the hammer down on it again. The sound makes me laugh. I hit the car again and again and again, making the dent deep and ugly, and I laugh harder and harder until I can't lift the hammer anymore.

What else can I smash—Grandmother's car, a window of the house, the mailbox, the front door? No. Something better.

She'll never miss it now.

I go up the stairs on my butt, pulling the sledgehammer and my crutches along.

I place the little porcelain girl in the middle of the floor in the yellow bedroom and bring the hammer down right on her face. I smash her until she's nothing but a pile of white powder.

She was sick of wearing that stupid smile all the time, anyway.

"Hello?" a voice calls from downstairs. I'm mid-swing, bringing the hammer down on that little girl one last time.

"Hey," the voice calls again. "This is the police."

They've finally come for me. I should be scared out of my mind. Instead, I'm giddy with excitement. It may as well be the Publisher's Clearing House Prize Patrol waiting for me down there with one of those giant checks for ten million dollars.

I hop out to the top of the stairs.

"Yes," I say, smiling. "I'm here!"

The police officer stands at the bottom of the stairs with his hands on his hips. "Come down here."

"Sure." I sit and bump my way down.

"Stand up."

This is it. The interrogation. And I'm ready. I'm going to spill it all, because it doesn't matter anymore. Whatever I've done, whatever mistakes I've made, none of it matters.

We stand eye to eye. He frowns at me, and I can tell he's trying to look mad and stern. But he doesn't even have any facial hair, no stubble. He can't be older than sixteen, which makes me start giggling again. I slap my hand over my mouth. It's never a good idea to laugh in a police officer's face.

"Is there something wrong with you?"

"Yes," I say. "Lots."

"Would you please tell me what's going on here? The neighbors called, said someone was smashing up the place."

"That was me," I say. "I was just...fixing a couple of things."

"Fixing what?"

I choke back more giggles. "My car. And a loose floorboard upstairs."

"Really," he says. "Have you been drinking, doing any drugs?"

Now that is just too funny. I laugh so hard that I have to sit back down on the stairs. "No, I have not been drinking or doing drugs." I squeeze the words out between my squeals.

He gives me a sobriety test then, makes me follow his finger with my eyeballs, and makes me touch my index finger to my nose with my eyes closed.

"See—cold sober. Always." I want to tell him to get on with the real questions. Where was I on such-and-such a date, at such-

and-such a time? Do I frequent the Green Hill Grocery? Do I know anything about a skiing trophy?

"I suggest you stop fixing things for a while. You're already injured, and you don't want to hurt yourself further," he says, real stern, pretending he's mad at me.

"O.K."

"Give the neighbors a rest. Keep it quiet."

"You bet."

I'm ready for the handcuffs.

He starts for the door.

"Is that it?"

"That's it. But I don't want to have to come back here again, understand?"

"I understand.

But I was ready. The truth was on the tip of my tongue.

20

My mother calls early in the morning to tell me Grandmother has died. Just like that. No preamble, no, "hello, my darling, how are you?"

"When? What happened?" I ask.

"Just an hour ago," she says, her voice flat. "She went in her sleep. I have so many things to do now — all the arrangements to take care of, the funeral home, the church. I'll have to call your aunts and the relatives."

Her excitement crackles through the phone.

"You know I was in the hospital, too, right?"

"Not now, Connie," she sighs, exasperated. "Can't you think of anyone but yourself?" Suddenly, I'm listening to a dial tone.

When she finally comes home at the end of the day, I'm in the kitchen heating a frozen pizza — a new pleasure since my stomach has started to heal for good. The screen door slams. There are footsteps in the hall. I peek around the kitchen door. My mother sits in Grandmother's chair in the den. After all she's done in the last few weeks, living at the hospital, hardly eating or sleeping, my mother looks perfectly composed, like she's been on an extended vacation instead of nursing her mother to her death.

I hide in the kitchen, wondering what to do. Is it safe to go out there? Will she strangle me or clutch at me? Will she soothe me, or try to hurt me? I don't know if I could tell the difference.

I sit at the kitchen table, trying to catch my breath without breathing too loudly. Maybe she doesn't even know I'm here. I could hide in this kitchen for days. It's a good plan; it could work.

The cloth napkin I put on the table for myself has Grandmother's initials sewn in the corner, a big curly "CG." She never stood up to my mother, and look what it got her.

Everything in her life turned out all twisted and wrong—even when she tried to do something right.

I expect a hug, a kiss, something. But when I stand in front of my mother, she doesn't even say "hello." I stand there forever, leaning on my crutches, before she even notices me.

She just looks me up and down, her mouth curled up like she's about to spit at me. For a moment, I think she is going to spit at me. But she looks away instead. Apparently, I'm not even worth the effort.

"What do you want?" my mother says.

My first instinct is to say "nothing" and hobble away. But then a booming echo, peppered with the tinkling of breaking glass, rumbles through my head. I smile at the sound of the sledgehammer crashing against metal and glass and porcelain.

"What are you smiling at?" my mother says. "Your Grandmother's dead—you have nothing to smile about."

"I just wanted to tell you that my ulcer is cured."

Her eyes become big and dark. Her fingers grip the arms of her chair.

"That's a lie," she says.

The smile slides off the bottom of my jaw. "No. It's not," I say. "And I won't ever run again, so you won't be collecting anymore of my trophies either."

"My mother is dead, and all you can do is say these awful things to hurt me." She crumbles into herself, rests her face in her hands and begins to weep. "You don't love me. You never loved me," she says through her tears.

At another time, this would've made me really sad. But now, I don't feel one way or another about it. I love my mother, but I'm tired. Tired of the ulcer. I'm even tired of running all the time. Why have I been running all these years, for myself, or for my mother?

The answer is hidden among so many lies. And I'm not even talking about Edward Henderson. That doesn't matter much to me. I had Papa, the best grandfather in the world, and I wouldn't have traded him for anyone. As far as I'm concerned, that's a lie I can live with.

It's all the other lies I need to face now. I can't run from them anymore. Even if I wanted to, I can't. It's going to take a full year for my ankle to work right. And then, maybe I'll be able to walk normally again. No more races. No more championships. I'm done with it.

A certain kind of person would say something to comfort her mother just now. But I don't. I don't think I'm that kind of person anymore.

The wake is open casket—the proper way. I sneak in early, before anyone has even arrived yet. Grandmother is dressed in a navy blue linen dress with matching shoes. There's a string of pearls around her neck and her hands are in white cotton gloves. My mother chose the outfit.

Her face is so caked with makeup I can see the granules of flesh-colored powder. Her cheeks and lips are too red. She never wore lipstick when she was alive. She never wore eye shadow either, but someone's put some pale pink on her eyelids. Not only is this practice really creepy, it doesn't strike me as a very healthy way to deal with death. The person in the casket's dead, not taking a nap.

I take the charm bracelet from my pocket and fasten it around her wrist. I'm keeping the box of Edward Henderson's things, but I don't need the key anymore. I plan to leave the box unlocked.

I took the bracelet from my mother's jewelry case—my last theft. It's...I don't know. I don't feel the need anymore.

Everyone comes to Grandmother's wake. There's a line around the block all evening during the calling hours. Being the oldest, my mother is first in the receiving line, then Elizabeth and Audrey and their husbands. I'm way down the end, last. I could stand next to my mother, but I don't. It's better for me to be at the end, where I can sneak off and sit down for a while. Standing on those crutches kills my armpits. My good foot keeps cramping.

My mother shakes each person's hand, smiles at them, and says a few words, mainly "Thank you" and "She was a wonderful woman." She doesn't cry, not even when people come up to her all teary. It's amazing. I don't even know these people, and I only started to know my Grandmother for that little while at the end, and I can't stop welling up every time some old man or old lady cries in my face.

There are lots of familiar faces at the calling hours, people I've seen around town, but the only people I know are Mable and Ethan and his parents. As soon as I see them among the crowd entering the funeral home, I sneak away to the bathroom and lock myself in for a while.

After Grandmother's in the ground next to Papa, my mother and her sisters and I stay at Grandmother's house for another week, fully emptying it. My mother wants to divide up Grandmother's things fairly, equally. Elizabeth and Audrey don't care. They don't want much of anything, just whatever was theirs to begin with. This surprises me. I thought they'd want all of it.

I hang out in the attic most of the time. The trunk and some other boxes are still there.

Picking through the hope chest one day, I start to cry a little—just a little. It's sad, what happened to Grandmother and Edward Henderson, and Papa even. It's a sad story. Then I notice Audrey standing in the doorway.

"I'm sorry," she says, turning to leave.

"No—it's O.K. Stay. Take a look around."

Audrey creeps over to me, and I wonder if I look that scared when I sneak around like that. I can't skulk anymore. Not with the crutches, anyway.

She picks up one end of a tablecloth that's lying across my lap. "It's beautiful."

"Grandmother made it." It took such effort to hide the hope chest all these years, and absolutely no effort for the words to slip out of my mouth. "This whole trunk's full of it."

"What's it doing up here, I wonder," Audrey says.

She doesn't know anything about anything that has to do with this trunk.

"Hiding."

Audrey shakes her head, puts her hand to her mouth. "She sure was a mystery." She sniffs a few times and wipes her eyes. "I wish I'd known her better. I wish she'd let me know her better."

"We probably all wish that."

"Not your mother," Audrey says. "Your mother knew her best. The two of them had some kind of understanding. They had their own secret club."

I blink at her. Am I in the right house? Is this my family? I want to remind her about the robes, how she and Elizabeth and Grandmother matched, and my mother didn't. And what about the birthday parties, the vacations—all those pictures with my mother shoved aside? But then I remember that she wasn't always shoved aside, and I am quickly lost in the tangle of truths again.

"It never bothered me that much, the way they got on. But Lizzy—she hated it. She was always vying with your mother for that top spot. But she never got it. Whatever was between your mother and Grandmother was always stronger. It always won out."

My mother and Grandmother did have a secret bond, all right. I want to tell her not to worry; she and Elizabeth have nothing to be jealous about. Their secret club wasn't so great.

"You should take some of this," I say, grabbing handfuls of the linens. "There are tons. Take some."

Audrey drops the tablecloth. "No. I don't want it." She wipes her cheeks again, sniffing the way people do when they collect themselves. "You take it. You obviously like it. You take it."

On the morning of my last day in Green Hill, I stand in front of my mother. She sits at the kitchen table, in what was Grandmother's place. And, like Grandmother, she pretends not to see me. She pours milk into her coffee, spoons some sugar from the sugar bowl into her cup.

I sit down next to her, leaning my crutches against the table. I put Edward Henderson's obituary down and push it across the table until it's right in front of her. Just her eyes move to look at it. They stop on the yellow square of newsprint for just a second before darting away.

She finishes her coffee, goes to the kitchen counter and pours herself another.

Edward Henderson stares up at her while she adds her milk and sugar.

She finishes that cup, pours another and sits back down with Edward and me.

Something in her has to give. Because if she can't give me something, some explanation or answer—I'll even take an excuse—now, with her real father's face in front of her, knowing that I know, then she'll never give me the truth about anything. And I don't know if I can go on like that. How do you go on like that?

"I know who this is," I say.

My mother gives me a look that used to make me wither.

"You don't know anything," she says, her voice a low growl.

My heart pounds so hard it rattles my ribs. Claiming liberty nearly chokes me. I take a deep breath. "I know who this is, and I know what you did to me."

My mother puts her hands flat on the table and pushes herself to her feet. She looks down at me, her eyes narrowing as she decides where to strike next.

"You don't know anything," she yells.

She snatches her coffee cup off the table and for a moment, I think she's going to pull her arm back and whip the cup at me. But the moment passes, and she storms over to the sink instead. She washes her cup, the coffee pot and the creamer. She wipes down the kitchen counter with a wet sponge, and then paper towel and Windex.

I lift the lid on the sugar bowl, a heavy ceramic affair meant to take the knocks of everyday use. It's still pretty full. I take the spoon out, put it on the table and replace the lid. I pick the bowl up in my hand and wait for my mother to finish her last pass over the counter with the Windex and paper towel.

The sugar bowl smashes against the cabinet right next to her head. Sugar flies everywhere, in her hair, all over floor and the nice clean counter.

My mother slowly turns around to face me. She looks down at her robe and brushes some sugar off it. She looks up again, fixes her narrow glare on me.

"Clean up this mess," she says.

The word rises up from somewhere deep inside me, like a bubble pushing up through my throat and filling my mouth.

"No."

My mother, more stunned by that one word than almost being killed by a flying sugar bowl, just blinks at me.

I put Edward Henderson's obituary back in my pocket and start to leave the kitchen.

"I said, clean up this mess."

I don't stop.

"Constance — I'm talking to you!"

I keep going, down the hall to the front door. The crutches don't hurt anymore, and my arms are so much stronger now. The doctors say my ankle is progressing well, and I'll be able to start real physical therapy soon.

Early this morning, before they left for home, Elizabeth and Audrey helped me put the rest of my things in my car. I repacked my duffle bag, which they put on the front seat with the box of Edward's things. They gave me food from Grandmother's pantry, too, some crackers and chips for the drive to the academy. I've decided to drive straight there, without stopping at home first. I think I'll stay away from home for a while. I'm not sure what to do now, but at least at the academy I'll have a place to live and a paycheck. It's a start anyway, a beginning to something, to something that's all mine, that I don't have to steal and hide away so it won't be snatched from me.

I push open the screen door.

"Where do you think you're going?" my mother says from the kitchen doorway.

I turn around to face her.

"I'm leaving."

"You can't leave me. You can't live without me."

"Watch me."

"What are you going to do without me? This is stupid."

"You're right, mom," I say. "This is stupid, and I've been too stupid to see what you've done to me all these years. I wonder now how I could've been so stupid."

It's just like those Monday mornings when I was in college. She's in her nightgown and robe, her fine brown hair all knotted and crazy. Her eyes are two dark holes in her face. Her shoulders are hunched, like an animal looking for a fight.

"There was never anything wrong with me, nothing that couldn't have been fixed a long time ago," I say. "But that's all over now. You can't control me anymore."

Just then, my mother melts. It's as if someone has pulled a plug and the current that was buzzing through her has drained out of her body. Her shoulders fall, her face softens, her head tilts to one side. Her hair even seems to relax. She raises her arms, reaches out to me.

"Connie," she says, sweetly. "You're upset. But you have to stop lying to yourself. You're going to have to accept that you're sick."

"I'm not lying to myself anymore," I say. "I'm not the one who's sick—you are."

In an instant, all the tension returns to my mother's body, her fingers curling into fists, her face contorting into a ugly mask.

"You ungrateful little bitch!" She hisses the words through gritted teeth. "How dare you!"

I can hear her breath, heaving in and out of her lungs. I always hated this moment more than the fits of anger or despair, this moment when I don't know what she's going to do next. But this time, for once, I'm not afraid. She's no longer a predator, but also not prey. She's nothing.

"No, Mom," I say, tears falling freely down my face, "How dare you?"

I leave her there, on her knees in the kitchen, trying to sweep all the sugar into a pile with her hands.

21

My first stop on the way out of town is the Green Hill Grocery. It's early, and most everything is still closed — of course — including the Grocery. I take one brown paper bag from my duffle on the front seat and leave it outside the door. There's a note inside with an apology for taking the items — the sunglasses, the perfume, the candy, and all those blush compacts. There's an envelope of money, too, to pay for the blush I used and therefore have kept.

I leave the scarves in a similar bag outside the antique store I stole them from.

I hope to leave Ethan's things in the same manner — unseen. All the cars are in the Matthews' driveway, but the house and the barn are quiet. No one is up yet. I park the car down the road a little — no need to wake them — and hobble down to the barn, gripping the third paper bag in my hand with the handle of one of my crutches. I follow a smooth strip of dirt on the very edge of the road to make my way to the barn. I pause at the bottom of the stairs. Still quiet. I put the paper bag on the bottom step.

A door creaks and then shuts. There's the thud of heavy boots on the landing at the top of the stairs.

I take a deep breath and look up.

"What are you doing here?" Ethan says. And for the first time since I arrived in Green Hill, he doesn't smile at me. This is the first time I've ever seen him without that gap between his teeth. I sort of miss it.

I can tell by his clothes, grease-stained shorts and an old shirt, that he's on his way to work. He holds a travel mug in one hand, a thread of steam pushing up through the drinking spout.

"I'm just leaving."

"Oh." He takes a ring full of keys from his pocket and locks the door. This is for my benefit, I'm sure.

He leans his back against the closed, locked door and takes a sip from his mug. I love coffee, and I used to drink it, even though it aggravated the ulcer. I salivate for Ethan's coffee. And with a jolt, I realize that it's not the taste I crave, but the pain it caused. Who would ever guess that living without pain would be such an adjustment? There are all kinds of addictions, and withdrawals for every one of them.

"Didn't think I'd see you again," Ethan says. He looks straight in front of him, not down at me. "The way you ran off…and then I come home to find my place is broken into and my mom's got you in the house, passed out on the couch and your foot blown up like a balloon."

"I can explain that," I say, not knowing how I will ever explain it.

"The police asked me, you know, if I had any idea who did it." He takes another sip of his coffee. "Of course, my mother finding you in the middle of the road right in front of our house did seem a little suspicious."

I pray I don't puke on Ethan's steps.

"But I didn't bother mentioning it to the police. It was just a coincidence, right?"

"Right," I whisper.

"And whoever it was didn't do any real harm. The only thing missing was my trophy, and I got that back." He sips his coffee. "Still, it was kind of mean, don't you think?"

My tongue feels too huge in my mouth. I swallow hard a few times.

"I'm sure whoever did it was just very confused and very stupid," I say. "Sometimes people do stupid things."

Ethan looks down at his feet then, flexes his scarred up knee. "Yeah, sometimes they do."

He walks down the stairs. I move to the side so he can get by.

"What's that?" he says, nodding at the paper bag on the step.

"Nothing."

He picks up the bag and starts to open it.

"You don't need to look at it now," I say, reaching for the bag, hoping to snap it shut before he can see what's inside. But I'm too slow, can't reach with the crutches propped under my arms. His hand is already in the bag.

My good leg feels weak and wobbly.

"My leatherman, the drill bits, my watch…"

"I can explain that."

"I don't believe it."

"There's an explanation for all of this."

He looks at me then, right in the eyes. Instead of hiding somewhere inside myself, I look back at him, my penance for what I've done.

"You found them," he says.

"Found them?"

"At your grandmother's. I must've left them there, dropped them in the grass or something?" His mouth starts to spread and there it is, that gap between his front teeth. Whatever Ethan knows or thinks he knows about me, I've been forgiven.

"Right—I...well...you must've forgotten them, or maybe they fell out of your pocket, or something."

"And what's this?" he says, pulling the check from the bag.

"For the lawn mower."

"I can't take this. That mower was on its last legs. It wasn't worth anything," he says, frowning.

"But I want to give you something for it."

"No, it wouldn't be right." He holds the check out to me on the palm of his hand.

I reach out, fold his hand around it and push his fist toward his body.

"I insist."

I hold onto his closed hand a moment more, for once not wanting to let go.

On my way out of town, I stop at the stone church. I put a check in the donation box in the vestibule, replacing some of the money I stole from the collection. Getting that fender fixed, so I could smash it again, was expensive. God will have to just trust that I'm good for the rest.

The Helping Hands is my last stop. Mable is at the door, opening up. She's all in blue again, just like the first day I saw her, a big, sweet blueberry.

"Oh, my," she says. "Your foot!"

"Yeah," I say, making my way toward her. "I needed a doctor after all."

"Are you all right?"

"Yes. I'm fine."

"You poor girl. Come in and see me."

"I can't. I'm leaving. I just wanted to drop off a few last things and say goodbye."

"Come in and say good-bye then. I can't stand saying good-bye in a parking lot."

I follow her into the store, which isn't exactly handicapped-friendly. I move slower than Mable as I weave my way through the tangle of used clothes. We sit in our usual chairs in the back room. Mable takes my hand. Her eyes get all watery.

"I wanted to tell you I'm so sorry about your grandmother."

"Thank you."

"It was so sad to see her go like that."

"Yes, it was." I have to squeeze the words past the lump in my throat that's sprung up out of nowhere.

"And I hope you can forgive me...for not telling you everything."

"It's O.K., Mable." I close my other hand around hers. "I understand."

"Friends?" she says, her cheeks pushing her glasses off the bridge of her nose.

The lump in my throat grows even larger.

"Friends," I say. "Now I've got to go."

She walks me to the door and gives me one of her bear hugs. I wrap my arms around her the best I can. It's not easy with the crutches, but it feels good to try.

She watches me from the door as I get into my car, which takes a few minutes with my ankle and the crutches.

"Wait," Mable calls. "I thought you had some things to leave!"

I tell her it's all in a paper bag by my chair.

As I pull out of the church parking lot, I stop to look at the mountain one more time. It's magnificent at the bottom of the hill. The sky is clear; the sun is warm; it's a perfect day for a climb. Not one reason to turn back.